Rhythm . . . tempo . . . let the blood flow. . . .

Let the matchless brilliance of Robert Cormier's new novel explode in your mind as you journey into the unforgettable world of the Complex and the soul of sixteen-year-old Barney Snow.

Inside the Complex, an experimental hospital, the Handyman treats Barney with "the merchandise" that shatters his memory with haunting illusions of his mother and deadly images of violence. Battling a private nightmare, Barney knows he must remain in "his own compartment," apart from the others: Billy the Kidney, weak and wheelchair bound; Allie Roon, nearly speechless and riddled with physical decay; and Mazzo—handsome, rich, and tragically devastated by his encroaching disease.

When Mazzo's twin sister, Cassie, with her pure blue eyes and irresistible beauty, comes to Barney for help, he can't refuse. But helping Cassie means befriending her brother—somehow reaching through Mazzo's bitterness and infernal determination to die—and giving Cassie daily reports on his condition. Entranced, Barney doesn't know that Cassie's own dark mystery makes her desperate for his support.

Amidst a whirlwind of passion for Cassie and the constant torment of hallucinations, Barney discovers the secret of the Bumblebee—daring, crazy, wildly compelling. In a riveting climax, Cormier reveals the core of his masterful literary vision and the heroic impact of a young boy's only hope.

The Bumblebee Flies Anyway

Also by
ROBERT CORMIER

Eight Plus One
After the First Death
I Am the Cheese
The Chocolate War
Take Me Where the Good Times Are
A Little Raw on Monday Mornings
Now and at the Hour

THE BUMBLEBEE FLIES ANYWAY

Robert Cormier

PANTHEON BOOKS
NEW YORK

Copyright © 1983 by Robert Cormier
Jacket painting copyright © 1983 by Norman Walker
All rights reserved under International and Pan-American
Copyright Conventions. Published in the United States by
Pantheon Books, a division of Random House, Inc., New
York, and simultaneously in Canada by Random House of
Canada Limited, Toronto.
Manufactured in the United States of America

First Edition
2 4 6 8 0 9 7 5 3 1

Library of Congress Cataloging in Publication Data
Cormier, Robert. The bumblebee flies anyway.
Summary: Sixteen-year-old Barney has only fleeting memories about his past but, as a voluntary patient at the institute
for experimental medicine, he knows he is different from the
terminally ill patients surrounding him. His involvement
with the bitter, slowly dying, Mazzo brings Barney hope,
pain, and a moment of heroic glory.
[1. Death—Fiction.   2. Terminal care facilities—Fiction.
3. Friendship—Fiction]   I. Title.
PZ7.C81634Bu   1983   [Fic]   83-2458
ISBN 0-394-86120-5   ISBN 0-394-96120-X (lib. bdg.)

To old pals
Jude Thaddeus, Martin and Anthony
and a new one
Max
with thanks

The Bumblebee Flies Anyway

1

THE day that Barney Snow saw the Bumblebee for the first time (although he didn't know it was the Bumblebee, of course) was also the day that Mazzo got the telephone installed in his room and Ronson received the merchandise for the Ice Age.

Barney was happy that he wasn't involved with the Ice Age. The last merchandise had been bad enough, and he was still feeling the effects. It had made him dizzy—more than dizzy: nauseous, his stomach spinning as fast as the whirling room, the walls slanting toward each other, shimmering and willowy, giving the room a strange surrealistic dimension. He had clung desperately to the bed as if it were a raft on stormy seas, riding it out, waiting, clinging to the collapsed sails that were the bed sheets. His temperature, however, remained stable, and so did his blood pressure. Which made the Handyman happy. And when the Handyman was happy, everybody was happy, although happy probably wasn't the right word. Finally, after eighteen hours, the dizziness abandoned him. The nausea also left. He lay weak and wan and listless on the bed, no strength at all in his body but filled with a sweet sense of having survived. Don't forget, the Handyman

3

warned, there will be aftermaths. The Handyman always laid it on the line.

Still in the aftermath stage, Barney was glad that the Handyman had put him on the shelf and had decided to concentrate on Ronson next. The Handyman explained that Ronson's merchandise—he did not use the word *merchandise*, of course—was a specific, calculated to produce an expected response. "This," the Handyman said to Ronson, "will make you go cold all over. Like ice. It will turn your blood to icicles." Ronson giggled in that way he had, but Barney did not respond, stayed on the sidelines. This one was Ronson's baby. Barney merely watched as they prepared Ronson for his excursion into the Ice Age. They took Ronson to Isolation, where the heat had already been turned up, although it had been a warm springtime. They provided thermal underwear, which Ronson kept calling thermonuclear underwear as he giggled. They brought in special blankets, which looked like ordinary blankets but, the Handyman explained, had been treated with a special kind of cold-absorbent chemical. Then they began to connect Ronson to all kinds of wires and sensors and such. Barney called all the paraphernalia used with the merchandise *doodads*. Zip-pa-dee doodads. Otherwise they'd scare the hell out of him. The nurse, Bascam, rolled up the sleeves and legs of the underwear and applied more doodads. A hole had been cut in the underwear in the area of Ronson's stomach. Bascam placed the final doodad right smack on his belly button.

Barney turned away. He had never watched a procedure before. The light reflected on the glass of the viewing window and he felt a little dizzy, a little woozy: the aftermaths. The Handyman hadn't encouraged Barney to

4

watch the procedure and hadn't discouraged him either. Free choice, the Handyman said, you have free choice here. A laugh, of course.

He left Isolation, left behind the spectacle of Ronson on the table, looking like some kind of giant insect, with strange antennae sprouting from him. And giggling away like mad. Ronson was tough, tougher than any of them, a fighter who'd won the Golden Gloves in Lowell two years ago, but he always giggled when it was his turn for the merchandise. A reaction, like the others. Allie Roon always wet his pants, which made it necessary for the Handyman to provide rubber underwear. Billy the Kidney whistled a soft tuneless birdlike melody. And Barney chewed the insides of his cheeks, his teeth gnawing at the flesh. Those first few moments of anguish always passed quickly, however. Allie's peeing, Billy's whistling, his own chewing stopped as soon as the merchandise began to work. Then you had other things to think about. Or sometimes, nothing. Depending. Sudden oblivion often waited after the needle plunged into the flesh: There was usually a needle where the merchandise was concerned.

Barney walked down the corridor, heading for fresh air. Bascam had said he could stroll the grounds today and smell the lilacs. Then she had blushed deeply and apologized. She had forgotten that he could not smell the lilacs or food cooking or anything else. His sense of taste had also been banished. Approaching Mazzo's room, he saw a stranger at the doorway, an outsider, dressed in outsider clothes, blue pants, tan jacket. He was carrying a package. Strangers were rare in the Complex. As Barney watched, the stranger opened the package and pulled out a telephone, like a magician on a stage. A sleek streamlined tele-

5

phone, green, one of the fancy ones. The stranger stepped into Mazzo's room. A telephone for Mazzo? Must be, Barney thought. Mazzo, the bastard.

Billy the Kidney came into view from the other end of the corridor. He was not in his wheelchair. He stood uncertainly, looking in Barney's direction. Billy the Kidney began to walk toward him, legs wobbly, knees bobbing. Billy had trouble walking. Had trouble doing anything. He had orders to stay in the wheelchair but constantly defied the orders, even though it was painful for him to walk. He placed one foot carefully after another now, like a child taking his first steps. He was grimacing, his tongue sticking out of one corner of his mouth, as if he was trying to remember how to operate his body, this strange mechanism of bones and muscles and tissues.

"Come on, Billy," Barney called. "Try to develop rhythm, for Christ's sake." Barney believed that rhythm was important. Tempo. Keeping time. Establishing a rhythm and letting it carry you. No matter what you did, it went easier if you placed your actions to rhythm. Like putting words to music. One-two, one-two-three.

Billy the Kidney had no rhythm. Or if he did, it was impossible for him to use it. He walked slowly and painfully, eyes wide with surprise, either at his ability to walk at all or because the pain was so startling in its intensity. Barney couldn't tell which.

"Rhythm, tempo," Barney called, clapping his hands. One-two, one-two-three.

Billy finally arrived at the spot where Barney was standing. His breath came in short gasps, his face was moist with perspiration.

"What's up with Mazzo?" Billy asked.

"I think Mazzo's having a telephone installed," Barney said.

Billy nodded. His eyes flashed as he balanced himself precariously, as if he were standing on a tightrope. The flashing in Billy's eyes was pain: Barney had seen it often enough.

Mazzo's voice boomed into the corridor. "Beautiful," he cried, "beautiful," his voice unnaturally loud, as if he were addressing an audience in a theater. "That's the most beautiful telephone I ever saw." Drawing out the word: bee-you-tee-ful. For the benefit of Barney and Billy, of course, but especially Barney. He'd evidently heard Barney's voice. He loved to shoot the works at Barney, even about a telephone.

"Jesus, I'd love a telephone," Billy murmured.

"Hell, who would you call?" Barney asked, knowing Billy had nobody to call.

"A lot of people, a lot of places," Billy said. "I had a phone one time." He began to whistle, the whistle of the merchandise, tuneless and without rhythm.

"Thanks a lot for the telephone," Mazzo called from inside the room, his accents exaggerated, the words drawn out in singsong fashion.

Billy saw the fury in Barney's eyes. "Play it cool," he said, touching Barney's shoulder, the movement throwing him off-balance so that he almost fell. He placed his hand against the wall for support.

"Cool, Barney, cool. He could be dead tomorrow." He pushed himself away from the wall with effort. Barney held himself ready to catch him if he fell.

"Let's get out of here," Barney said. "I'll get your wheels and we'll take a stroll outside."

"Fine," Billy said, balanced again.

Mazzo's voice came to them once more.

"You mean I can call anywhere? Anyone? Anytime?" Loud, taunting, loathsome.

Barney ducked quickly past Mazzo's room, not wanting to give him the satisfaction of knowing he'd heard him talking about the telephone. And he didn't want to look back to see Billy the Kidney standing there like some kind of wounded bird who was caught between land and sky and belonged to neither anymore.

They picked up Allie Roon on the way, and the three of them proceeded to the Northeast Exit. The nurse who signed them out didn't pay much attention to them. She was small, with delicate wrists and high fragile-looking cheekbones. Her pointed chin was set in determined fashion. She checked their names on the roster, avoiding eye contact. Like all the nurses and attendants outside their own immediate section, she seemed to pretend that they did not exist. Barney had been puzzled by that attitude at first and a bit angry. Until the Handyman had explained that it was difficult for some people, even nurses and physicians, to confront youngsters in a place like the Complex.

They signed their names, Allie Roon needing help as usual. Barney held the pencil while Allie did his best to move it, trying to control his fingers, his hand, his wrist. The signature was grotesque, covering three lines on the roster. The nurse looked annoyed.

"Allie Roon ought to be allowed to use an *X*," Billy the Kidney said.

The nurse laughed, a startling sound of sudden merriment. The laughter transformed her face, softening the harsh angles, making the cheekbones glow. Old Cheekbones. Billy the Kidney looked stunned: Had it been that funny?

Barney pushed Billy in the wheelchair toward the doorway. Allie Roon walked ahead of them. Or rather, jangled. Allie Roon always danced to some unheard melody, some unknown rhythm. But a depraved rhythm, ever changing, fast then slow then fast again, not at all like the rhythm Barney sought in his daily life. Allie's every moment was spasmodic, especially his hands: His hands were spiders forever climbing invisible webs. He seldom spoke, and when he did speak he stammered, the words emerging torturously in a shower of spit. Allie was the youngest person in the Complex, just a kid, twelve or thirteen. But he had an old man's face, wizened and worried, as if he'd lived a century or more. Barney knew about Billy's rotten kidneys, but he did not know the cause of Allie Roon's condition. Actually, he didn't want to know. The Handyman was right when he said that it was best if they lived in separate compartments. Don't become intimate with each other, the Handyman lectured, and forget about the past and future. There are no guarantees about the future even for the man walking down the street this morning in the best of health, the prime of life. And the past—forget the past; it is as dead as yesterday's weather forecast. Concentrate on *now*. Remember, the Handyman said, you are all in transit. I hope it's not rapid transit, Mazzo had said. Mazzo was quick: You had to allow him that much. But a real bastard, quick or not.

The air outside was beautiful. Barney lifted his face to the sky, letting the spring breeze freshen his cheeks, twitching his nostrils, seeking aroma. Billy the Kidney did not respond to the outdoors. He sat slumped in the wheelchair, studying his feet. Allie Roon danced ahead, doing

9

something that was a cross between disco and a rhumba and was neither.

The grounds surrounding the Complex were shabby and wore an air of neglect. The lawn had not been mowed since last fall and still contained winter's leftovers: twigs and branches, scraps of old newspapers, debris blown from the street, probably tossed from passing automobiles. He looked at the building itself, six stories high, faded red brick, sagging black shutters, the exterior giving no hint of the efficiency within. Billy the Kidney, who always knew everything about the Complex, said it was the original Monument Hospital, which was abandoned when a new structure was built on the other side of town. It was rescued from neglect when the Handyman and his associates moved in and began to operate the former hospital as a facility for experimental medicine. The Complex wore an air of mystery, like an old convent. The roof slanted toward the front of the building in a steep pitch at the astonishingly sharp angle of a ski jump. Unlike most buildings, which had either flat roofs or two-gabled roofs, this one resembled a lean-to, giving the Complex an alien, angular look. Across the street two huge tanks rose against the sky, dwarfing the abandoned building between them. The building had once been a chemical plant. Fire had ravaged the structure, and it stood in disgrace now, charred and blackened, the windows and doors bandaged with wooden boards.

"I like this neighborhood," Billy the Kidney said, coming alive again.

"This isn't a neighborhood," Barney scoffed. "A neighborhood has houses and people."

"Maybe that's what I like about it," Billy said. "I saw too many neighborhoods and too many people all my life.

All those foster homes and strangers who were supposed to be my brothers and sisters but weren't. And no privacy at all. The Complex may be like a hospital, but at least I got my own room and privacy."

"You're making a speech," Barney said, fidgety suddenly. Tempo, rhythm, he told himself. "You're also coming out of the compartment."

"Know what's the matter with you, Barney Snow?" Billy asked. "You're cold. Your heart is as cold as your name."

"I just think we ought to stay in our own compartments," Barney said. "Like the Handyman says."

"He's not the Handyman," Billy said, anger making his voice tight, lips pressed against his teeth. "Why do you always call him that? His name is Doctor Edward Lakendorp. Why do you always call things by what they're not? Like the merchandise. It's not merchandise, for Christ's sake. It's medicine."

"Chemicals," Barney said. "Drugs."

"What's the difference?"

"A lot of difference," Barney said.

"Look, Barney, I don't want to go poking around in anybody's private life. But isn't it natural to be a little curious, a little human, especially in this place? I think this is exactly the time to invade each other's privacy, no matter what the doctor says. We hardly know a damn thing about each other."

Barney was watching Allie Roon. The kid danced near the fence, arms and legs moving vigorously, as if he were being buffeted by the wind. The fence was high, ten or twelve feet in height, wooden slats solidly fitted together, fortlike, impregnable. Allie Roon looked up at the fence as he danced, measuring the height with his eyes as if he intended to climb it.

11

"Hey, Allie," Barney called. The wind took Barney's voice and magnified it, booming it through the air.

"What do you say, Barney?" Billy asked, squirming in the wheelchair, shivering a bit.

"About what?" Barney asked, still looking at Allie Roon. Allie had stopped the dance, although his arms still twitched. He continued to gaze up at the fence.

"About the compartments. Getting to know each other. Like Allie Roon. Who is he? Where does he come from?"

"This isn't a Lonely Hearts Club," Barney said, watching Allie Roon, who had started to climb the fence. Not climbing, of course, but trying to gain purchase on the wood. His legs began to work like pistons, but he wasn't going anywhere.

Barney walked toward him. "Hey, Allie, I got a better idea," he called. Allie stopped his efforts and turned toward Barney, waiting for him to get there. He was a light-haired boy with freckles. The freckles moved when he twitched. They moved now as Barney approached.

"If you want to see what's on the other side, let's walk down to the end of the fence," Barney said. "It's easier that way." He pointed toward the sidewalk about fifty feet away. He looked back at Billy the Kidney. "Want to see what's on the other side of the fence?" Barney called.

"It's a junkyard," Billy yelled. "You see one junkyard, you've seen them all." He brooded now, slumped in his chair.

"Come on," Barney said to Allie Roon. Allie nodded. Or at least Barney thought he nodded: It was hard to tell with all that twitching. Anyway, Allie dutifully followed Barney toward the sidewalk, still dancing as he went, an improbable figure, the old man's wizened face and the boyish freckles. A lilac bush grew against the fence, the purple clusters so heavy they made the branches droop. Barney hurried past the bush. He saw a trailer truck lumber by on the street, belching blue exhaust. Justice, kind of. He couldn't smell the lilac, but he couldn't smell the exhaust, either. And these days he couldn't smell the odors in the Complex, which got so bad sometimes they took away your appetite.

Allie tripped and Barney helped him regain his balance. They reached the sidewalk, arm in arm, Allie's bones moving beneath Barney's fingers. Barney was disappointed to find that the fence continued along the street, unbroken by any entrance.

"Wait here," Barney said, loosening himself from Allie's grip. He began to climb the fence, his feet finding support somehow in the small spaces between the slats. The exertion cost him a lot, but he thought, What the hell. The Handyman would be furious if he saw Barney climbing the fence so soon after the last merchandise, but Barney kept climbing, developing a rhythm now, matching his beating heart to the rhythm of his breathing and the movement of his body. He reached the top, straddling the fence, his heart accelerating dangerously and his breath coming fast, but he felt triumphant as he clung there, gathering his strength. Looking down, he saw Allie Roon gazing up at him, a smile on his face, all twitchings gone. The first time he'd seen Allie Roon smile: His face lit up the way a streak of lightning brightens the sky. He realized that Allie Roon hadn't really wanted to see what was on the other side of the fence. He'd wanted to climb it. Barney felt noble, as if he had completed a mission for Allie.

Barney surveyed the scene before him: the junkyard in all its desperate glory. Acres of junk, a wasteland of abandoned cars and trucks and vans and buses, a metal graveyard. The vehicles were rusted and busted, sagging, some without wheels, as if sunken into the earth, or maybe sprouting from the earth like evil growths. Barney sniffed the air and, despite his inability to smell, could swear the smell of decay and desolation filled his nostrils. He realized this was the rear of the junkyard. No trees grew in the junkyard, no bushes, no shrubs. No one in sight. No living thing anywhere. Barney swiveled his body and looked over his shoulder at the Complex. Despite its shabbiness, it looked respectable compared with the junkyard. But the junkyard had spare parts and the Complex didn't.

Turning again, Barney spotted the red sports car. The small car drew his attention because it stood upright and complete, its color vivid in contrast to the mottled and ruined cars surrounding it. Yet there was something strange and off-key about it. He squinted against the sun, studying the car—it looked like an MG he had seen once—holding on to the fence as the wind rose again, and the image of the car grew in his mind, not this car down below but the other one: What other one? *The one with him inside, out of control on the slanted street, going down down down and fast faster faster, his hands gripping the wheel, knuckles white, foot pumping the brake pedal but nothing happening and the speed gathering, accelerating, the hill slanting steep, steeper, car careening crazily, rampaging now, streetlights flashing on the pavement, pavement wet, engine roaring, whining. The car was filled with his screaming, a scream of horror, loud and high and terrible. His cheeks were taut, stretched, drawn back like the astronauts' during blastoff. When he spotted the girl at the curb, ready to step into the street, in the path of the car, his scream rose an octave and his eyes leaped in their sockets, threatening crazily to spill out onto his lap. The girl stepped off the curb, not fifty feet ahead, the car hurtling toward her, impossible to stop the car, Jesus, the horn howling now although he wasn't conscious of blowing it and the girl looking up as the car hurled toward her, her mouth an oval of astonishment, her . . .*

Barney found himself clutching the fence, his legs scissored against the rough wood. His fingers trembled as he loosened his hold. His breath came in terrifying gasps and his heart threatened to explode from his body. He tore his eyes away from the MG in the junkyard. A voice reached him dimly, Billy the Kidney's voice: "Get down from there, Barney. Barney, get down." He looked down to see Allie Roon still grinning at the bottom of the fence. Gaining confidence, he swiveled to search for Billy the Kidney, saw him in the wheelchair, his mouth open and his voice reaching Barney like an echo in mountain passes. "Come on, Barney. You'll catch holy hell. . . ."

Barney needed no further urging, because he wanted to get down from there and feel the earth beneath his feet, feel his heart getting back to normal, feel his breathing becoming regular. Slowly, methodically, moving one hand and one foot at a time as if he were descending a precipice, he managed to reach the bottom without emergency. His heart was still beating very hard, though, dancing in his body the way Allie Roon danced as they made their way to Billy the Kidney in his wheelchair.

"Jesus," Billy said. "You looked like you were frozen to the spot up there. What were you doing, anyway?"

"I spotted a car in the yard. An MG. It looked almost like new. I was studying it," Barney said, grateful that his breath was coming regularly now and his heart was slowing down.

"It's getting cold," Billy said. "Let's get inside."

Barney looked back at the fence and shivered, a chill rippling across his flesh. He had had the nightmare before, the car and him in it and the car slanting down the hill headed for the girl, but it had never happened in the daytime, not while he was awake. Was it possible to have a nightmare while you were awake?

Allie Roon danced ahead, but slowly now, in a sad parody of a waltz. Billy the Kidney brooded in the wheelchair as Barney pushed him along.

"You sure nothing happened to you up on that fence?" Billy asked.

"Nothing," Barney said, making his voice flat, final, so that Billy would stop asking questions.

But he knew he had seen something.

What he didn't find out until later was that he had seen the Bumblebee for the first time.

2

MAZZO would probably die first, but there were no guarantees. Actually, it was a toss-up among all of them—Mazzo and Ronson, then Billy the Kidney and Allie Roon. Surprisingly enough, Ronson was responding to the merchandise while the others remained unchanged. There wasn't supposed to be any response, of course, in the sense that improvement could be expected. And a cure was out of the question. Looking at Billy the Kidney, Barney often winced at the fact of Billy's imminent death, the certainty of it, the complete absence of hope.

Observing Ronson now in Isolation, still in the Ice Age, silent and unmoving, all the wires and doodads intact, Barney was depressed. He pictured in his mind Ronson in the ring, sleek and slender and swift, jabbing away at an opponent, connecting with a right and then a left as the crowd cheered, and later standing with his hands over his head, the winner.

Turning away, he encountered Bascam, who had padded through the doorway, a computer printout in her hand. She ignored Barney as she studied Ronson on the table and then looked at her watch and checked something on the printout, making a mark with her pen. Ronson was

17

also being watched in Observation in another part of the Complex, all of his reactions and movements recorded on a panel of monitors, under constant surveillance.

Bascam was tall and thin and as impersonal as a thermometer. Her body revealed no contours beneath the green uniform. Her graying hair was pulled into a tight bun at the back of her head. He had never seen her register an emotion: She never smiled or frowned or laughed or displayed happiness or sadness. Maybe you needed to deaden your emotions in a place like this. Yet she had blushed with embarrassment this morning when she'd suggested that Barney smell the lilacs. It was good to know that Bascam was human after all. He wasn't always sure about the Handyman.

Downstairs now, Barney spotted Billy the Kidney in his wheelchair near Mazzo's room. Barney was held by the expression on Billy's face. Sad. No, not sad. What then? He groped for the word and found it: wistful. Billy was looking toward Mazzo's doorway with a wistful woebegone expression on his face. Like there was something in Mazzo's room that he wanted more than anything else in the world and couldn't have.

Sensing Barney's presence, Billy turned around, spotted Barney, and instantly blushed, the glow a vivid contrast to his usual yellow pallor. Now Barney saw something else on Billy's face: guilt.

"What's going on?" Barney asked.

"Nothing, nothing's going on," Billy said, swiveling his wheelchair around so that Barney couldn't look into his eyes.

"What are you hanging around Mazzo's room for?" Barney asked, lowering his voice so that Mazzo couldn't hear.

Billy shrugged, still turned away, his face still scarlet.

18

Everybody hung around Mazzo's room. Doctors and nurses and the aides. They couldn't do enough for Mazzo, even though his disposition was rotten and he was always moaning and groaning and bitching. And belching and farting.

"That telephone," Billy said, sad and wistful.

"Jeez," Barney said. "Who would you call if you had a phone? You said yourself there's nobody out there to even write a letter to."

"I got a lot of calls I can make," Billy said. "A lot of people I can call. There's a whole bunch of people to talk to."

Barney didn't reply. He didn't want to find out anything personal about Billy. And vice versa.

"I had a phone at my disposal last year at this other place I was before coming here," Billy said, still not looking at Barney and his voice whispered and confidential. "The phone was in a small office that nobody ever used and I discovered it by accident. I'd sneak in there and make my calls.

"I'd call, oh, the local radio station and make a request for a song, although I didn't have a radio—the station had a request number in the phone book. Or I'd call the police station downtown and tell them I was new in town and ask the location of a street, like I wanted to visit there. Then there were the Dial numbers."

Billy's voice grew dreamy now. "The Dial numbers were nice. I found them in the phone book. Dial-A-Prayer and you'd hear a pretty good sermon. Or at least a voice, even if it was recorded. Then there was Dial-A-Diet. That was operated by the board of health, I think, and they gave you menus for certain kinds of diets if you had a disease or a special physical condition or something. The diets

19

sounded terrible, but it was nice hearing a girl or a woman talk. They always picked people with beautiful voices. Then there were the wrong numbers."

Billy shook his head in fond remembrance. "Those wrong numbers. See, I'd pick any old number from the phone book and dial it and somebody would answer and I'd try to fake them out, you know. Pretending I was trying to find my Uncle Louis, say, who used to live at that address, and I'd sometimes get a conversation going. I was pretty good at it, too, Barney."

Barney thought of Billy the Kidney sitting in a hospital trying to make contact with the outside world. Dial-A-Diet, for Christ's sake.

"You didn't make one of those obscene phone calls, did you, Billy?" Barney asked, joking, keeping his voice light, wanting to keep everything light and bright.

Billy looked at him in dismay. "I'd never do anything like that. I didn't take advantage of the phone, either. I never made long-distance calls. I always kept it local. I just wanted to hear some voices at the other end of the line."

Stop it, Barney thought. I don't want to start feeling bad for anybody, not Billy the Kidney, not anybody. He knew tricks about not thinking certain things, but you couldn't control what other people thought or said. Tempo, rhythm.

"Listen, Billy, if you want a phone so much, then why don't you ask the Handyman to put one in for you?"

"No money," Billy said. "I checked the Handyman. He said you need money for everything extra here. He said the grants don't even cover operating expenses. I don't have any money. But Mazzo's loaded. His family is rich. They can afford a phone."

"I don't have any money either," Barney said, puzzled suddenly. Why is it that some people have money and others don't? Why aren't Billy the Kidney and I rich like Mazzo? Some things he knew, and he knew he wasn't rich, knew he was as broke as Billy the Kidney.

"Let's see," Barney said, snapping his fingers, rhythm, tempo, but keeping his voice low. "If you can't have a phone of your own, there ought to be a way to get you the use of one."

Billy perked up, eyes shining, not the flashing of pain but something else, expectation.

"There's got to be a way," Barney said.

"You think so?"

"I know it. Let me work on it, Billy."

Billy sighed, the spell broken, the brightness gone. "Hell, Barney, how can you get a phone, even the use of one?"

"Look, Billy, how long have I been here in the Complex?"

Billy frowned, thinking. "Four or five weeks, I guess. I remember the day you came. It was raining cats and dogs. End of March or first part of April. You ran like a bat out of hell from the car to the door. Know why I remember?"

"Why?" Barney asked, curious about how other people saw him. You see yourself only in mirrors, and mirrors don't show everything.

"Because everybody arrives here in an ambulance. On a stretcher. With IV's and things. But not you. Not Barney Snow. You got out of this big black car and you ran into the place. You actually ran." Billy fooled with the controls of his wheelchair. "Jesus, Barney, for a while there I really hated your guts. Nobody is supposed to *run* into this place, like he's warming up for the Boston marathon."

21

"But you learned to love my terrific personality, right, Billy? Even though . . ."

"Yeah," Billy said. "Even though." Voice flat, gone dead.

Even though I'm not going to die but you are. And the others, too: Little Allie Roon and poor Ronson in the Ice Age and Mazzo, the bastard.

"Is that why Mazzo hates me so much?" Barney asked.

Billy squirmed in the wheelchair. "What the hell, Barney. Mazzo's not the greatest guy in the world. But he's rich and handsome and had everything going for him. He was a star athlete. And now he's . . ."

"I know," Barney said. "He's going to die." But me, not rich and not handsome and not much going for me, I'm safe. Barney used his old trick and turned off the thoughts, not wanting to dwell on who was going to live and who was going to die because sooner or later he would have to confront the fact of Billy's death and he didn't want to do that. "Let's get back on the track, Billy. What we were talking about? I've been here exactly six weeks tomorrow. And in that time, Billy, have I ever conned you? Ever lied? Ever been a phony?" Maybe with other people but never with Billy.

"Not that I ever found out," Billy said, becoming aloof now and not going all the way with Barney. The talk of Barney's arrival here, the running, had brought out the difference between them. I'm still the alien here, Barney thought, almost an enemy.

"Okay, then, let me tell you this: I will get you a phone. A phone at your disposal. That's a promise. And Barney Snow does not break promises."

"Ah, you don't have to promise anything," Billy said.

"I know, I know. But I'm promising anyway," Barney said, wondering why he was doing it.

Mazzo's voice interrupted them: "Who's out there?" Whining and querulous. "I know somebody's out there. Who's out there spying on me?"

"Who wants to spy on you, you bastard?" Barney yelled back.

"Is that you, Barney Snow? Is that you out there spying on me? Eavesdropping?" A spoiled, little boy's voice.

Barney looked down at Billy. "Want to see that telephone up close? Hold it in your hand? Hear the dial tone?"

Billy grinned, sheepish but eager, a child's grin. We're children here, Barney thought, we're all children. Orphans, in fact. Stripped down, nothing guarding us but our skin. And skin no protection at all. "Come on, Billy. Let's pay Mazzo a visit and see that telephone."

They went into Mazzo's room, Barney pushing the wheelchair. Christ, but Mazzo was handsome, and the thing that was killing him had not diminished his beauty. In fact, the disease seemed to heighten it, accenting the line of his jaw, emphasizing the delicate structure of his cheekbones and forehead, enhancing the startling blue of his eyes, even more striking with the fever dancing in them. His flesh was splotchy, blotches like healed burns scattered on his face and forehead. His blond hair was thin, limp with perspiration, scalp pale and scaly. But through it all shone his unaccountable beauty. Despite the disease and its ravages. And his rotten disposition.

Mazzo eyed them suspiciously from the bed. Barney forced a smile. "Hi, Mazzo."

"What do *you* want?" Mazzo asked, nasty as usual.

Barney paid no attention to Mazzo's attitude; it was par

for the course. "Just thought we'd drop by and say hello."

Mazzo directed his attention to Billy. Billy was staring at the telephone, eyes wide with enchantment. The instrument hung on the wall above and to the left of Mazzo's bed, within easy reach. One of those one-piece jobs, the dial imbedded in the receiver itself.

"Hey," Mazzo said, catching on. "That's why you're here. You want to see my telephone." *My* telephone. Just like he always said *my* room, *my* bed. As if he owned the whole world.

"It's a beautiful instrument," Barney said admiringly. "I was telling Billy about it. My father worked for the phone company and told me all about them. This one you've got is a beautiful piece of work. What they call a self-contained dial." He was making it all up, of course, spinning his wheels, marveling at his ability to lie, to improvise at short notice.

Mazzo looked at the telephone, studying it as if he had never seen it before. "A telephone is a telephone," he said finally.

"No, this one's different," Barney said, stepping forward and lifting the phone off its hook. The dial lit up as he held it in his hand. He could hear the dial tone, a thin strand of sound connecting them with the rest of the world outside. "Here," he said, handing the phone to Billy. Startled, Billy reached up and pressed the instrument to his ear.

"Put it back on the hook," Mazzo commanded. "It's a goddamn telephone, not a toy. It's to call people up on, not to play with. You look stupid with that phone on your ear without a call to make."

Billy handed Barney the telephone with regret, and Barney replaced it on the hook. What a bastard Mazzo

24

was. But he got away with it because of his beauty. Nurses hovered over Mazzo, despite his grunts and groans, as if they wanted to preserve his beauty as long as possible, as if his beauty was so rare and radiant that the world would be left desolate by its going.

Mazzo smoothed the sheet with long, thin fingers. Artistic fingers. Barney's were short and blunt. "I didn't even want the phone," Mazzo said. "The goddamn thing is no use to me."

"You made a big production out of it when it was installed," Barney said.

Mazzo smiled, an astonishing thing, giving an additional sparkle to his eyes, softening the jawline. "That was for your benefit, Barney."

"Well, what have you got a phone for if you don't want it?" Barney asked.

"My mother, that's why," he sneered. "She wants me to have a phone so she can call me. I won't let her in this lousy place, so she wants to call. She's already called once, but I didn't answer the damn thing. I let it ring. I hate the sound of the thing but I let it ring. I don't want to talk to her."

Barney winced at Mazzo's remark, recalling his own mother. Or trying to recall her. Since he had begun taking the merchandise, he sometimes found it hard to concentrate. Like now, when he tried to summon his mother's face and couldn't. Or when you are blinded momentarily by a flashbulb, and able to see everything but that bright spot left by the flash. That's the way it was now as he thought of his mother, unable to summon her face clearly but remembering how she always wore a lot of jewelry, junk jewelry, and she made music when she walked, you could hear her coming a mile away. But he couldn't bring back her face at this moment. One of the aftermaths. Which was why he was glad he wasn't having any more merchandise for a while.

"Okay, you guys, now that you've seen the phone, get out of here," Mazzo said, dismissing them, closing his eyes as if that would make them disappear. Barney realized for the first time how much Mazzo's eyes contributed to his beauty. With eyes closed Mazzo seemed ordinary, good-looking maybe, but nothing special. Some people, babies especially, are beautiful when they sleep. But not Mazzo. Did the nurses wake him up at three in the morning just to see those eyes light up his face?

"Listen, Mazzo, can we do anything for you?" Barney asked. "I mean, is there anything you want?"

"In return for a phone call?" Mazzo asked, sarcastic, eyes still closed. Mazzo was not so dumb.

"I mean it, Mazzo. If there's anything I can do, name it."

Barney knew his words sounded ridiculous. What could he do for Mazzo that nobody else could do, that Mazzo couldn't do himself with all that money?

The telephone rang, surprising and startling, out of place here in the hospital room. Billy leaped in the wheelchair. Mazzo grimaced, pulling the sheet up around his neck. Instinctively, Barney's hand went to the telephone. A phone rang, you answered it, like a law of nature.

"Don't touch that phone," Mazzo said, his voice flat and deadly.

The ringing continued, loud, insistent, shrill. Rang and rang. "She knows I'm here and she knows I can't get away and that's why she lets it ring," Mazzo said, eyes closed again.

The hell with it. Barney picked up the phone. "Cinemas One and Two," he said, singsong fashion, into the mouthpiece.

The sudden silence left a small echo ringing in Barney's ears. And out of the echo he heard a sigh and then a sound he couldn't identify. Somebody crying maybe? He was sorry now that he had picked up the phone, but he couldn't stop for some reason. "Cinemas One and Two," he said again, with rhythm this time, tempo. "Want to know what time the movie starts?"

A small click and then the dial tone buzzed in his ear. Barney replaced the receiver on the hook. He didn't look at Mazzo and he didn't look at Billy the Kidney, either. He looked at the floor, wondering why he had answered the phone, for Christ's sake. Don't let it ring again, Barney thought, because there is nothing I can do to help.

The telephone did not ring. Without saying anything and still not looking at Mazzo, Barney pushed Billy the Kidney out of the room and down the corridor. It wasn't until he arrived at his own room that Barney wondered why Mazzo didn't simply leave the phone off the hook.

3

DID YOU FUNCTION NORMALLY IN THE PAST 24 HOURS?

Barney stared at the words, uncertain about how to answer.

REPEAT.
REPEAT.
DID YOU FUNCTION NORMALLY IN THE PAST 24 HOURS?

Again Barney waited, studying the words on the video screen, wondering what was normal, after all. He knew that the question would be repeated exactly twenty-five times, and if he still didn't answer, the screen would grow blank, setting off an alarm somewhere, summoning either the Handyman or Bascam or someone else as if a state of emergency had been declared.

REPEAT.
REPEAT.
DID YOU FUNCTION NORMALLY IN THE PAST 24 HOURS?

What the hell. Barney pressed the button marked YES. There were three buttons that could be pressed in response to the questions: YES, NO, and one containing a question mark. The Machine, of course, was programmed to ask questions requiring either an affirmative or negative reply. The question mark was for use only when the inquiry wasn't clear. Then there would be a pause, a humming sound as if the Machine were actually thinking things over, and the question would come back phrased differently. This always gave Barney the shivers, and he'd tell himself that there probably was someone sitting at a keyboard in another part of the Complex typing the questions. The Handyman assured him that this was not the case. The apparatus, he said, was sophisticated enough to carry out its own reprogramming and to modify its approach to the answer it sought. He could also go on at length about the operation of the Machine—the thousands of doodads that meshed together in precise and marvelous sequences—but it was all too complicated for Barney to understand or bother about. All he knew was that each evening at seven he came to this small windowless room, little larger than a closet, and faced the Machine. Next question.

Barney anticipated what the next question would be, or at least its essence. After all these nights he had learned the sequence, and although the wording was slightly changed, the substance of the questions remained the same.

DID YOU EXPERIENCE PAIN IN THE PAST 24 HOURS?

Barney pushed the NO, button.

DID YOU EXPERIENCE PHYSICAL DISCOMFORT
IN THE PAST 24 HOURS?

Which was another way of asking the pain question again. Or was it? The Handyman was cute about pain, though. He never used the word. He preferred a word like *discomfort* or its many variations. *This may make you uncomfortable for a bit.* Or: *You may feel a twinge from this.* Or: *This may be distressing for a moment or two.* But never *pain.* He let the Machine use the word, but Barney had never heard it on his lips.

NO, Barney answered again.

WAS YOUR ROUTINE ALTERED IN THE PAST 24 HOURS?

This question and its variations always touched off a reaction in Barney, depending on what kind of mood he was in. Sometimes it amused him. What would happen if he answered   YES? Yes, my routine was altered because I only went to the john twice today instead of three times. Could the Machine handle that kind of answer? Billy the Kidney claimed it could. Billy said Barney was lucky because his responses were those of a normal person in good condition. "Take the pain question," Billy had said. "Answer   YES   to the pain question and the merry-go-round starts. What kind of pain, and a long list to choose from. The location. How often. How long. The intensity, by degrees. Wow."

REPEAT.
WAS YOUR ROUTINE ALTERED IN THE PAST 24 HOURS?

Barney was tempted to fool with the answer, to push   YES   to see what would happen. It would also break the monotony. But the Handyman had warned him at the outset against that kind of stuff. The Handyman had said that anything but the truth would foul up the project. And foul up Barney's place in it.

"But why use a machine when anybody could ask these questions?" Barney had asked.

"It saves staff time," the Handyman explained, "and it gives us complete access to the information by storing it. I can summon anyone's history and receive it in a matter of moments. Actually, this particular unit is a diagnostic tool—it is capable of coming up with evaluations of the data it receives from patients."

"But why me?" Barney had asked. "All I do is answer: no pain, nothing abnormal, no change in routine."

"It's a requirement we must fulfill. As long as you are receiving drugs, you must be monitored. Knowing the reaction to the drugs—and even *no* reaction is a reaction of sorts—is vital. It is why you're here, Barney."

REPEAT.
WAS YOUR ROUTINE ALTERED IN THE PAST 24 HOURS?

He thought of the moment on the fence today when he had seen the car hurtling down the hill. Hell, he'd been *inside* the car, and it hadn't been a dream or a nightmare, it had been happening at that moment. The car, the steering wheel, the wet pavement, the slanting street and the girl stepping off the curb. That wasn't normal, was it, to have a thing like that happen in broad daylight? Yet he knew that there was no way he could tell the Machine what had happened in a series of YES and NO questions. The Machine handled only objective data, the Handyman had said. Subjective matter like dreams were covered in personal interviews. Barney had told the Handyman about the dream of the car—it had occurred three or four times in the past few weeks—but the Handyman had only shrugged and made a note in Barney's case history. If it keeps recurring and if it bothers you, we'll get someone in to discuss it, he had said. Barney knew who that someone would be: a psychiatrist. He wasn't in love with the idea of talking to a psychiatrist.

REPEAT.
REPEAT.
WAS YOUR ROUTINE ALTERED IN THE PAST 24 HOURS?

Barney pressed the NO button and watched the word appear on the screen.

The Machine hummed its tuneless song again and then fell silent and blank. A short session this time. He felt disappointed. This always happened when the questions ended, as if somehow he had failed a test.

Suddenly he was tired. He left the room and passed through the silent corridor, past all the doorways—doors closed, red lights glowing above the doors—of poor Billy the Kidney and pathetic Allie Roon and Mazzo with the telephone that he didn't want but Billy the Kidney did.

Barney took a chance as he swung Mazzo's door open slowly and quietly. The patients weren't supposed to be disturbed after the staff turned the red light on. A small lamp burned on a table near Mazzo's bed. Mazzo was an indistinct form under the blanket. Letting his eyes get accustomed to the dimness of the room, Barney waited, not breathing, not moving, listening for footsteps in the corridor. He heard the hum of the machine Mazzo was connected to, the ping of his heartbeats being monitored. He could not see the telephone: It was lost in the shadows.

"Mazzo," Barney called softly. "I meant what I said. If there's anything I can do, let me know. I can get around this place and you can't."

No response. Or had there been a slight movement in

32

the bed, a small stirring, and had he seen a flash of perspiration on Mazzo's forehead as he moved?

Barney waited a moment, then withdrew, closing the door gently.

The corridor was empty, the red lights glowing. Silence, except for the hum of a motor somewhere in the walls. Odorless and colorless, the walls a drab gray, the ceiling a dull white. He felt lonesome, suddenly.

What am I doing in this place, anyway? Barney asked himself.

But he knew what he was doing in this place, after all, Barney thought as he viewed himself in the mirror. Each night before taking the capsule and slipping into the bed, Barney inspected himself in the mirror, as if to confirm his presence here in the Complex, to reassure himself that the figure in the mirror was actually Barney Snow. It was easy to lose your identity in an institution, in a place where everything was planned and scheduled and arranged ahead of time. The merchandise, which he had received three times since his arrival, often left him woozy and vague, although there had never been any pain involved. Of course, the merchandise was the reason he was here. And also the fact that he was the balancing factor, the stabilizer, the norm by which to measure the abnormal. On his arrival he had been told by the Handyman that he would also serve another function here, the subject of later tests that would be designed specifically for him. Spare me the details, Barney had said. Medical terms scared the hell out of him.

Barney squinted at his reflection in the mirror. He wished he were good-looking like Mazzo. He thought of all the worlds he would have conquered, all the girls he would have impressed. He knew that it took more than good looks to be successful at anything, but the good looks at least got you up to bat. Barney had seldom gotten up to bat. He was not tall, about five six, and slightly bowlegged. Hair cut short to keep it out of his eyes. Adolescent acne spotting his cheeks like small wounds healing. Good eyes, though. He didn't need glasses. Snappy brown eyes.

Barney heard the squeal of Billy the Kidney's wheelchair and turned to find him rolling into the room.

"You're going to catch hell cruising around this time of night," Barney warned. Actually he was glad to see Billy, glad to see anybody in the evening, when everybody went under wraps early and Barney had nothing to look forward to but television, in which he couldn't summon interest, and then the annihilation brought about by his nightly capsule.

"What are they gonna do? Kick me out?" Billy said. "I couldn't sleep, even with a pill."

Barney sat on the bed. "What's eating you, Billy? Like today, outside. You were in a lousy mood. . . ."

"Maybe it was the junkyard," Billy said, rolling the wheelchair back and forth, back and forth.

"What about the junkyard?"

"It reminded me of all the cars I stole. . . ."

Barney had to suppress a laugh. Of everyone he had ever known, Billy was the least likely car thief. Small and shriveled in the wheelchair, his face innocent and young, Billy reminded Barney of an altar boy. "You stole cars?" Barney said, trying to hide his astonishment.

"Sure, for a whole year," Billy said, pride in his voice.

"How many cars did you steal?"

"Twenty-four. I counted them, kept track of them. On a board in my room, a bulletin board I made out of a cardboard box. That time I lived outside Philly for two years

34

with the same family. I marked off the steals on the board. But nobody knew what I was doing. I'd steal a car and mark it up. Had codes for the names. Like a Monte Carlo was the Phillies. And a Malibu was the Yankees. I named the cars for baseball teams. Everybody thought I was a big baseball fan, keeping those names up on the board."

"So tell me. What did you do with the cars you stole? Sell them to the Syndicate?" Barney still wasn't taking it all seriously, figured Billy was telling tales to pass the time.

"Nothing. I didn't do anything with them. That's why I never got caught or got into trouble. I'd just steal them and take a ride. Go someplace for an hour, maybe, get away from that place I was living. I'd drive around and then bring the car back near where I took it, because it'd be a long walk back if I left it out in the boondocks."

"How did you learn to steal cars?" Barney asked, curious now because he was becoming convinced Billy was telling the truth. Billy was too innocent to be a liar.

"I learned from a friend of mine. He served time in tough places. He knew all about stealing cars, punching out, the switch, everything. And other stuff. Like always take cars in the movie parking lot or at a restaurant where you know the people are going to be busy for a while. Never outside stores in a shopping mall where the owner could come out any minute." The wheelchair continued to rock back and forth.

"You never got caught?"

"Never. That's because I didn't really steal the cars. I borrowed them."

"That was a big risk, just for a joyride."

Billy leaned his head against the back of the wheelchair and closed his eyes. His pallor was terrible in the lamplight, yellow and deadly. "Jeez, it was nice, driving along.

35

I'd open all the windows and let the breeze blow in. I'd turn the radio up loud. Once I took a car that had CB stuff, and I turned the knobs and dials and heard all these voices out there calling to each other. It was beautiful."

Barney didn't say anything. He couldn't remember the last time he'd been in a car, and sent his mind back for the memory but encountered only that nightmare car slanting down the street. At the same time he thought of the MG in the junkyard, shining and spanking new in the middle of all those ruined cars and trucks.

"Remember this afternoon how I said I saw that car, how it looked like new?" Barney said, raising his voice a little because Billy's eyes were still closed and he wasn't moving and Barney wondered whether he was dead, whether he had died quick, just like that, the way the Handyman said it could happen. Then Billy's eyes fluttered open and Barney breathed a sigh of relief.

"I remember," Billy said. "Know how long you were on top of that fence? Like you were frozen, a statue? Hell, I started counting after a while, and I counted to one hundred and twenty-five. Which is a hell of a long time if you take a breath between each number."

"I want to see that car again," Barney said.

"Why? What's that car got to do with you?"

"I don't know," Barney replied, his hands tracing patterns on the sheet. He didn't want to tell Billy about the nightmare of the car, wondering whether the nightmare would be set off again if he saw the MG once more from the fence. "I don't know, but I've got to see it again."

"We'll go out tomorrow, Barney, if neither one of us gets a treatment. I'll act as a lookout."

"Great, Billy, great," Barney said.

And then Billy seemed to be overcome by a huge weariness that made his body droop. As if suddenly his bones and muscles had turned to wax and the wax was melting. Billy's head fell forward on his chest and he rested it there a moment. Then he whispered: "Think ... I'd ... better ... get ... to ... bed."

Barney pushed him back to his room, the wheelchair whispering through the dim corridor, the door to Billy's room swiveling open noiselessly. Barney helped Billy to get into the bed. Billy's breath was coming hard again, and when his eyes fluttered open, the flashing was in them.

Barney patted Billy's shoulder.

"See you tomorrow," he said softly.

"May—be ..." Billy said.

Barney was sorry suddenly that he hadn't come out of the compartment for Billy, poor Billy who wasn't sure that he'd wake up tomorrow morning.

May—be.

The syllables echoed within Barney all the way to his room, as he prepared for bed and took the capsule and then slipped in between the cool sheets. He lay quietly, waiting for the Handyman's capsule to bring obliteration. The last thing he was aware of was the vision of that red car in the junkyard, and then he plunged suddenly and sweetly into sleep, grateful for the Handyman's knowledge of the stuff that brought oblivion.

But sometime in the night he was in the car again, hurtling down the slanted street, and the girl stepped out from the curb and this time he almost ... almost ... saw her face and then his own screams awakened him.

Or had he been awake all the time and didn't know it?

4

THE Handyman summoned him to the Hit Room during breakfast the next morning. Bascam delivered the message as Barney ate the nothing food. "He wants to see you after you've finished eating," Bascam said, touching his shoulder, making Barney jump. Sometimes Bascam gave him the creeps, appearing out of nowhere on her rubber-soled shoes, gliding like a ghost through the Complex. He wondered if she was married and had a family, whether she ever left this place: She always seemed to be around, night and day.

Barney relaxed at the table after Bascam left. He knew that the Handyman would not have allowed him to eat breakfast if he were scheduled for new merchandise today. On the days when merchandise was administered, the diets were under strict control, with preparations beginning at least twenty-four hours in advance. Barney pushed the food around the plate. Fried eggs and bacon, but the food could have been cardboard as far as Barney was concerned. He had lost interest in eating since his taste buds had failed to work, and he ate simply to keep up his energy, to fill a cavity in his body.

The sound of the knife and fork hitting the plate echoed loudly in the dining room. Barney always ate alone, the only person in Section 12 to eat regularly. Billy the Kidney and Mazzo and Allie Roon took nourishment in their rooms, in a variety of ways, through plastic tubes, IV's and such. Mealtimes did not exist for them; food was only another element to be introduced into wasting bodies. Barney was constantly dismayed by the futility of it all, even though the Handyman had tried to explain the situation at the Complex to him. The conversation had taken place shortly after Barney had arrived and learned that the Complex was not a treatment center, that Billy and Allie Roon and Ronson and Mazzo were doomed to die.

"How about a miracle?" Barney had asked. "Or some kind of hope, some kind of long shot?"

"I have never witnessed a miracle," the Handyman had said. "Nobody here is looking for such a thing. Or even a cure. This is the last place in the world to come for that. Although what we do here may someday produce a miracle."

"Then why aren't guys like Billy and Ronson and even Mazzo beating their heads against the wall? That's what I'd be doing. Pushing the panic button. That's what most people would be doing."

The Handyman paused as if trying to find the right words. Barney called him the Handyman in order to avoid the word *doctor*. Doctors scared him to death. Doctor Lakendorp looked so much like a doctor—always dressed in green hospital garb—that Barney resorted to his old trick: providing a more suitable label for things that he feared or worried about. Like *merchandise* for drugs. Barney called the doctor the Handyman because a handyman is skilled and clever and Dr. Lakendorp was expert at his job, skilled with needles and drugs and all the paraphernalia of medicine. Barney felt secure with him but never completely comfortable. Why? He wasn't sure. Maybe because the doctor kept himself at a distance, behind an invisible wall. Small and compact, he held himself stiffly erect all the time, as if trying to compensate for his lack of height. His movements were precise, formal, almost like a figure on a music box. Short beard and mustache neatly trimmed, black hair so neatly combed it seemed to be painted on his skull. Brilliant green eyes. He did not speak with an accent, but his speech was so formal and proper that it was obvious English was not his native tongue.

"Let me explain first what we do here, Barney," the Handyman said. "This is not a hospital or a clinic or a hospice, although it has come to be called a clinic simply because people have a need for labels. This is a facility for experimental medicine. We deal here with patients of limited life expectancy."

Meaning people who were dying, Barney said, automatically translating the Handyman's words.

"We operate here under strict codes and regulations that must be scrupulously observed."

Barney didn't say anything. He was sorry, in fact, he had started this conversation. He had the feeling that the less he knew about this place, the better off he'd be.

"For instance, my boy, we have only volunteers here. We must obtain informed consent. The subjects must know exactly what awaits them here. For our part, we must operate under the code which insists that the well-being of the subject takes precedence over everything else. We must also avoid all unnecessary physical and mental suffering. The risks to the subject must never exceed the

40

humanitarian aspects of the situation. And, of course, the subject is always free to withdraw from the project."

Subject, project. Cold words to chill the bones.

"But you haven't answered my question, doctor," Barney said, cutting through the Handyman's terrible words to get at what he really wanted to know. "Why aren't Billy and Allie and Mazzo in a state of panic? Have they been drugged? Put on tranquilizers so that they don't know what's going on?"

"The only therapy they receive, Barney, is involved with experimental procedures," the Handyman said. "However, these are terminal patients, and they have reached a certain state of existence." The Handyman arched his back, craned his neck, as if weary suddenly but not wanting to admit to the weariness. "All terminal cases display similar characteristics. People who have learned that there is no reprieve, that their conditions are irrevocable and irreversible, proceed through a succession of stages. Panic, at first. Then perhaps rage. And then: Why me?" Those eyes fastened on Barney. Like X-ray eyes, Barney thought, as if they could see into your innermost being. "Then there is the stage of denial, when they trick themselves into thinking that a terrible mistake has been made. There is something in human beings that whispers secretly to them that they are personally immortal, that other people die, but not them." Eyes almost sad now, brooding. "Some argue with God or whatever deity commands their belief, offering prayers, good works, bribes, anything to get well, to find out that it has all been a mistake. And then at last a kind of resignation, like weariness after battle. Acceptance. And with this, calm. They may fret about other aspects of their lives, but they have come to terms with their limited expectancy."

"The tests," Barney said. "Why are they putting themselves through the tests? They could be home or someplace with friends."

"Who can accurately know other people's motives?" the Handyman asked. "Perhaps they want to contribute to mankind. Serve a useful purpose. Give meaning to their final days. I do not question their motives. I cannot deal in imponderables. I deal in results, effects. I need subjects for the work we are doing, and they are provided for me. I do not question, do not go beyond that."

What kind of monster is he? Barney thought.

Perhaps sensing Barney's revulsion at his words, the Handyman continued, voice almost gentle. "I cannot allow myself to become involved, my boy. The subjects are made as comfortable as possible. Our medical teams provide therapy, both physical and psychological. As director, I am ultimately responsible for the well-being of our subjects. But you must remember that we are primarily investigators here. We must view our subjects objectively. Must keep a certain distance. As you must also do, Barney, if you are to remain here. We all have separate compartments and must remain within them."

That was the first time the Handyman had used the word *compartment,* but not the last. Barney was glad to have taken the Handyman's advice, had minded his own business during his stay here, not allowing anyone to get too close to him. Even Billy the Kidney, who hated to be left alone. Although he and Billy had become friendly and spent a lot of time together, Barney didn't allow any intimacies, turning him off when he became too personal about himself or curious about Barney. Maybe I'm becoming a monster, too, Barney thought.

*   *   *

He pushed the plate away, the bacon and eggs half eaten but his stomach satisfied for the moment. He left the dining area and headed down the corridor to the elevator that would take him to the Handyman's office on the second floor. He felt the immensity and the mystery of the Complex all around him. The six-story building covered the equivalent of a city block, but Barney was familiar only with Section 12, the pediatric area he occupied with Billy the Kidney and Ronson and Allie Roon and, of course, Mazzo. Section 12 was isolated from the rest of the facility, although Barney occasionally caught a glimpse of a passing gurney on which a patient lay, heading for merchandise or an operation, he didn't know which and never asked questions.

The Handyman gave him the run of Section 12 and imposed few rules or regulations. When he was not involved with merchandise, he was allowed to establish his own daily routine. The Handyman, in fact, encouraged all the patients to come and go when they were able to. Billy the Kidney had good days during which he could maneuver his wheels all over the place or even try to walk. Other times he remained in bed, pale with exhaustion, unable to visit even the Recreation Room with its black-and-white television set and the old books that smelled musty and dusty and the outdated magazines. "We have no funds for luxuries or comforts here," the Handyman explained, "but then most of the patients here are past the need for luxuries." Sometimes Barney hated the Handyman.

The Complex was Barney's home for the moment, but he disliked a lot of things about it. The sound effects, for instance. Blips and bleeps of cardiac monitors, the rattling of bottles and jars and tubes that contained fluids he didn't even want to think about, phones ringing in the distance with the sound of emergency, bedside machines, like the one to which Mazzo was connected, that hummed or groaned, their dials and gauges glowing green in daylight or darkness. He tried to shut his ears to the sounds but couldn't, of course.

Nobody bothered Barney. The nurses passed him by as if he did not exist, focusing their attention on the patients in need of their care. They attended to Barney with the same care when he received the merchandise, but he always recovered quickly and the nurses withdrew swiftly and efficiently, their attentions always required elsewhere. Barney didn't mind, was glad to see them go off.

Now he knocked at the door of the Hit Room, paused, then swung it open. He called it the Hit Room because this was where the Handyman hit patients with news of the next merchandise. The Handyman sat behind a simple wooden desk, its surface bare of furnishings, like a butcher's block before the day's work begins.

"You did not have to knock," the Handyman said. "I was expecting you."

"I was knocking for luck," Barney said.

The Handyman locked his hands together and rested them on his desk. He studied Barney as if he had never seen him before. This was a ritual, this scrutiny, and Barney always endured it silently, patiently. The Handyman and his X-ray eyes.

"Luck is a useless word," the Handyman said. "It is especially meaningless here."

Barney didn't say anything. He always let the Handyman take the initiative. And the Handyman seldom lost time getting to the point. He didn't believe in small talk, never discussed the weather or the state of the world or

44

anything except what went on here in the Complex, as if no other world existed.

"You've been here forty-two days, Barney, and have undergone three tests. Three tests, three affirmative responses. By affirmative, I mean that your response has either confirmed our knowledge of certain conditions or, as in one test, added specific new evidence to our knowledge."

Barney was mildly curious: What conditions? What knowledge? But he didn't ask any questions. He had made a bargain with the Handyman when he had first arrived. I will do whatever you want, whatever is required of me, but don't tell me too much. I don't want to know the details.

"So, my congratulations, Barney. You've more than lived up to expectations."

For some reason Barney felt pleased beyond words, although he felt that he had done nothing to earn congratulations, had only lent the Handyman his body for short periods of time.

"And now we come to a new stage," the Handyman said. "What we spoke about when you first arrived. These tests you've undergone were only preliminary to a series that's scheduled for you. To start forty-eight hours from now. Thursday, at nine in the morning."

"You said the other tests were preliminary. You mean only warm-ups? Like spring training before the real season starts?"

"Exactly, Barney." A flicker of a smile.

Barney thought of the three times he had taken the merchandise. Never pain but the apprehension, the nausea, the dizziness, and the aftermaths. "Boy, doctor, those were some warm-ups."

"The importance of a procedure isn't measured by its physical effects, Barney. A routine procedure can sometimes cause major discomfort." There he goes again, Barney thought, avoiding the word *pain.* "And remember, we never expose anyone to more than he can absorb or endure. We know your far horizons, Barney, just as we know your limits. The tests, in fact, proved what we suspected."

"What did you suspect?" Barney asked, not sure that he wanted to hear the answer.

"That you would be ideal for the experiments you were brought here for."

"So tell me about them," Barney said, investing his voice with a bravado he did not really feel, telling himself to let the blood flow, tempo, rhythm.

The Handyman still sat there, hands clasped on the desk, not having moved since Barney entered the room. While Barney was conscious of having squirmed and fidgeted in his chair and now was letting his arms dangle at his sides, letting the blood flow.

"We're about to begin a series of procedures involving the brain," the Handyman said as if he were a teacher addressing a classroom, and Barney only casually involved. "Specifically, the memory. It's an exciting departure for us. As you know, we are involved in experimental therapy here, but thus far it has been confined to the physical, not the mental. Now we explore new territory."

The Handyman smiled again—he was breaking some sort of record today—but Barney realized that his eyes didn't change with the smile. They remained the same, dazzling in their intensity and brilliance but hard and cold.

"The brain, Barney, remains uncharted territory for the most part, one of the last frontiers to be explored. Outer space is another frontier. The brain is inner space, a land of many marvels about which we know only too little. We know less about the brain than about any other region of the body, but there has been some advancement in knowledge in recent years. In particular we have witnessed the effects of chemicals on the brain. I'm sure you've heard of mind-altering drugs, Barney. They range from tranquilizers that doctors prescribe to relieve the anxieties of their patients to sophisticated drugs that have changed the course of treatment of the mentally ill. These drugs have opened the doors to research into the chemistry of the brain."

The chemistry of the brain. Barney felt self-conscious suddenly, thinking of his brain: How do I think, where do thoughts come from? He could feel the blood gathering in his hands as they hung limply on either side of the chair.

"Then there's another side of the drug picture," the Handyman said, moving for the first time, unclasping his hands, the index finger of his right tapping the desk lightly. "This is the exciting aspect of developments, Barney, the positive, constructive side. If these new chemicals can help afflicted persons, why can't they improve the performance of normal people? Can they improve mental ability? Increase the capacity to learn, to assimilate, to remember? Some progress has already been made on these fronts, however limited it has been. But now we must push even further."

He looked fondly at Barney, the way a teacher might look at a favorite pupil.

"Your involvement, Barney, will involve memory. We are going to introduce elements into your system that will affect your memory."

"You mean make me some kind of genius at remembering things? I could be great on quiz shows, win all kinds of money."

"We are attempting to do just the opposite, Barney. We will obliterate your memory. A portion of it, anyway. We will introduce a condition similar to amnesia. Temporary, of course, a matter of two or three hours."

"What do you mean, similar to amnesia?" Barney asked, beginning to chew the inside of his cheek.

"Don't look so apprehensive, Barney," the Handyman said. "Let me explain what will happen, and you will see that it is quite a simple matter. The fear of the unknown is always dissipated when knowledge arrives."

Barney thought: tempo, rhythm.

"Let us consider, Barney, what a wonderful thing memory is," the Handyman continued. "It's the ability not only to remember but to be able to reproduce what has been learned or experienced. This is called retention.

"There are two kinds of retention. First, short-term. Remembering information for a brief time, after which the information is discarded. Say, a telephone number you looked up and have no further use for beyond that one call. Or the name of a person you meet casually and never see again."

The Handyman paused. Barney didn't say anything, was trying to figure out where all this gobbledegook was going.

"Long-term retention is a complex operation, however," the Handyman said. "It involves memories of your earliest days. And it also involves retrieval." Frowned at Barney, then went on to explain, voice hurrying a bit. "Retrieval is the ability to pull information out of the memory, information that has been stored there for a length of time."

Barney nodded, wanting the Handyman to get down to

48

specifics and yet not sure whether he wanted to hear all the details.

"There's a lot more, Barney—for instance, unconscious memory, in which we retain mental impressions of something that is so unbearable to recall that we repress it. Psychiatrists are usually concerned with this repression. There's also the screen, in which one memory—or an image—is used to shield another memory."

"What kind of memory stuff are you going to try on me?" Barney asked, impatient finally with all the explanations.

"Short-term," the Handyman said, looking pleased at Barney's question. "We will blot out an area of memory with a chemical that is a new compound. You will be tested while the compound is active in your system. There should be no physical effects."

The blood had gathered in Barney's hands, and they dangled at his sides like ripe fruit.

"What's it going to feel like, doctor? I mean, will I wake up and find that I won't know who I am or anything? My name, my address? I remember once when I got lost in a department store when I was just a kid. My mother was there one minute and not there the next. I wasn't tall enough to reach the counters. All I could see were legs. And my mother gone, vanished. I started to scream, not only because I had lost my mother but because I didn't know who I was. Without my mother to verify who I was, I was lost." The terror of that moment came back now to Barney as if it had happened yesterday or last week; lost, without identity, nameless. His screams reverberating in his ears, his spine rippling from a chill, until his mother was suddenly there, clutching him, sweeping him into the soft folds of her coat, kissing and hugging him—and he was suddenly restored to the world, he knew who he was, he was little Bunny Snow and his mother loved him and he was safe and secure in her arms.

"Control is the key, Barney," the Handyman said. "The experiment will be conducted in controlled circumstances by a scientist who is one of the world's leading theorists in the field. We're not abandoning you to the mercies of a rogue chemical, Barney. You have seen our processes here. Rest assured that we keep your welfare in mind at all times, and we must proceed as always according to the rules and regulations of experimental medicine."

Barney was afraid his hands, pulsing with the blood now, were going to drop like fruit to the floor.

"We have four tests indicated for you, Barney, each affecting certain aspects of memory, each providing us, we anticipate, with more knowledge to further studies in the field. It is a pioneering effort, and you are one of the pioneers."

"Tell me one thing, doctor," Barney said.

"Anything you want to know that will put you at ease."

"Can you guarantee that my memory will come back? That the part you block out will return? Once you said there are no guarantees in the work you are doing. When you were talking about Billy and Mazzo and Ronson and Allie Roon—you said there were no guarantees."

"But we are dealing with disease in their cases, Barney. Terminal illness. Irreversible conditions. Their diseases control their lives and even affect the tests. With you, it's different. *We* have control. In dealing with memory study, *we* are setting the rules, establishing the conditions, determining the patterns."

"Can you tell me what memories you're planning to blot out?" Barney asked, lifting his hands to the arms of the chair, letting them rest there, letting the blood flow free again through his body.

"I prefer not to, Barney. Any preknowledge on your part might affect your thought processes at the time of the experiment."

"How about this expert? Who is he?"

"His name is Dr. Emile Croft, and he is eminent in his field. He will administer the chemical and observe your reactions, but I will be involved personally with you in the procedure. While you are under the influence of the drug, I will be your contact, interrogate you, be a link between Dr. Croft and you. This is one of the reasons we brought you here early, before commencing the tests. We wanted someone—in this case, myself—with whom you are familiar to be involved."

Barney was tired suddenly, not a physical tiredness but a weariness of his mind, as if he'd been doing too much thinking.

"We will talk again before the test begins, Barney. In the meantime, follow your usual routine. Take advantage of our relaxed rules. Try to get some fresh air. Try to relax. You don't need any particular physical preparation and no advance medication. Perhaps a light diet, mostly liquid, within twelve hours of the beginning. And we will suspend your evening sessions with what you call the Machine, until later."

"Fine, doctor," Barney said, rising, conscious that the Handyman was terminating the conversation. The inside of Barney's cheek was raw and stinging. He hadn't realized he had done that much chewing.

"This will be a great adventure, Barney," the Handyman said, flashing one of his stingy smiles.

It wasn't until he was in the corridor that Barney realized he hadn't mentioned the incident on the fence, how the nightmare of the car had become a daylight nightmare, if such a thing was possible.

He hesitated, almost went back, but didn't.

Maybe the new chemical would take the nightmare away.

5

PERCHED on the fence, knees pressing the weather-roughened wood, Barney focused on the MG, marveling at the sleek low lines and the gleaming scarlet hue. It looked out of place in the junkyard, an alien among the disreputable wrecks surrounding it. He squinted against the sun, narrowing his eyes. Movement caught his attention at the far end of the junkyard. Two men walking in his direction, picking their way across the junk-strewn lot. Barney hugged the fence, tightening his legs against it, trying to make himself small as he huddled there. Which was ridiculous, of course. How can you hide sitting on top of a fence? To his relief he saw the men moving away, back toward the front of the place, too engrossed in their conversation to notice Barney. He was at least five hundred feet away, in any case.

The presence of the car was baffling to Barney. Why was it here? As he lifted his head, the world tilted slightly. Not the world but himself, assailed by sudden dizziness. Would the nightmare of the car slanting down the hill begin now? He should have stayed inside the Complex, shouldn't have come out here, climbed this fence, vulnerable, unprotected. He closed his eyes—worse with his eyes closed—

opened them and saw that the world was stationary once again. No nightmare. Here and now, Barney Snow in command.

But the MG. He had to get a closer look, touch the car, establish its reality. He felt a kinship with the car: It was like him, different from the other vehicles in the junkyard just as he was different from the other patients in the Complex. Both aliens.

He swung one leg over the top of the fence. Crazy, don't do this. Did it anyway. Now he was sitting on the fence top, balancing delicately. Swung his body around, let his legs drop, used every bit of strength in his arms to secure a hold while his feet sought support on the fence. And found it somehow. Barney let himself down tentatively, carefully, proud of the way his body functioned, smoothly, easily, doing what he commanded it to do: Get down from the fence.

On the ground Barney tested the earth beneath his feet, heart pounding, breath coming fast. Felt the solidness of the ground and realized he trusted nothing these days, not even earth. He began to walk carefully toward the MG, picking his way through the yard's debris, abandoned carburetors and batteries and other stuff he couldn't identify. He felt as if he were making his way through a battlefield long after the bombs had exploded and the soldiers had fled, taking the dead and wounded with them.

The wind began to rise, whistling through the abandoned cars, a door banging hollowly nearby, its clangor like the sound of doom. Stop the dramatics, Barney, he told himself. He slipped in a puddle of grease, lost his balance and reached out to a sagging station wagon for support. A rat scurried out of the car, spurted between Barney's legs and fled the scene.

Barney stopped short as he approached the car. Felt his jaw drop open, like in a comic book. The MG was a fake. Not a car at all but a mock-up, made of plywood, the doors and hood and the other parts held together by screws and hinges. He kicked at the phony car in anger, feeling tricked and betrayed. Up close, he saw that the paint was somewhat faded, although it looked fresh and new compared to the wrecks that surrounded it. The interior was unfinished, thin boards serving as the front seat and the floor. The steering wheel was fastened to an aluminum shaft, the wheel itself small and out of proportion to the rest of the car, probably taken from a child's toy automobile. The dashboard was another piece of plywood, but someone had cleverly drawn a speedometer, gasoline gauge and other dials on it to give the dash the appearance of reality.

Grudgingly, Barney admired the handiwork that had gone into the making of the car, the care with which the various parts had been screwed together. He kicked one of the rear tires, the way people did in used-car lots. The tire was real but smaller than an ordinary one, maybe a tire from a motorbike.

Walking around the car, stroking the smooth wood, he wondered what the hell it was doing here. Who built it? And why? The front bumper was simulated silver, dull in spots, but still glinting in the sun. Barney noticed a label attached to the bumper. Squinting, shading his eyes from the sun, he bent down and read the faded print.

MONUMENT VOCATIONAL
HIGH SCHOOL
WOODWORKING DEPT.

So that was the big secret. A bunch of kids in a trade school had built the car as part of a course and then either sold it or turned it over to the junk dealer once its usefulness was over.

Barney looked around the junkyard, at row upon row of abandoned vehicles in various states of ruin. No sound here but the wind moaning as it moved through the empty cars. Glancing at the mock automobile once more, he felt sad, as if he had lost something. Or had finally learned how a magician made the rabbit appear from the hat and it turned out to be not magic after all.

Let's get out of here, he told himself. And he began running toward the fence, slipping and tripping, as if chased by ghosts or goblins. As he began to climb the fence, he realized that the Complex was almost cheerful—almost but not quite—compared to this terrible place where the only inhabitant was a gray rat lurking in the ruins.

Billy the Kidney wheeled into view at the door of Barney's room.

"Mazzo," Billy said, eyes flashing, but not with pain this time. Something else.

Mazzo's dead, Barney thought, held suspended for a moment, breathless, emotionless. Emotionless? At someone's death? Had his emotions gone the way of his sense of taste? He cringed, felt the horror of being without any feeling whatsoever. And then the emotion came: poor Mazzo, such beauty and promise, gone. All of this in a split second.

"Where've you been?" Billy asked. "I've been looking all over. Mazzo's been screaming for you for an hour."

"That sounds like Mazzo. Screaming."

"You know Mazzo," Billy said.

Barney raised himself from the bed. He'd been resting after his foray into the junkyard, thinking of the fake car and the merchandise waiting for him in two days. When he closed his eyes, the car gleamed beautifully in his mind.

"Did he say why he wants me?" Barney asked.

Billy shook his head.

Barney established himself on the floor. "Let's go and see what he wants."

Billy swiveled away. "He wants to see you alone. He told me: Send Barney in here and then take off. Like I'm a servant or something." A wound in Billy's voice.

Barney watched Billy wheel through the doorway, head down, arms working like mad, knowing Billy was angry and sulking but nothing he could do about it.

Bascam was leaving Mazzo's room as Barney arrived. She avoided Barney's eyes, looked sheepish, hurried away. As if she'd been caught doing something wrong. Maybe Bascam was like all the others, stealing into Mazzo's room at all hours, basking in the glow of his beauty.

"Where the hell have you been?" Mazzo asked angrily as Barney approached his bed. But not going too close. He didn't want to get too close to Mazzo.

"Out," Barney said.

"Out where?" Unbelieving, of course. Figuring, Where could Barney Snow possibly have gone?

"Just out. What business is it of yours?" Not giving an inch.

Mazzo sighed, shaking his head, the violet eyes brooding, face blotchy, moist with perspiration but handsome all the same. Christ, I wish I looked like that, Barney thought. All that beauty wasted.

Mazzo remained silent, seemed to be contemplating something very mysterious and interesting on the bed sheet. Barney waited. He was in no hurry. Glancing at the telephone on the wall, he wondered if Mazzo was waiting to hear it ring. Did Mazzo want him to go into his song and dance again? Why didn't he just take the phone off the hook? Take everybody off the hook?

"A bargain," Mazzo said finally, drawing his eyes away from the sheet and looking directly at Barney, turning the full force of those brilliant, fevered eyes on him.

"What kind of bargain?"

"Billy wants to use my telephone, right?"

There he goes again, Barney thought, putting his stamp on everything. *My* telephone.

"Right."

"Okay. Every afternoon at two, they wheel me to the third floor for the chemicals. It takes about an hour. During that hour, from two to three, Billy can use the telephone." Mazzo closed his eyes, grimacing a bit, as if the words had cost a huge effort. "But no long-distance calls. Strictly local."

"Right," Barney said, wary now, wondering what Mazzo required in return. Mazzo was not the kind of guy to do anybody favors, especially if they involved Barney Snow.

Silence deepened between them. A door opened and closed in the distance, followed by the whisper of footsteps. Mazzo's machine alternately hummed and bleeped. The curtains were half drawn and Barney stepped away from the bed, receding into half shadow. Mazzo's eyes strayed around the room, looking everywhere but at Barney. Barney waited, patient. It was Mazzo's move. Let him move.

Finally Mazzo sighed again, perspiration dancing on his forehead and cheeks. The sigh carried all the tragedies of the world in it, as if he alone were burdened and nobody else. Take it easy, Barney told himself, take it easy. Mazzo could be dead by this time tomorrow. Or even an hour from now. Let him sigh.

Mazzo reached over to the cluttered table beside his bed, his hand prying among the bottles and tubes and basins. His hand was slender, long fingers bestowing grace on whatever they touched. Those fingers lifted an envelope from the table and extended it toward Barney.

Barney reached for the letter, but Mazzo snatched it back. "Wait a minute," he said. "You don't have to read what's in here. I'll tell you what it says."

Barney caught a glimpse of handwriting on the envelope. Blue ink, delicate and spidery.

"It's from my sister," Mazzo said. "She's coming here to visit me. This afternoon." He held the envelope between thumb and index finger at one corner, as if it were a specimen to be slipped into a plastic folder and used later as evidence. "She's a witch, my sister," he said, a hint of a smile on his face. Not quite a smile, but a softening, a gentling of his features. "She's not really a witch, of course, but she can, like, cast spells over people. Charm them, soften them up. Then come in for the kill." His features hardened again, the ghost of a smile gone. "That's why she's coming here. To soften me up."

"Why does she have to soften you up?" Barney asked.

Mazzo looked annoyed at the question. Then decided to answer.

"She wants to talk me into allowing my mother to visit me here and hold my hand while I check out. That's what she wants." He held the letter toward Barney again. "Smell that?"

Barney sniffed, twitching his nostrils, faking it, not wanting Mazzo to know that his sense of smell was gone.

59

"See?" Mazzo asked. "Nothing. If it smells of anything, it's soap. Good strong soap. No perfume, no cologne. She doesn't use the stuff, doesn't need it."

Mazzo dropped the letter onto his chest, silent again, brooding.

"She sounds spooky," Barney said.

"She is spooky," Mazzo said, but the gentleness was in his face again and his voice caressed the word, turning *spooky* into something beautiful. "She's my twin. Which makes me spooky too, I guess. She's got this one thing she could always do. Twist me around her finger, make me do anything she wants. I thought I was safe from her. She's been away. But now she's out and coming here."

That was the longest speech Barney had ever heard from Mazzo's lips, although he didn't seem to be speaking to Barney at all.

"You say she's out now," Barney said. "Where's she been?"

"Let her tell you if she wants," Mazzo said, turning to Barney as if just discovering his presence here. "The point is that she's coming here. To soften me up for my mother. And that's where you come in, Barney. Where you keep your end of the bargain."

"What do you want me to do?" Barney asked, genuinely puzzled.

"I want you to be here. I don't want to be alone with her. I don't want to give her a chance to work me over, give me the business. I want you here, standing right where you're standing now."

"What good will that do?"

"Let me worry about that."

"What if she doesn't want me here?"

"It's what I want that counts," Mazzo said, the old Mazzo once more, all gentleness gone. "This is my place, not hers. Okay, I have to let her in here. She's my twin sister. I owe her that much. One visit. One shot at me. And then no more." He sank down on the bed, shriveling himself into the sheets, as if trying to make himself disappear. "But I've got to get through that one visit."

"And what do I do?" Barney asked, reluctant to get involved. Especially in a family thing. He wanted to stay in his own compartment and stay out of other people's compartments.

"Just be here. Be here and follow my lead. When she starts getting to me with the old magic, I'll start talking to you. Answer me back. Agree with anything I say. Pretend she's not here."

"This is crazy. I'll feel like a nut."

"It doesn't matter how you feel," Mazzo snapped. "And it isn't crazy." Then slowly, craftily, tauntingly: "Don't you want Billy to use the phone, make his phone calls?" Talking as if Barney were seven or eight years old.

The telephone rang and Mazzo leaped in the bed, as if someone had applied an electric shock. He placed his hand on the phone and held up his other hand to Barney in a traffic-stopping gesture. His lips moved and Barney could see him counting silently: one, two, three . . . Finally he lifted the receiver, pressed it to his ear. Listened grimly, eyes half closed, lips tight, cheeks taut. Then he slowly took the receiver away from his ear and replaced it on the hook. Sank back down on the bed, tugged the sheet up to his neck.

"What was that all about?" Barney asked.

"You ask too many questions."

"I didn't ask to come in here," Barney said. "Talk about spooky. That was spooky what you just did. Answer a phone and not say anything."

"My mother, that's who it was," Mazzo said. Pausing, then: "I told her she could call me once in a while. Only if she didn't say anything. No conversation. She can listen to me breathe. That's all she wants to know, anyway, that I'm still alive."

Mazzo, you bastard.

"Answer me something, Mazzo," Barney said. "How come you get all this special treatment? A telephone in your room. Your mother calling. Your sister coming to visit. Nobody is supposed to have visitors here. What's going on, anyway?"

"Haven't you heard, Barney?" Mazzo asked, the old nastiness back in his voice. "Money talks. And my mother has the money. This place exists on grants, bequests, stuff like that. When she knew I wanted to get in here, she bought my way in. Sat down and wrote a check. Money buys everything."

Barney didn't say anything.

"Well, almost everything," Mazzo amended.

For a moment there Mazzo had seemed like a nice guy, someone you could like.

"Why the hell did you want to buy your way into this place?" Barney asked. "It's not exactly the Ritz."

Barney remembered the Handyman's explanation about why patients came to the Complex. To help mankind, he said. To serve a useful purpose. He had never questioned Billy the Kidney or Allie Roon about their reasons for coming here, not wanting to invade their private compartments, but he sensed a kind of nobility about them, even though they seemed helpless and pathetic most of the time. At least they didn't gripe or complain or bitch the way Mazzo did. What was Mazzo doing here?

"Look, Barney," Mazzo was saying. "Don't worry about me. All you have to worry about is being here when my sister comes. You do that and I'll let Billy use my phone for a week. Every day."

Barney squirmed. Damn it, he had his own problems.

"A week, that's a long time in a place like this," Mazzo said. "A lifetime, maybe."

He knew he couldn't disappoint Billy.

"What time is your sister coming?" Barney asked, giving in.

"At three thirty. After my trip upstairs."

Barney blew air out of the corner of his mouth. "Okay," he said. And wanted to get out of there. He realized that he had a tendency lately to flee from places, from the Handyman's office and the junkyard and his own room and now Mazzo's room.

"What's her name?" Barney asked from the doorway, over his shoulder.

"Cassie," Mazzo said, lifting his head with effort. "We're not identical twins. She's not at all like me."

"Good," Barney said. "That's the best news I've heard all day."

Barney chewed the pencil, frowning, looking down at the pad of paper on the table before him, one of those blue-lined paper schoolroom pads. He wrote his name carefully on the paper, printing the letters, using capitals. BARNEY SNOW. He studied his name for a while and then looked up, contemplating this room that was his home in the Complex.

Not much of a home. Dull green walls, bare of decorations. Venetian blinds admitting slashes of light in an uncurtained window. Steel bed with a gray blanket turned down to reveal part of a once-white sheet. The table at which he sat, a sort of improvised desk, was unadorned, and the single drawer was empty. The brown tile floor had no carpet.

The bureau standing beside the window had been painted a lackluster gray and contained his few possessions—a couple of shirts, socks, underwear, a striped tie, a few paperback books whose titles he couldn't remember, a wristwatch that didn't work anymore. Two jackets—one zippered, the other a sports type of jacket—hung in the closet along with two pairs of trousers. He had arrived here traveling light, bringing very little from that other place. That other place. He didn't want to think about it. Tempo, rhythm. Think of here and now.

There's so little of me here, he thought, and realized how easily his entire existence could be obliterated along with his memory.

He fumbled in his trousers for his wallet and didn't find it, remembering now that he had turned the wallet and his money—four one-dollar bills and some change—over to the Handyman for safekeeping on his arrival. No need for money here, the Handyman had said.

A wallet, however, would provide proof of identity. He remembered filling in the identity card that came with the wallet. But without it he had nothing to prove who he was. Suppose he woke up somewhere upstairs, his memory wiped away, not knowing his name, not knowing who he was?

Chewing the pencil again, imprinting his toothmarks on the yellow surface, he thought: Maybe I'd better write down my age, too. If they wiped away his name, they'd probably wipe away other things as well. Barney printed his age: 17. Well, not really his age. He wouldn't be seventeen until July, but this was close enough.

He added his weight: 134.

And his height: 5'6".

He decided this was enough. It was the kind of information that would spring to his lips if anybody asked him who he was. It was also the kind of basic information he would need to jog his memory into remembering other things if the experiment went wrong.

Satisfied, he folded the piece of paper carefully in half, tore it along the folded edge. Folded it again and tore it once more. Then again, until there remained a small square upon which he'd written the information. He then folded this piece of paper a final time, reducing it to the size of a postage stamp, making it easier to hide.

Next problem: where to hide it?

He looked around the room slowly, considering possible hiding places. The closet? Under the mattress? Wait—the bureau. In the pocket of one of his shirts. . . .

The absurdity of the situation struck him. If he hid the paper somewhere in this room, how could he remember where if they took away his memory?

Damn it.

He was disgusted with himself. He was slipping, losing his grip.

Forget it, toss the ridiculous little piece of paper away.

But he couldn't.

He didn't entirely trust the Handyman's experiments, aware that there was always an element of risk. He had to do something in the face of this latest risk. Leave evidence of his identity behind, someplace, *someplace* where he could find it if things went wrong. In case they wiped his memory away and couldn't bring it back.

It would be terrible to wake up and not know your name, not know who you were.

Rhythm, tempo. Let the blood flow.

Come on. Where could he hide the paper? Someplace out of sight but easy to find.

Now a new possibility appalled him. Suppose they didn't take him back here but kept him upstairs, in isolation? What good would a hidden note in his room be?

And then the solution came. Simple, beautiful.

He'd carry this small square of paper with him. On his person. His body.

Wait a minute, let's be logical now. Start from the beginning. He'd be wearing certain articles of clothing during the treatment if standard procedure was followed. A green "Johnny" that buttoned in the back and came to your knees. Shorts, no undershirt. No place to hide anything. He remembered spy stories in which secret agents swallowed pieces of paper containing important information. Which was impossible in this case, of course, pointless.

He looked down at his body, a body he had never taken any pride in before he came to the Complex, too aware of his shortcomings, the slightly bowed legs, his arms too long for his height. But here, compared to the others wasting away, whose bodies were deteriorating day by day, he had felt good about himself for the first time, realizing that even beauty, like Mazzo's, wasn't any use if you couldn't live.

Barney drew up his shirtsleeve, saw the array of puncture wounds from the needles. A Band-Aid covered the most recent puncture. And Barney suddenly saw the perfect hiding place for the small piece of paper: under a Band-Aid. He would fold the paper until it was small enough to fit beneath the small bandage, the feel of the paper certain to call attention to itself when he awoke. There was a chance that the doctor might discover it first, but he had to take that chance. And he'd reduce the risk of discovery by applying the Band-Aid to the inside of his thigh. Or some other place. Between his toes, maybe?

He had a feeling that this act of subterfuge would prove futile, that it was impossible to fool the Handyman. But it was worth trying. Sitting here in this forlorn room, he felt almost as if he didn't exist. But at least he could cling to his identity, his name, and do something about it.

"I am Barney Snow," he said aloud, enunciating carefully.

His voice echoed in the air.

There was no answering voice to say: Yes, you are Barney Snow.

6

*H*ERE she comes," Mazzo said.

Barney heard heels clicking in the corridor. Ordinarily, the passage of feet in the halls of the Complex was quiet, muted, footsteps like whispers as patients and staff ghosted by in rubber-soled shoes or slippers. But the heels he heard now were like small staccato shouts, alien in this place, threatening somehow.

Barney stood away from Mazzo's bed, his back to the window. The open venetian blinds laddered the room with sunlight, filling it with a false kind of cheer. Barney squinted, studied the apprehension on Mazzo's face. He should be happy to see Mazzo looking worried, but Barney himself didn't exactly feel at ease. He didn't want to be caught in the crossfire between Mazzo and his sister.

The sound of heels grew closer, a rhythm established, as if she were the drum majorette in an invisible parade. Then the footsteps faltered, became uncertain, and stopped altogether just outside the door. Was she gathering her wits to prepare herself for the meeting with her dying brother? The silence continued, and Barney heard, in the silence, the sound of Mazzo's quick sharp breaths.

Barney blinked, and as if by magic, Mazzo's sister stood

in the doorway. Her beauty struck him like a physical blow. Or like a small explosion deep inside him, shifting his bones and muscles and tissues the way earth is moved deep below by a shock wave. His first impression was of blue everything: dark-blue blazer, powder-blue sweater, eyes startling blue, not the cold and distant blue of the sky but a warm melting blue. Those eyes swept the room, resting for a moment on Mazzo, the bedside paraphernalia of basins and tubes, the machine to which Mazzo was attached, and finally Barney. He lost himself in those eyes, felt lifted and exalted. Maybe she was a witch, after all. Her short blond hair, almost boyishly short, caught the sunlight and spun it into gold.

She regarded Barney with a sad kind of amusement, shaking her head slightly. "I know who you are," she said, her voice surprisingly low and husky.

Barney was startled. His cheeks grew warm, his heart bounced crazily in his chest. He wanted to say: "Who am I?" As if she knew secrets he didn't know. But he didn't say anything, felt he'd stammer like Allie Roon if he tried to talk.

Mazzo rescued him. "And I know who you are," Mazzo said to her. "You're the same old Cassie. But what did you do to your hair?"

She turned away from Barney and directed her attention to Mazzo. Barney, too, looked at Mazzo, surprised at the tenderness in his voice when he spoke to his sister. A different Mazzo suddenly.

She ignored the question about her hair, shrugging slightly as if an answer wasn't worth giving. Leaning forward a bit, she studied his wan figure in the bed as if trying to determine whether this was really her brother or an imposter.

"You don't look so bad," she said, the sultry voice emerging again, like the voice of a blues singer Barney had heard one time on the radio. "You've lost some weight. Your eyes look like you're on something. But you look pretty good, considering."

"I'm dying, for Christ's sake," Mazzo said. "So it doesn't matter how I look. How I look has nothing to do with it." But this wasn't the old Mazzo talking. This new Mazzo used the same old bitter words, but when he spoke them to his sister, they were softened somehow, gentled.

"I was just trying to cheer you up," she replied. "Would it make you feel better if I said you look terrible, that it's hard to believe you used to score touchdowns and hit home runs for good old Stanley Prep?"

Her own voice had a kind of bantering now, matching Mazzo's new voice—the voice Barney had never heard before—and it seemed to him that Mazzo's and Cassie's voices were more important to them than the words they used, the voices like a code between them.

Barney studied them as they talked. They were twins, of course, and bore a certain resemblance to each other. Both blond, fair skinned, Cassie beautiful and Mazzo handsome although the disease had ravaged his flesh and features. Mazzo lay in ruins, like someone beaten and robbed and left abandoned, while Cassie's beauty was vibrant and compelling. Barney felt younger suddenly than his sixteen years. Mazzo and Cassie were probably twenty or so, but Barney felt like a kid beside them. God, he wished that he was older.

"Time for introductions," Mazzo said, calling to Barney, summoning him from his thoughts. "Barney, this is my sister, Cassie."

"Hello, Barney," she said, glancing at him. Then back to

70

Mazzo: "Still up to your old tricks, aren't you, Alberto?"

"What old tricks?"

She laughed, a throaty kind of laugh, as husky as her voice.

Looking at Barney again—God, she was beautiful—she said: "You see, Barney, Alberto's always needed a buffer. Even as a kid in school. He'd get into trouble and bring some kid home with him." To Mazzo again: "Remember the time you totaled Papa's Porsche the day after he bought it? Lucky you weren't killed. And when you came home that day, you brought home some kid you'd met in the emergency room at the hospital. Your buffer. Like your friend here."

Mazzo closed his eyes. "God, how I loved to drive," he said wistfully. "Nothing better, Cassie, than sitting behind the wheel, top down, the motor throbbing, the wind whistling by. The road before me and the car eating it up. The Porsche and the TR6 . . ."

"You wrecked the TR6, too," she said, mock-scolding him.

They had forgotten Barney now, caught up in each other, and Barney felt out of place, like a spy eavesdropping, listening to secrets.

"I shouldn't be dying in bed, Cassie," Mazzo said. "I should have died before all this happened to me, bombing down the Mass. Pike, ninety miles an hour. And then boom. In a blaze of glory. Not like this."

And now he was the Mazzo that Barney knew. Bitter and resentful. But why not? "This rotten place with its stink and crap. And I'm part of the stink and the crap."

"Take it easy, Alberto," she said. "Take it easy." Moving to his bedside, removing her jacket at the same time. Her movements were thrillingly sexual to Barney, the way she raised her arms, the fullness of her breasts, the lips wet and slightly parted. He had not been aroused, had not felt a longing for a girl, for such a long time that he couldn't remember when. Sex was absent from the Complex; no place here for love or lust or desire. Cassie Mazzofono brought it all back, however. The old stirring again, but the stirring mixed with an aching, because a girl had never loved him. He had a dim memory of kissing a girl at a party, but he'd never really held a girl in his arms, never caressed a breast or darted his tongue between parted lips to meet another tongue. In his bed at night, yes. Vivid images conjured up. Playboy centerfolds recalled. But never in reality. Looking at Cassie now, he felt the old aching, along with a new sadness. And wasn't sure why. But did know, really, although he hated to acknowledge it. The *why*: knowing he could never attract a girl like Cassie Mazzofono. Not a girl like that. He meant nothing to her: why should he? He was only a buffer, a stooge. She'd barely glanced at him. Probably wouldn't recognize him if she met him in the hallway tomorrow.

"I suppose Mother sent you here," Mazzo was saying. "What is it, a plot of some kind?"

"We're not in a conspiracy, if that's what you mean. She told me to tell you that she loves you. But you already know that."

"Do I?"

"Yes. You should. She doesn't want to interfere in your life. What you've got left of your life. She finds it hard to let you go. She finds it hard to accept what's happening to you. But if you keep giving her the cold shoulder, she'll find it impossible, Alberto."

Alberto. To Barney he'd always been Mazzo, always

would be. As if nobody in the world but Cassie had the right to call him Alberto.

"Don't try to con me, Cassie. Don't try to soften me up," Mazzo said. "It won't work."

Red blotches had appeared on his face, angry blotches, as if the anger in his words was being expressed by his body, the way pictures in a book illustrate the text.

"Where was she when we needed her?" Mazzo said. "Caught up in her own little world of the country club. What she did to Papa, who wouldn't hurt a soul on earth. She killed him, Cassie."

"He died of a heart attack," Cassie said.

"Screw the idea of a heart attack. He died because he was stabbed in the heart. By what she did. Divorcing him like that."

Cassie blew air out of the corner of her mouth, patient, as if she were saying words she'd said a thousand times.

"We can't be the judges, Alberto," she said. "We don't know what it was like for them. Somehow the marriage fell apart. And then Papa died. Nobody can prove there was a connection. They were like night and day. Maybe they shouldn't have married in the first place. But they did. And we were born. She's our mother. We're her children. Twins, for God's sake. And we almost killed her when we were born. I found out later that she almost died."

"There's no *almost* in my case, kid," Mazzo said. "Look, I was a good son to her for a long time. But the rules are changed now. I don't want her around for my final moments. I don't want anybody around."

"Does that include me?" Cassie asked.

"Yes," Mazzo said, the word no louder than the sound a leaf makes touching earth after tumbling from a tree.

I've got to get out of here, Barney thought. I don't want to be listening to this.

As if she had read his mind—a touch of the witch, maybe—Cassie Mazzofono turned toward him and said: "Why don't you go?" Not a question, not a suggestion, but an order. Delivered gently but an order just the same.

Barney looked at Mazzo, but Mazzo was up to his old trick, studying the sheet as if he could find answers there, as if the world didn't exist outside the bed he occupied. In the absence of any protest from Mazzo, he felt free to go, having kept his end of the bargain.

Yet as he moved toward the door, he felt a sense of loss. And something else. He didn't want to leave without saying something to Cassie Mazzofono, anything, establishing himself as a person in her eyes. As Barney Snow. Not just a stooge, a buffer.

He waited for something to happen as he arrived at the door. An intervention. Mazzo calling back or Cassie curious about him: *What did you say your last name was?* But he knew that nothing would happen. He was a cipher in their lives, zero, nothing. He took a good long look at her. But her eyes were on Mazzo. He left the room without saying good-bye. They probably wouldn't have heard him anyway.

At the far end of the corridor he found Billy the Kidney waiting. Out of his wheelchair, leaning against the wall. Eyes flashing with more than pain.

Billy told him that Ronson was dead, had died suddenly in Isolation, all functions ceasing even as the nurses monitored the actions and reactions of his body.

Ronson was in the Ice Age forever.

7

"WHO is that masked man?" Barney asked, trying to keep it light, to cover his nervousness as he sat in the barber's chair.

"Not the Lone Ranger," the Handyman answered behind his own mask. Barney was surprised that someone like the Handyman had even heard of the Lone Ranger. He never connected the Handyman with the world outside the Complex. "Actually, Barney, this is Dr. Croft, whom I told you about. He will carry on the demonstration."

Demonstration, Barney noted. Instead of *experiment* or *test.*

Dr. Croft loomed over Barney and the chair, a tall thin man, face hidden by the surgical mask. Except for his eyes, which were gray and flat and expressionless.

"You are in good hands," the Handyman said from somewhere to his right. Barney couldn't see him now and did not move his head. Could not move his head. His head was enclosed in a kind of helmet, doodads connected to his temples. The chair was not a barber's chair, of course, and resembled a dentist's chair more than anything else but wasn't that, either. Straps bound Barney's arms and legs.

75

He'd felt a surge of claustrophobia when his arms were first pinned down but fought the feeling of being trapped, letting the blood flow, tempo, rhythm.

"This is for your protection," the Handyman had explained. "We have secured your arms and legs to keep you stationary." As usual, Barney figured, the Handyman was using words like *secured* and *stationary* as a smokescreen, more double-talk, and he let it pass, wanting to get it over with, whatever the Handyman and Dr. Croft had in mind.

"Let me tell you what is going to happen, my boy," the Handyman said. "Dr. Croft will administer a drug. A routine injection in your left arm. You will grow drowsy, a not unpleasant sensation, and then fall asleep. While you are asleep, we will administer other drugs. These you will not feel or know about. You will not be in this chair at that time. You will become conscious in sixty minutes. In a room on this same floor. You will be under observation for a period of forty-five minutes. You will then be interrogated for perhaps thirty minutes or so, depending on your responses. You will then sleep again for several hours, the sleep induced by the introduction of a final drug into your system. You will be in no physical danger. There will be no distress of any kind." He recited all this as if reading from a blackboard to a backward pupil.

"During the questioning," Barney asked, "will I know who I am?" Barney wriggled his toes and felt the small wad of paper he had hidden under the Band-Aid in the crease next to his big toe on his right foot. He felt good, knowing the slip of paper was there. Felt crafty and clever. Gave him confidence and lessened the panic he ordinarily felt when new merchandise was injected.

"I will know who you are, Barney. I will be questioning you."

"You didn't answer my question, doctor," Barney said, feeling a flicker of panic now despite the Band-Aid.

"You always said to spare you details, Barney. I was only complying with your wishes."

"I don't want all the details. I just want to know if I'll remember anything. Like my name."

"You will not remember your name. But consider this: You will also not remember not knowing your name. When you finally awaken after the demonstration is over, you will not remember the interrogation. But you will awaken with a sense of well-being, as if you have emerged from a long, restful sleep."

Barney swallowed, his throat dry, mouth parched. "Like when someone's been hypnotized?"

"Exactly," the Handyman said. "You must remember, my boy, what I promised when you first came here. We never demand more of you than you can provide or sustain. We know your capacities from earlier tests. We know how far to go, how long to go. You must trust me in this."

Now Dr. Croft stood before him, the masked man, gray eyes, bushy eyebrows. "You'll be just fine," he said, in a Texas drawl slightly muffled by the mask. "Try to relax, boy."

Somehow the doctor's accent, bringing back the memory of a thousand cowboy movies, took the edge off Barney's concern. He closed his eyes, let his body sag and go limp, submitting himself to whatever was needed as he always did, loosening his bones and muscles, feeling himself drifting, drifting, softly, gently.

The prick of the needle was like a dart hitting his flesh.

He waited, eyes still shut.

Heard the beating of his heart like a punching bag hit by a boxer.

His hands clutched the arms of the chair, fingernails digging into the plastic or leather or whatever it was.

Then, it came.

First the roaring. From far off, like a storm gathering or a tidal wave forming or a volcano rumbling just before it erupts.

The sound coming closer. Like a thousand jets rocketing through the air, shattering windows. And Barney, thinking ridiculously, I'm glad I don't wear glasses.

The roaring increased.

Not the passing jets now.

The roaring nearby. Close. Inside him.

I am roaring.

He began to spin and needed to open his eyes, to see what was happening, but he couldn't. He found it impossible to make his eyelids move.

And suddenly he was glad he couldn't, because he began to spin. Still sitting in the chair, strapped in, but spinning all the same. Spinning and whirling and, wow, twisting, too. In the air, here, everywhere. Body melting and flowing and always moving, moving.

He was glad that he was fastened in the chair. Otherwise he'd be actually flying through the air.

But wait.

That's what he was doing.

Off and away.

Swirling and twirling, like he was orbiting the planet in a dizzying, dazzling flight.

Then

he

tumbled

into

oblivion. . . .

8

THE boy opened his eyes. There had been an explosion of light but no aftermath of smoke and rubble, the way there would be in a real explosion. For a moment the light was blinding, and he raised his hand to protect his eyes, blinking furiously. Then the light became less intense, not blinding anymore, regular daylight. Funny, there were no blind spots in his vision, the way it usually happens when a flashbulb pops or you look at the sun too long. Then he knew why, of course. The explosion of light had occurred inside him, not outside.

He was glad to find that he could move his head, and was surprised that this small act pleased him so much. He looked around cautiously, warily, and wondered why he should be so cautious. Nothing threatened him here. He was in an ordinary room, chairs placed against three of the walls, a coffee table holding various magazines and two glass ashtrays in the shape of maple leaves. Like a doctor's or dentist's waiting room. Impersonal. No one had ever lived here. An oval mirror on the wall to his right reflected a painting on the wall to his left. The painting showed a mountain scene, flat, without distinction, like a picture on a calendar. His couch faced the door, which was closed. A television set stood in the center of the room. Not a television set, really: There were no dials or switches. A monitor, then. The screen was dull green and blank.

He felt as if he should get up from the couch and test his body, to see if his arms and legs and the rest of him were in good order. He didn't know why he felt he had to do this. But something vague and elusive troubled him. The way it happens when you awaken from a bad dream and don't remember what the dream was but know it was terrible, threatening, leaving a shadow over your life.

Placing his feet tenderly on the floor, he stood up. He wriggled his toes in the slippers. The slippers were gray and fitted him tightly, almost like socks. Standing up, he was suddenly weak and giddy and his head began to throb. He sat himself down again, slowly, letting the sections of his body change positions to accommodate the sitting posture. He knew at once what was the matter. He felt like his body was in separate sections, held together loosely, was aware of his arms and legs being distinct from his torso, and his head a further extension of his body. Each of the separate parts connected by bones and tissues and muscles and veins and arteries. He didn't like to think of all those connections. Suppose somehow they ceased to work, became disconnected? Would his arms and legs drop off, clatter to the floor, and lie there in disarray? Ridiculous, of course. They would not fall off, but they could cease to function, something wrong with the connections, like a telephone out of order but still connected to the wires.

He tried not to move, did not want to disturb the network of elements that held his body together, even though he knew nothing could happen. He just didn't want to take a chance. He might get a headache. It felt good not to have a headache; he had a dim memory of a blinding headache just a moment ago when the light had exploded in his eyes.

The room was chilly. His eyes sought a thermostat but found none. The color of the walls was orange, but a soft orange, soothing to his eyes, a sort of brown orange, dull brown, not brown really but beige, a muted kind of beige, so muted that it was almost colorless, certainly nothing as vivid as orange; why had he thought the walls were orange when clearly they were almost without color, bland, blank, except for the mirror and the painting?

He waited for someone to come in the door, to swing the door open and greet him. He would bet any amount of money that someone would come in at any moment now and explain all this and tell him he could go. He turned his head, left to right and then right to left again, appealing to the walls. Go where? He had a feeling he was being observed by the walls or someone on the other side of the walls with the power to observe him, and they could answer the question.

Where would he want to go, anyway? An answer to the question presented itself, inside him, inside his head. He could feel the answer coming and then another question but he didn't want the answer to come, didn't want to go inside, didn't want to probe. He didn't want to close his eyes, either, because he wanted to be here, here and now, in this room, with familiar things he could identify: chairs, magazines, the mirror, the painting, the coffee table, the monitor. He would check the magazines later to see what kind they were. He could see them clearly from this couch, but he did not care to identify them at this moment because he would have to squint his eyes to make out the names and faces on the covers and he didn't want to take a chance with his eyes or any part of his body at the moment. He would simply sit here and wait and not move, and certainly he would not go inside himself.

The monitor hummed and the screen glowed with a soft

light at the edges and then a bright blankness. A face emerged from the blankness. The face filled the entire screen. The face and the ears and the black hair and mustache and beard. The neck disappeared somewhere out of sight below the monitor, invisible, extending probably to the floor and through it to the ceiling of the room below and then through *that*. It amused him to think that.

"Hello," the face said. Not the face but the mouth of the face. The lips moving.

He looked without recognition at the face, knowing it well all the same, feeling secure now that he wasn't alone in the room anymore. No one had come through the door, but the man on the monitor was as good as someone actually in the room.

"Hello," he answered.

"How are you feeling?" The voice of the monitor was well modulated, even, not loud or soft but just right.

"I'm feeling fine," he said, but the response was automatic, wanting to please the man and win his approval. He didn't want to think of his body or about how he was actually feeling. That would mean going inside, and he didn't want to go inside.

"No discomfort?"

"No."

"No distress?"

For some reason he wanted to laugh. No discomfort, no distress. The idea of no discomfort and no distress amused him very much, although he did not know why.

"You look just fine," the face said.

Puzzled, he asked: "Can you see me?"

"Yes." The face nodded. The entire head joined the nod.

"How?"

This was his first question. He really did not want to ask questions. It seemed important not to ask questions.

Maybe just this one question. But no others. Because one could lead to another and another. And he didn't want to start asking things. Danger lay that way. Asking things and going inside himself, which also was a danger.

"We have many methods of scrutiny. Of observation. You know that, don't you?"

He nodded in agreement. Of course he knew. He didn't know how he knew, but he was certain that he did. It wasn't important to put it into words or even to think about it much. The knowledge was there, inside him. He could check out the knowledge if he wanted to, but that would mean going inside and he resisted the impulse. He wanted to stay outside. Definitely.

The man spoke again: "I am about to present you with three words. And I wish you to react. It doesn't matter how you react. You won't be judged by your reaction, but it is important that you do so."

He was eager to react, to please, to keep the conversation going. He concentrated on the face on the monitor screen, concentrated on the lips, watching for the small dartings of the tongue when he spoke.

"Go ahead," he said.

"Snow," the mouth said.

"White," he answered, quickly, distinctly, proud of his swift answer.

The face was blank, waiting. Wasn't *white* enough? He paused, knowing he would have to go inside to think of more answers. But he didn't have to go far: The answer was there at the top, close to *white*.

"Rain," he said eagerly, watching for the reaction, but the face was still blank, no expression, a kind of waiting in the eyes. Ah, the eyes. Now for the first time he noticed the eyes. He had been concentrating on the mouth and the lips and the sly appearances of the tongue because the voice had been important. But now he realized the eyes were important, too. The eyes could speak. A silent language, but they could speak, after all. He looked at the eyes now, studying them, brilliant and green but also cold and remote.

"Rain," he repeated, to give himself time to go inside just a little, just a little bit, just to dip under the surface to bring up enough to satisfy the doctor.

"Cold, doctor," he said.

The doctor's eyes glowed suddenly, their brilliance intensified. He had hit pay dirt, said something that had caused the doctor to react. He felt proud. He said it again: "Cold." That had been the word the doctor had been waiting for. *White* hadn't been right and neither had *rain*. But *cold* had done it.

But now something disturbed him, something from inside him, and he was afraid he would have to go deeper inside to find out what it was. He didn't know what it was. But it frightened him. *Cold.* He tosssed the word about in his mind like a ball he was juggling, and the picture amused him, the amusement holding off the other thing beneath the surface. And then, of course, he saw what it was: *doctor.* He had said *Cold, doctor.* The man on the screen was a doctor, although it was impossible to tell from looking at him. There were no clues. He did not know whether he wore a doctor's uniform or not because he could see only the face. What did doctors wear anyway? In here the color was green, the surgical gowns were always green. In here . . .

"The second word."

"Yes," he said, grateful for the doctor's voice. He'd been about to go inside but the voice had stopped him.

"Car."

"Automobile."

The doctor merely looked at him, blank again, the eyes without any signal, any clue about whether *automobile* was right or wrong. But if he'd been right, then the eyes would have glowed again, and so he felt he was wrong and he tried for another word, but cautiously, as if his brain was tiptoeing.

"Tires," he said.

The doctor waited.

"Hill."

Blink. Saw a hill distinctly. Wet pavement. Motor roaring. Blink. Inside the car: him. At the wheel. Rain on the windshield. Blink. Blink again. Nothing.

But something.

The doctor stared at him from the monitor. He didn't like the way the doctor stared at him. There was something in the stare that gave him the willies, the chills.

"Am I doing all right, doctor?" he asked, his voice small in his ears, almost a whisper so that he wasn't sure the doctor had heard him.

"You are doing just fine," the doctor said, his voice reassuring.

"Was *hill* the right answer?" he asked.

"There are no right answers or wrong answers, Barney," the doctor said.

Barney nodded, glad to hear that he could not possibly fail the test.

"Close your eyes, Barney. Relax."

Barney did as the doctor asked. He closed his eyes, his eyelids fluttering a bit before they settled down. The eyelids were heavy now, pressing down on his eyes.

"Try to sleep, Barney," the doctor said, the words reaching Barney separately, apart from each other, *try,* and the pause in between as *try* lingered in the air and then *to* sounding big and hollow like a stone being dropped into a chasm from far above, echoing as it struck bottom deep below, *sleep*, booming in his ears, like a big drum struck by a huge hammer, and then *Barney*, the name like a shout from afar. *Barney, Barney*, somebody calling him to come outside and play after supper in the soft summer night in the school yard, *Barney, Barney*, the voice far-away, faraway, fading.

But who is Barney?

Barney who?

The name raced in his mind, unattached to anything, like a word in a foreign language he didn't know. Barney, Barney. Panic caused his flesh to quiver, the small hairs to raise on his arms and legs. He was afraid to open his eyes. Yet he wanted to open them in order to get outside, outside himself; otherwise he would be trapped here inside, inside where the terrible thing lurked, the thing he knew was there but could not put a name to, the question he was afraid of asking.

Barney who?

Not that question.

What question?

Who am I?

Worse: What am I?

His eyes flew open and he stared in horror at the room in which he found himself: the chairs against the walls, the closed door, the mirror reflecting the painting, the blank television screen in front of him. The room was like that painting: flat, two dimensional, as if he could reach out and touch the wall across the room from him by barely extending his hand. What am I doing here? Where do I belong? He looked down to check out his arms and his chest and stomach, lifted his hands to inspect them, looking for clues maybe. He wanted to look into the mirror but didn't think he could rise from the couch without falling, his legs untrustworthy, certain to buckle and let him plunge to the floor, where he would stay forever.

I am me . . . me . . . the word screaming inside him as if from eternity. He was out of context with the world—what was the world? What was this room? What was he here?—not *who* but what? *What was he?* This was the source of his terror, the horror that whistled in him like winds howling in a tunnel.

He was alone, cast adrift, lost, unrelated to anything. He shut his eyes again, pressed to keep them shut, raised his hands to his eyes to keep them shut, feeling his body trembling, staring into a vast emptiness that was as bad as this alien room he was in, trying to hold on, afraid he was being swept out to space, separated from earth, defying gravity, crashing through the orbit to limits past anything known . . .

. . . and then he was in the car again, at the wheel, slanting down the street, the rain pounding on the windshield, glistening on the pavements, the motor roaring in his ears, a siren now sounding in the night, the hill slanting crazily, dizzyingly before him, his foot on the brake pedal but the car still rushing downhill until he saw her again stepping out from the curb, her face turned to him for the first time and he bent forward to see that face even as he screamed for her to *Look out, look out* until he crashed into a mirror that broke into a thousand fragments, sending pieces of himself, splintered and jagged, across the face of the night.

9

*H*E awakened as if from a long and restful sleep, stretching his arms and legs luxuriously, yawning mightily and lazily, a small part of him unwilling to leave that sweet dark haven.

Opening his eyes, he saw Billy the Kidney in his wheelchair near the bed, bending forward, concern on his face.

"You okay, Barney?" Billy asked.

Barney grinned, filled with a sense of well-being. Most days he woke up from troubled sleep with memories of that car slanting down the hill or haunted by dreams he couldn't quite remember but that left him uneasy and apprehensive.

"Sure, I'm okay," he said. Noticing the furrow of worry wrinkling Billy's forehead, he said, "What's the matter? You look like you've seen a ghost or something."

"I was worried, that's all," Billy said, rocking the wheelchair back and forth. "I mean, after what happened to Ronson. And then you with the new medicine. They kept you upstairs two whole days."

Now it was Barney's turn to frown, as he pondered the lost days and hours. He closed his eyes and saw the masked face of Dr. Croft and those gray expressionless eyes looking down at him. And he remembered spinning off into dark terrifying depths. Out of the darkness came that strange restorative sleep.

"Two days?" Barney said. "It was supposed to be only a few hours." Had he slept for, like, forty-eight hours? No wonder he felt rested.

"Bascam said everything was going along fine," Billy said, "but you never can tell about her. You sure you're okay, Barney?"

"Fit as a fiddle," he said, keeping his apprehension under control, not wanting Billy to become upset. "Tell me about Ronson."

"There's not much to tell, Barney. He died and they took his body away. One minute he was here and the next gone." Billy's voice mournful, doleful.

Barney was about to say *Poor Ronson* but didn't. Maybe Ronson was better off now, wherever he was. Anyway, he was irritated by Billy's sorrowful face and voice. He was tired of sadness, death, and dying.

"Come on, Billy," he said. "Cheer up. Maybe Ronson right this minute is boxing away someplace, winning the championship." Ridiculous, of course, stupid, but Billy nodded in agreement, like a small child satisfied with a fairy tale at bedtime. "Tell me about the phone. Did you get to use it?"

Billy nodded, eyes flashing, easily diverted.

"Yesterday. Mazzo didn't have his treatment the day before."

"Who did you call?"

Billy turned shyly away. "Oh, a few people. I called the police department and told them I was a stranger in town and needed to look up some long-lost relatives. I gave them some names of streets, said I was parked on Main Street, and the cop told me how to find the streets I wanted, starting from the center of town. I kept him talking, oh, about ten minutes, I guess, although he was interrupted once or twice when his other phone rang. I could hear the police radio in the background, voices and static and stuff. It was kind of nice."

He fell silent, still shy, and Barney waited patiently.

"Then I tried a few wrong numbers. Tried to get a few conversations going but no soap. Then I hit pay dirt. I got an old lady on the phone. I asked to speak to Gladys. Gladys was the name of a lady in one of the foster homes who used to buy me candy. Anyway, this old lady's name was Gladys, too. She said nobody ever calls her, she keeps the telephone for emergency purposes, in case she has to call a doctor or the police. She said she almost dropped when she heard someone calling for her, not calling for her exactly but using her name. We talked for ten or fifteen minutes at least. She was some talker. Told me her whole history. She was born in Iowa. . . ."

Barney tuned him out, the way he did sometimes with the Handyman, because as Billy talked he began to get flashes, swift sudden images in his mind, the way pieces of dreams occur later in the day, long after you've awakened. Not only images—the disembodied face of the Handyman, an office with a dentist's chair, a television screen that was blank but somehow threatening—but the aura of the dream or whatever it was, a feeling of being lost and alone, panic shouting through his veins and arteries, as if he had been abandoned by the rest of the world on a bleak, uninhabited planet out in space somewhere. The images passed quickly before his mind's eye, like a series of doors being opened slightly and closed swiftly to allow only a glimpse of what was beyond and even that glimpse gone before he could tell what it was. Then the flashes stopped, the final door slammed shut for good, the panicky feeling gone, and he was here again with Billy, who was still talking about the old lady named Gladys.

Billy's face darkened now as he talked. "Then I asked her if I could call again because it was nice talking to her, like talking to my own grandmother and there was this long pause and when she spoke again she sounded suspicious and began to ask me questions about myself and what could I tell her? I mean, I'm a rotten liar and I couldn't tell her the truth, so I kind of stammered and didn't know what the hell to say and she yelled at me. Young man, she said, what are you after? Are you trying to put something over on an old lady? And she slammed the phone in my ear."

Christ, Barney thought, does everything have to turn out lousy all the time?

"How about Dial-A-Prayer?" Barney asked. "Or Dial-A-Diet?"

"They're not in the book anymore," Billy said, looking away from Barney and then back again and fooling with the wheels. "I wasn't going to tell you about the old lady, Barney, and how it turned out that way. I mean, I appreciate the way you got the phone for me." Pause, spin of wheels. Then: "I'm not going to use the phone anymore. I should have known better. That was okay when I was a kid, but not now. . . ."

A shadow fell across the doorway. Barney looked up to see Bascam standing there. He was glad to see her, to have her interrupt Billy's sad lament, and felt instantly guilty.

"Dr. Lakendorp wants to see you," she said. Face as blank as a mannequin's in a store window.

Barney got out of bed, eager to get away from Billy and also eager to see the Handyman, to find out about those fugitive hours. As he placed his feet on the floor, he remembered the Band-Aid he had attached to his foot.

Wriggled his toes now. Discovered the Band-Aid was not there. He was a bit shaky as he stood up, and he felt Billy watching him warily. Bascam helped him with his slippers, kneeling stiffly before him, and then assisted him with his bathrobe. As he turned, a flash: The masked doctor bending over him, eyes as flat and emotionless as those of a fish in a tank in an aquarium. He blinked, flash gone, doctor's face vanished.

Bascam did not offer any further assistance and he was grateful. He followed her down the corridor to the elevator, gaining strength as he went along, tempo, rhythm, letting his blood flow free.

The Handyman extended his hand in greeting and Barney realized immediately that it wasn't merely a greeting. He looked down at what had been deposited in his hand in a swift deft movement: the Band-Aid and the crinkled piece of paper containing the notations of his identity.

"Clever of you, Barney."

Barney looked away sheepishly, realizing he could never outwit the Handyman.

"You are very resourceful."

Barney blossomed with the compliment, having detected a note of admiration in the Handyman's voice. Which he had never heard before.

He motioned Barney to seat himself. Barney shoved the Band-Aid and the piece of paper into the pocket of his robe. Settled himself in the chair and awaited the Handyman's verdict.

"How did I do?" Barney asked finally, breaking the silence, the Handyman having outwaited him.

"You did fine, my boy," the Handyman said. "It was we, perhaps, who were amiss."

Amiss. A strange, goose-bumpy word. What did he mean by it?

"We miscalculated."

Miscalculated. A word worse than amiss. Don't tell me any more, Barney wanted to say, while knowing that he had to hear more, had to find out what the Handyman meant.

"You mean by having me out for two days instead of a few hours?" Barney prompted. By *out* meaning lost, blank, a cipher.

"Yes. That. Although I must admit that we decided to administer additional sedatives to keep you immobile for a while."

"Why was that necessary?" Barney asked.

"At one point during the questioning you exhibited signs of anxiety."

More word games.

"You mean I panicked?"

"We did not realize we would be so successful. You are an admirable subject, Barney, with perfect responses. Because of this, we detained you perhaps too long. The neurons involved—"

Barney stopped him. A word like *neurons* set off alarm bells in his body. "In plain English, doctor."

"Yes, of course," the Handyman said apologetically. "We are seeking to determine whether memory control can be pinpointed, whether one facet of memory can be removed while others are not. In other words, a carefully selected erasure. In fact, think of this therapy as erasing part of a video tape."

"Were you successful, doctor?" Barney asked, feeling beads of perspiration gathering on his forehead and the back of his neck.

"Eminently," the Handyman said. "During questioning—which, of course, you cannot remember and are not meant to remember—the control was precise. To an astonishing degree, my boy."

"Why did I begin to panic?"

"You became fatigued. We were so caught up in your responses that we extended the interrogation beyond our original schedule. We then made a judgment that you needed a transitional period before being restored to normalcy."

All these words gave Barney the chills, caused the sweat on his flesh to turn cold.

"Am I normal now?"

"Completely, Barney," the Handyman said heartily. "I must point out, however, that there will be aftermaths."

As if the Handyman possessed some terrible power of suggestion, Barney was suddenly swept with dizziness, the desk between them shifting as sands shift in a windstorm. He grabbed the edge of the desk for support, afraid he might pitch forward.

The Handyman moved quickly. Up from the chair and around the desk, quicker than Barney had thought it was possible for him to move. Barney felt strong hands grip his shoulders.

"Vertigo?"

The Handyman's voice boomed in his ear.

"More than that," Barney managed to gasp, gripping the desk tightly, seeing his knuckles turn bluish white.

"What, my boy?"

"I can't remember all of a sudden," Barney said.

"Can't remember what?" The Handyman's voice low, almost intimate in Barney's ear, but loud at the same time, reverberating in Barney's mind like an echo growing in volume instead of diminishing.

"Everything. Who I am."

He turned to the Handyman in sudden confrontation, saw his eyes like green moons, the pores of his flesh like mountain craters.

"I'm Barney Snow. I know my name. But nothing else. I don't know anything else." Lost in a void, in an aching emptiness. Panic whistled through him. He wanted to run, get out of here, away from the Handyman and those eyes. "Where did I come from? How did I get here? Who am I?"

"Think," the Handyman commanded. "Concentrate." His voice snapping against Barney's ear, sharp and crackling. "Think of your mother. She . . ."

His mother's face blossomed in his mind's eye, so beautiful, so lovely. And the tinkling bracelets that accompanied her wherever she went.

The tinkling bracelets filled the emptiness in his mind: He could almost hear them. He also felt the hot sting of the needle in his arm and realized that Bascam had entered the room and had somehow rolled up his sleeve and given him a shot while the Handyman held him firmly on the other side. He let himself go limp, to flow with whatever was joining his blood from the needle—tempo, rhythm—clinging to the face of his mother, her tinkling bracelets, closing his eyes, letting his mind fill with her so that everything else could be obliterated, especially the panic.

After a while he felt his heart beating normally. He looked lazily around for Bascam but she had departed, as silently as she had arrived. The Handyman was once more behind the desk. Barney sought his eyes, was glad to see the doctor regarding him in his usual manner. Emergency over, if it had been an emergency. Whatever it was, done with, for now anyway. The sense of well-being he had known this morning on awakening filled him again, a feeling of drift, letting go.

"Now what were we talking about, doctor?" he asked, languid, the words coming out of his mouth like bubbles from a toy pipe.

"We were just finishing, Barney," the Handyman said. "I had been saying how well you performed during the test."   .

Barney remembered now, played back in his mind what the Handyman had been saying about erasing tape, his memory like a tape being erased. But it didn't matter, really, nothing mattered as he remained in the chair, but not completely in the chair because part of him was floating beautifully and languorously somewhere else. Crazy, of course, but he let that other part of himself float away if it wanted to.

Later, when he had returned to his room, he bent over to take off his slippers and he was in the car again, behind the wheel, the wet street slanting before him, the cobblestones glistening with pelting rain, windshield wipers slapping back and forth, the motor roaring in his ears, lights flashing, horn blowing, louder than before, louder than ever, and then that figure stepping off the curb as the car approached and he pressed the brake pedal but nothing happened, the car would not stop, was gathering speed until . . .

He found himself face down on the bed, clinging to the pillow, gritting his teeth, tears running down his cheeks, his hands aching from holding the steering wheel so tightly, fingers singing with pain from clutching the wheel.

He stayed that way until sleep finally came with enfolding arms and his mother's face passed before his eyes just before he trickled off into sleep like rain sluicing off a sloping roof.

10

"**Y**ou have a visitor."

Barney looked at Bascam in surprise, testing her words, stalling before making a response, adjusting himself to the morning light that filtered through the slats of the venetian blinds. He dimly remembered falling asleep the night before after the nightmare of the car—he would definitely speak to the Handyman about it today—but remembered nothing else. The digital clock said it was 8:45. Late for him.

"Who is it?" Barney asked, knowing visitors were not allowed here, although an exception had been made for Mazzo. Another exception seemed unlikely. Especially for him.

Bascam managed a dim smile. A feat for her.

"You'll see," she said.

Barney was mystified and a bit apprehensive as he followed Bascam down the corridor, which was quiet and hushed in the morning hours when wasted bodies were preparing for another day.

"Is it an emergency?" he asked.

"Not an emergency," she answered.

Who could it be? He wasn't like Mazzo, had no mother

97

out there or a sister like Cassie. Tempo, rhythm, he told himself.

"Is it bad news?" he asked, trying to keep up with Bascam's brisk stride.

"Depends what you mean by bad news," Bascam answered glancing briefly over her shoulder. Poker-faced as usual, impossible to tell whether she was serious or not.

Bascam left him at the end of the corridor without another word. Barney walked toward the reception room near the exit to Section 12. He nodded at Old Cheekbones, who merely stared at him as usual and then resumed whatever she'd been doing at Barney's approach, bending over the papers on her desk.

Barney turned the corner into the reception room and there she was.

Cassie Mazzofono.

His heart leaped. Literally. Rose in his chest, taking his breath away. She stood there, sun catching her blond hair, spinning it, making it dance on her head, which was ridiculous, of course. But Cassie Mazzofono was so beautiful, so vibrant in that beauty, that she made Barney think crazy thoughts like that, made him glad that he had somehow found his way here to the Complex.

"Don't look so surprised," she said in that husky bantering voice. She was wearing blue again, a light-blue raincoat, unbuttoned to show a blue blouse and dark skirt. Her blue eyes were warm, inviting.

"And don't look so worried, either," she said. "I'm not going to bite you."

"You looked as if you wanted to bite the other day," he said.

"That was the other day. Come on in, sit down."

"I'd rather stand," he said, unsure of himself, delighted

with the fact of her presence but also wary, on guard. "Does the doctor know you're here? We're not supposed to have visitors."

"He knows I'm here," she said, removing her raincoat and folding it over the back of a chair, every movement beautiful. "He's not happy about it, but he knows."

"Why isn't he happy?"

She sighed. "Because I'm indulging in a bit of blackmail. My mother made a substantial donation when Alberto was admitted here. And she's still providing funds. A place like this always needs money."

"And you told the doctor that if you couldn't visit here, she'd stop the money," Barney said, still standing there, wondering what to do next, what to say next.

"Well, I didn't put it that bluntly, but yes, that was the message," Cassie said.

"He didn't say anything to me about a visit."

"He agreed only last night. It was probably too late to notify you. And I came here early today before he changed his mind."

"But what do you want with me?" Barney asked. Wanting to know and yet not wanting to know too, simply because as long as he didn't know, anything was possible. She could say: I fell madly in love with you at first sight the other day. Age doesn't matter. I want you to perform heroic deeds for me. Impossible, crazy, Barney told himself. But she was here in this room, wasn't she? Which he would have considered impossible yesterday.

"Relax, Barney," she said. "You don't mind if I call you Barney, do you?"

He shrugged, feeling inadequate and defenseless standing here in his robe and slippers, still shaky from the last merchandise.

"Call me Cassie."

"Cassie," he said, the name light and bright on his tongue.

"Come on, sit down," she urged.

She led him to the chairs near the window in the full morning sunlight. The chairs were uncomfortable kitchen-type chairs and the room bare of adornment, like his own bedroom, dingy walls, curtainless windows, venetian blinds fully opened to let in the daylight. She made the room seem anything but dingy, however. He sat across from her, conscious suddenly of his body, his hands and feet, as if he'd just learned he had hands and feet, wondering what to do with them.

She shivered a bit, hugged her arms to her chest. "God, I hate this place," she said. "It gives me the creeps. It's the last place on earth I want to be."

"Then why did you come back?" he asked, honestly curious.

"To see you."

"Why me?"

"Because you're different from the others here. Everything and everyone is so hopeless here. But not you. I sensed that right away in Alberto's room. And later he told me you weren't like the others. You're here for different tests."

Barney soared with delight. She had recognized him for what he was, different, his own person, not anyone else. But he was still puzzled. "And that's why you're here? Because I'm not like the others?"

"It's kind of complicated, Barney," she said. Then paused, shook her head the way a puppy shakes off water, touched her cheek with fingers that were surprisingly small and blunt. He loved to see her move, every move-

100

ment graceful and endearing to him. "Okay, I hate this place but my brother's here. And he won't leave this place alive. You're here, too. Alberto said you're a fixer. He told me about the telephone deal you arranged for that boy in the wheelchair. He also said you're a tough guy."

"I'm not so tough," he said. "But in a place like this you have to protect yourself. So you act tough sometimes. The doctor says we have to live in separate compartments, that we shouldn't get to know each other. A guy by the name of Ronson died a few days ago. But it wasn't too bad because I never got to know him. Didn't let myself get to know him."

"But you got friendly with the boy you arranged the telephone for," she said. "You found out how much he wanted a telephone."

Barney felt uncomfortable. "Billy needs cheering up sometimes. But I don't let him get too close."

"How close would you be willing to get to my brother?"

That was it: the windup. And then would come the pitch. He felt let down. She was not here to see him, after all, just as he had known it from the first moment.

"What do you mean?"

"I mean, would you visit with him, get to know him better, become friendly with him? Cheer him up?"

"Nobody can cheer him up," Barney said. "He doesn't want to be friends with anybody. Me and him, we don't even get along."

"Would you try to get along with him if I asked you?" Her eyes were fastened on him, the gorgeous eyes that opened up worlds for him. "Actually, I don't know how communicative he will be. He seems to have taken a turn for the worse since I first saw him here. Feverish, barely talking. But, would you try?"

Barney wanted to say: I would do anything for you. Especially if you looked at me the way you looked at him, as if I was somebody special in your eyes. Hell, she didn't have to love him. Just admire him a little, trust him.

He had to stall a bit. "Tell me what this is all about." Again, wanting to know and yet not wanting to know.

She sighed, as if she'd been running long and far and finally had reached her destination.

"It's like this, Barney. My brother doesn't want either my mother or me to see him anymore. He was always proud and independent—he doesn't want us to see him this way. He's never forgiven my mother for what she did. Divorced my father, and he died shortly afterward. Alberto says he died of a broken heart." She paused, sighed again. "Anyway, he made me promise not to come here again, not to visit him. He said we could telephone him once in a while. But that's all. And he was so full of pain and misery that I gave him my promise, my word of honor. But I want to know how he's getting along. Dr. Lakendorp isn't very communicative, resents my presence here like I said, says he can give me reports from time to time. But I don't want a doctor's report. That's like reading a temperature chart. I'd like to know how Alberto's doing. The little things. What he talks about. How he feels. And also this—I hate to think of him alone all the time. I'd like to think he has a friend. Someone like you." She looked directly into Barney's eyes now. "Someone like you, Barney. Alberto tries to act the wise guy and so do you. You're more alike than you think you are. I thought maybe you could become friends. Or friendly, at least. And I figured I could drop in every day or so and you could tell me about him."

"Like a spy," Barney said, oddly touched, having to say something.

"A tender kind of spy," she said.

God, she was beautiful. He would do anything for her. And he realized at that moment that if he agreed to be her spy, then he would see her when she came for his reports.

"Of course, I'm hoping Alberto will change his mind and let my mother and me see him eventually," she continued. "I'm sure that will happen, but until . . ."

Suddenly, her words faltered, the way her footsteps had faltered outside of Mazzo's room that day. She touched her forehead with a trembling hand, turning her face away. As she did so, Barney saw that her eyes had changed, looked shattered, as if someone had struck out at her, delivered a blow to her face and eyes.

He leaped to her side, grabbing her shoulder.

"Migraine," she said. "They hit like lightning. This place . . . I had a terrible one after I left the other day."

"Can I get you a pill?" Barney asked, aware of his hand on her shoulders and her flesh beneath her sweater, hating himself for thinking of her body at a time like this. "They must have migraine pills here."

Shaking her head, Cassie said: "I have a special prescription at home. Maybe I'd better go along. . . ." She looked up at Barney, smiling wanly, a bit pale, eyes with that shattered look.

"Sure I can't do something?" he asked, feeling helpless, knowing there was nothing he could do. He had released her from his grip, and stood there awkwardly.

She rose to her feet and slipped on the raincoat. "I'll be all right," she said. "The first stab is always the worst." Another attempt at a smile. "Sorry, Barney."

"Look, Cassie, I'll do it. What you say. I'll talk to Mazzo ... your brother. Visit him every day." As if his words could cure her, take away the headache.

"Thank you," she said, the husky voice tender. "I'll be back in a day or two. . . ."

She was gone a moment later, but Barney lingered in the room awhile, basking in the memory of her visit, her voice, the feeling of her flesh beneath the sweater, reluctant to leave this drab and dreary room that she had turned into a place of utter beauty for a few minutes.

Cassie paused outside the doorway, lifting her face to the fresh air, forehead throbbing with pain. Her old adversary, her ancient foe.

Walking on wobbly legs, she made her way to her mother's station wagon. Felt a sense of guilt as she walked. That poor kid, Barney Snow. Using him that way. Aware of how he looked at her, all that longing and desire in his eyes and taking advantage of it. Yet had to do it.

In the car she leaned her head against the seat, trying to relax a bit before driving home. She felt miserable. And going home to her mother would not help the situation. As she groped for the car keys, she allowed herself a small wave of triumph. At least she had accomplished her mission, had gotten that boy to keep in touch with Alberto.

Alberto, Alberto, she thought as she switched on the engine and felt its surge of power. If you die, what becomes of me?

11

*L*ATER, Barney couldn't remember the precise moment he had made the breakthrough with Mazzo. Looking back, he saw that there was a series of small advances into Mazzo's world and his confidence, tentative and stumbling, as he groped, unsure of himself, but determined to carry out his mission. A mission for Cassie. Cassie was the key. Once he began to see Mazzo through Cassie's eyes, as the brother of the girl he loved with such delight and such despair, a different Mazzo began to emerge. Barney saw Mazzo's vulnerability and desperation. Having seen Cassie in the full bloom of her beauty and loveliness, Barney realized the extent of Mazzo's deterioration. No wonder he was bitter and hateful. No wonder he turned his face away from visitors, no wonder he swore and growled and didn't care whether he farted and belched in the presence of anyone who might be in the room. He had been young and handsome and rich, and now he was an emaciated figure in the bed, his beauty in tatters. Barney felt moved with compassion as he watched Mazzo, pale and perspiring on the bed, no longer combative, subdued by the disease or the drugs, wondering how he could reach him. At the same time he didn't want to reach him. He dreaded the visits to

Mazzo's room. There was such an air of despair and defeat that Barney was afraid it would also invade him, as if Mazzo suffered from a disease contagious enough to affect him.

He made himself visit Mazzo, however, for the sake of Cassie. He developed a habit of dropping in several times a day, at odd hours, between treatments and visits by nurses. At first Mazzo was uncommunicative, brooding, immersed in his small private world, barely acknowledging Barney's presence. Barney tried to begin conversations but received no response at all, other than negative reactions. Sometimes Mazzo closed his eyes, shutting out Barney. Other times he turned away, hunching himself into the bedclothes. Barney did not give up. He had pledged his word to Cassie and he would see it through. He had only one weapon, and he used it in every way possible. Talk. His voice. He would wear Mazzo down with words.

He talked. Kept up an endless monologue of jokes and stories, telling Mazzo what was happening in the Complex, or at least what he observed. Barney had always been crazy about talking-animal jokes and he told every one he knew, embellishing them, drawing them out, making short jokes into long ones. If the kangaroo strolled into a barroom and ordered a martini, Barney painstakingly described the barroom, going into a thousand details while leading up to the punch line. Sometimes he didn't think the punch line mattered, because Mazzo never reacted, didn't laugh, didn't smile, didn't show impatience as Barney spun the tales. And Barney began to realize that Mazzo's lack of reaction was a plus sign. He never laughed at the jokes, but he never told Barney to shut up, get out, don't come back.

Getting out of bed in the morning, Barney went to the

small table and drew up a list of topics to bring to Mazzo's room. He made up an entire biography for Bascam, from the time she was born (the only baby in the world who didn't cry when slapped by the doctor) to the fact that she had eighteen children at home and that's why she never smiled. Barney knew the material wasn't that funny, not funny at all, in fact, but it gave him a chance to fill the room with his voice, to bounce the words off the walls and ceilings. Mazzo said nothing, did nothing. Barney sometimes became discouraged and thought: The hell with it. Let the silence fall. He'd stand beside Mazzo's bed, wanting to shake him into responding, tired of the sound of his own voice, bored and impatient. Then he'd think of Cassie and see her face and those dancing eyes before him, and he'd say: "Hey Mazzo, did I ever tell you about the giraffe who got the sore throat and . . ."

Desperate one afternoon, empty of ideas, tired of the sound of his own voice, he saw Billy being wheeled by on the way to a treatment. Billy waved feebly. "Did you know Billy the Kidney was an expert car thief?"

He spoke to the air, having grown accustomed to a lack of response from Mazzo. But he noticed now that Mazzo stirred at the question, turned and looked at Barney, a glimmer of interest in his eyes.

Barney pounced on the topic of Billy's car thefts. Told him about Billy's exploits, how he stole the cars and the rides he took, elaborating a little, exaggerating a bit, but not too much. He didn't want to lose credibility with Mazzo now that he had finally gotten a response after all this time. Talking about cars, he was afraid that he might induce his nightmare to return right here in Mazzo's room, but he kept on talking anyway and the nightmare didn't come.

107

Finally, topic exhausted, he fell into silence.

Mazzo's lips moved. He uttered words Barney couldn't understand. He leaned toward Mazzo, inclining his head.

"I like cars," Mazzo croaked, voice hoarse and broken.

Barney's hopes rose at this first response. Mazzo had given him a topic to explore further: cars.

He didn't really know much about cars, so he pummeled Billy the Kidney with questions about them. Billy didn't know a hell of a lot, but at least he'd driven a variety of them, knew their names, knew about four-wheel drive and stuff that was too technical for Barney to follow. Barney took a lot of this information to Mazzo, improvising again, spinning his wheels as usual, making up stuff about car races, describing at length a drive he told Mazzo he had taken in a green MG, which Billy said was the best car he ever stole. Barney played games, too, with the information, telling a weird science-fiction tale of how the MG's joined forces with computers to take over the world, juggling the words, his mind racing and his tongue trying to keep up with it. Having run out of both words and ideas, he stood breathlessly at Mazzo's bedside, feeling as though he'd just finished a long and arduous run. Mazzo lifted his hand, summoned Barney closer. "You're crazy," Mazzo said. But there was no venom in his voice, and his eyes did not have their usual hard glitter. It was as if he had said: "Thanks, Barney."

One morning Barney was seized by an aftermath as he told a long story about an elephant who happened to wander through a supermarket, a variation of the giraffe in the barroom joke. He paused in midsentence—"The clerk turned around as the elephant raised its . . ."—as dizziness assailed him. His eyes suddenly could not focus, and he held on blindly to the bed, his fingers grabbing the sheets for support in a world dissolving under his feet. Let the blood flow, rhythm, tempo, holding on, holding on, getting a flash of the nightmare car slanting down the hill, his hands on the steering wheel and the car out of control on the wet street, rain splashing against the windshield and the wipers going back and forth, rhythm, tempo. Then the dizziness receded, his eyes focused again, sweat ran down his cheeks into the corners of his mouth, salty and warm. But he was normal once again. His heart still raced a bit and throbbed in his ears, but that was par for the course following an aftermath.

He looked up to see Mazzo, half propped up on one elbow, studying him, as if Barney was a stranger he'd never seen before.

"A reaction," Barney said. "From the merchandise they give me. It happens once in a while."

For the first time Barney saw a look of concern in Mazzo's face. Barney thought: It's as if he's discovering that I'm human too, that you don't have to be dying in this place to be a good guy.

Then Mazzo lowered himself again and closed his eyes, shutting Barney out once more.

The final breakthrough came one evening as Barney sat beside Mazzo's bed in one of the wooden chairs. There was not a comfortable chair in the entire Complex, it seemed, and the beds were not exactly luxurious either. Bascam had been annoyed when Barney had showed up at the door to Mazzo's room.

"You here again?" she said.

Barney didn't bother to answer. Bascam stole one more secret look at Mazzo and departed without another word. He and Mazzo remained silent. Frankly, Barney didn't feel like talking. He could still hear the echo of his earlier words coming at him from the corners of the room. Mazzo seemed to be dozing. Then he spoke, said something Barney didn't understand.

"What did you say?" Barney asked.

Mazzo spoke again, words muffled, unintelligible.

Barney leaned across the bed, turning his head so that his ear was close to Mazzo's lips.

"Any . . . more . . . after . . . maths?" Mazzo whispered.

Barney couldn't believe his ears. Mazzo the bastard was not only talking but asking about Barney's condition.

"No," Barney said.

Mazzo nodded. "Good," he said.

"Listen," Barney said, "the aftermaths aren't bad at all, really. They come and go and last only a minute. Hell, they're nothing compared to the nightmare—" He caught himself but too late. Christ, he'd done so much talking in this room that now it was second nature to babble about anything and everything. Even the nightmare of the car. Which he hadn't wanted to tell Mazzo about, tell anybody about.

Mazzo's eyes were fixed on him, fevered and blazing.

"Nothing," Barney said, answering the eyes' demand. "The nightmare is nothing."

Mazzo continued that fixed demanding stare.

"Nothing, I said, Mazzo. Nothing."

Mazzo fixed his face in a don't-give-me-that-crap expression.

Barney didn't say anything. And then he thought: If Mazzo wants to know, why not tell him? He'd been trying to get his attention day after day without spectacular results. Now here was Mazzo actually wanting to communicate.

Barney told him. About the car and the slanting street.

The rain and the wind. The roaring motor and the wheel in his hand. The girl emerging from the mist, stepping off the curb. The car hurtling toward her. The moment of awakening at the point of collision.

Mazzo pondered the story for a long time, saying nothing, apparently deep in thought. He began to question Barney, wanted to know all the details. How the steering wheel felt in Barney's hands, the effect of the speed on his body, how fast he thought he was going. Barney did his best to supply the details, surprised finally at how vivid the details of the drive were, brief as it was, dream that it was. Satisfied with the details, Mazzo fell back against his pillow. After a while he said: "Boy, how I'd like one last ride." Wistful, full of longing.

Barney realized that Mazzo had been living that ride through him, relishing the details so that he could re-create the wild ride in his own imagination.

He looked down at Mazzo, so pathetic in the bed.

"Know what, Mazzo? You're going to have that last wild ride."

Even as he spoke, he knew that it was crazy, a ridiculous promise, like telling Billy the Kidney he would get him a telephone. Why do I keep doing things like this? Yet he'd gotten Billy the telephone, hadn't he?

Mazzo looked at him, confused. Childlike. Then, hopeful.

"You are going to have that one last ride, Mazzo."

Barney's thoughts flew wildly. There had to be a way to get Mazzo into a car. Despite all the medical paraphernalia that surrounded him, the doodads connecting Mazzo to the machines. Despite the odds. He pictured a wild scene: dispatching Billy to steal a car downtown and then he and Billy smuggling Mazzo out of the Complex and into the car for a final ride careening the city streets. Make it a green Porsche, he'd tell Billy the Kidney. Ah, ridiculous. Because Billy was in no condition to steal a car, to say nothing of walking out the door. And Mazzo would never leave this place alive.

But it would be beautiful, wouldn't it?

He looked at Mazzo again and Mazzo had closed his eyes, seemed to be sleeping but Barney knew he wasn't.

Barney felt somehow that he had let Mazzo down.

His sense of smell returned.

While eating breakfast one morning, he realized he could taste the eggs. One moment he was methodically chewing and swallowing the food merely to satisfy the dull gnawing in his stomach. Scrambled eggs, bland, which he used to douse with ketchup to make them palatable. But he hadn't bothered to do so here at the Complex after losing his sense of taste. Why bother with ketchup or even salt or pepper or anything else? But now the taste of the eggs came alive in his mouth, flavorful, delicious in fact. He gulped the cold milk, and was surprised to find it tasty. He'd always preferred chocolate milk.

Breathing deeply, inhaling luxuriously, he brought the air of the Complex into his lungs and was instantly plunged into the smell of the place. Not one smell, really, but many of them blurred into a pervasive odor, elusive, hard to pin down, a nameless smell with an undertone of unpleasantness. Maybe the smell of sickness itself.

Pushing himself away from the table, he decided to drop in on Billy the Kidney and Allie Roon. He had been neglecting them lately because of his concentration on Mazzo. Cruising along the corridor on his way to visit them, he sniffed broadly and comically, his nostrils quivering, and he laughed with delight. Even that peculiar smell of the Complex did not spoil his delight. Maybe that's what happens when you get back something you thought you had lost forever.

Cassie came to the Complex almost every day, late in the afternoon when the sun began to lose its brightness and a pale ivory light softened the harsh edges of the day. Barney waited for her at the exit, ignoring Old Cheekbones, who did not know she was being ignored, of course, because she paid so little attention to his comings and goings. Barney's breath quickened when he saw Cassie coming up the walk, arms swinging, head held high, movements fluid and utterly feminine, blond hair catching the failing light. There was always that marvelous moment when she reached the door, saw him there, and smiled. For him alone.

In the bare reception room that she transformed into a place of comfort and ease by her presence, she never asked: "How is he?" No need. She settled into the straight-backed chair, placed her hands in her lap like a dutiful child, lifted her face to Barney as if in supplication, and waited. For that single splendid moment no one else existed in the world but them, in the dying light. Barney had never known such intimacy before, with anyone. He never touched her, dared not get too close, and yet felt closer to her than anyone he had ever known.

At first he tried to fake it, in an attempt to give her encouraging news, dredging through the evidence of his visits with Mazzo to provide an optimistic report, to tell her that yes, he seemed a little better, more comfortable, less resentful of his predicament. Until she said: "Cut it out, Barney Snow." In that husky wise-guy voice. "I need the truth. I can make up my own fairy tales. But tell me the truth about Alberto."

So Barney told her the truth, although strangely enough there wasn't much to tell, really. Mazzo's condition seldom fluctuated. He never seemed in great pain, although occasionally he was seized by a spasm that glazed his eyes and caused him to stiffen in the bed, his veins bulging like thin ropes beneath his flesh. Most of the time he drifted in a sort of haze, half dozing. Cassie groped for details, relentless in her questioning, sharp eared and pitiless, exact in her demands. Wanting to know, for instance, how pale Mazzo was, the exact shade and tone of his flesh. *White, Barney? How white? Bone white? Snow white?* Barney searched for the right words—how white was bone white, anyway?—wanting to give her the truth she sought. *Spasm, Barney? What kind of spasm? How painful?* How could you describe somebody else's pain? But he tried. For her sake. Wanting to please her, keep her coming to the Complex.

The best moments happened when the questioning was over and they sat in the room across from each other, Barney reluctant to let her go, seeking various ways of keeping her there. Sometimes she rushed off as if late for an appointment, other times she lingered awhile as Barney tried to make conversation. A pathetic kind of conversation, full of stops and starts, pauses and painful silences. He tried to get her talking, asking her about the outside world. Remembering that Mazzo said she was *out* now—jail? (impossible)—he carefully asked her: "Do you go to college?" And before she could answer, he asked, crazily, another question: "Do you like movies?" Stupid. She hesitated a moment and said: "I'm in between right now." What did that mean? And: "I haven't been to the movies for a while." She looked away from him, avoiding his eyes for the first time. She was holding something back, of course, but he didn't press her for further information, grateful to be sitting with her, basking in her presence.

The breakthrough, when it came, was sudden and unexpected, not slow and gradual as it had been with Mazzo. It happened the day his sense of smell returned. It added a new dimension to his attraction to her. Mazzo had said she didn't use perfume or cologne. The scent that she carried was distinct, however. Some sort of soap. She smelled well scrubbed and clean, the way clothes smell when they've been flapping in the wind. Drinking in that heady scent of cleanliness, he shared his news with her, how he was able to smell again. Told her that all his senses seemed sharpened, sunlight more dazzling, sounds louder in his ears, not louder but clearer, more defined. Which was crazy, of course.

"Not crazy," Cassie said. "I read somewhere that a person who wears glasses can't hear as well when he takes the glasses off."

For some reason this struck them both as absurdly funny, and they burst into laughter.

"You smell good, Cassie," he said, carried on the waves of the shared laughter. "No perfume or anything. Just you."

"Not me," she said. "What you smell is soap. From the Hacienda. I took some home with me."

"The Hacienda?"

"Not really a hacienda. I call it that because it's made of stucco and looks like it belongs in Mexico somewhere and not New England." Her chin tilted challengingly. "It's a convent, that's what it is. And not exactly a convent, either. A novitiate."

Barney got a flash of nuns praying, candles burning, a memory from school days. *Out now* . . . What Mazzo had said.

"Isn't that a place where you go to become a nun?" Barney asked. Walking a tightrope.

"The others did, I didn't. I just wanted to get away."

Barney waited, afraid to say anything else.

"I hated my life," she said at last. "And didn't know why. At first I blamed it on my mother and father—the breakup of their marriage. And then Papa dying on us. Dying on Alberto and me. Alberto was luckier. He was always away—summer camps, prep school. I was at home, hated Monument High but also hated that preppie world Alberto liked. I had so much hate in me. I think for a while I hated my mother, too. My mother, you see, is a very private person. Or cold, like Alberto claims. He says all those generations of Yankee blood have turned her into a museum piece." She seemed to be ruminating now, scarcely aware of Barney's presence. "They shouldn't have married in the first place, of course. He was the hot-blooded Italian with a talent for making money. Alberto said it was like that old Robert Frost poem. "Fire And Ice." Know which is stronger, Barney?"

He leaped a bit at being discovered by her again.

"No," he said, his voice a whisper.

"Ice, anytime. Papa's fire went out, but my mother's ice never melted. Although I heard her crying in her room the night we learned that Papa had died out in St. Louis on a business trip. Heart attack . . ."

She shook her head, as if awakening from a reverie.

116

"My God, Barney, this sounds like true confessions. I'm sorry to be going into all this." She shivered a bit. "This place. It does things to me."

"I like to hear you talk, Cassie," he said. Her name on his lips was beautiful. Like music he was composing as he spoke.

"I have to be going," she said, suddenly in a hurry, as if surprised to find herself still there. And she was gone in a minute or two, gathering her things together, hastening from the place as if some terrible fate would overtake her if she stayed any longer.

A pattern became established after the breakthrough. She'd arrive, usually in a rush, breathless, and settle into the chair, peppering Barney with questions about Mazzo, the same old questions, really, about pain and attitude—*Is he still unhappy? Does he say much? Is the pain very bad?*—and Barney assured her as best he could. She was insatiable, as if looking for a clue that would give her the secret to Mazzo's illness when actually there was no secret. Finally she'd sit back, at ease in the chair, almost languid in the gathering dusk—they never put on the light—and then sometimes she'd talk, usually in answer to a question that Barney had prepared beforehand.

Taking a deep breath, Barney asked: "Why doesn't he talk to your mother on the telephone? He always answers but never says anything."

Cassie lifted her shoulders and let them fall. Have I gone too far? Barney wondered.

"He thinks he's punishing her," Cassie said finally, an air of wonder in her voice as if she was finding out the answer for the first time. "But what he's trying to do is punish the world by doing that to her." Crossing her legs, the nylon catching the hallway light, she said: "Oh, Barney, you should have seen Alberto before all this. He was a marvelous athlete. We used to cheer him on, first in Little League and then in football in prep school. The way he swung a bat, or threw a pass. A natural athlete, Papa said. Alberto and I are twins—he was born a minute before me and always called me his kid sister and I didn't mind—but we're not alike in many ways. I go around as if I've got two left feet, drop things, never was sure what I wanted to be, never sure about life. Alberto was always sure. I'd follow him around like a kid sister should. I used to love it when we were kids and got the flu together or measles and had to stay home. We'd drive my mother or the housekeeper—good old Mrs. Cortoleona—crazy. . . ."

Barney could have sat there forever listening to that lovely husky voice, becoming for a brief time a part of Cassie's life, sharing those childhood moments. Often he felt as though she had forgotten his presence and was speaking to herself, expressing thoughts she had never said aloud before, that awe and wonder in her voice. Most of the time she didn't really answer his carefully prepared question, but it didn't matter. What mattered was that the question touched off one of her monologues, and Barney was a rapt listener, absorbing her words, making them a part of him and recalling them later at night in his bed as the capsule carried him off to sleep.

"Summers were best of all because we'd go riding out in Lunenburg, me on the gelding Papa bought me—Marbles, a marvelous horse—and Alberto on Majestic, his favorite steed—he always called them steeds, never horses—and we had such fun. Or swimming. The summer before the trouble began with my parents was a golden summer. Alberto and I and some kids from town—Sarah Golden and Melanie Brooks and Joey Northrup—we rode and went to the circus and watched the sunrise once from Mount Wachusum and then drove all the way into Boston for breakfast at the Copley. Joey was older, had a license and his father's Mercedes. Gee, what times." Her voice trailed off, wistful, a little-girl quality about her again that never failed to move Barney, to make him nostalgic for things he'd never known. "And then my mother and father separating and Alberto going away and . . ."

That final *and* hung in the air, like a promise unfulfilled, like the flash of lightning before the thunder explodes in the sky. But she fell into silence, didn't keep the promise, no thunder, either.

He sensed a mystery about her and pondered this after she left the place, and he stood there watching her going down the walk, sorry to see her disappear into the evening's darkness. Why did she really come here day after day? What was she looking for?

Sometimes she seemed weary, appeared distracted, listless, asking the questions as usual but mechanically, as if she were only going through the motions. In those moments her eyes also seemed lusterless, as if covered with a film that dimmed their brightness. Other times her eyes had that shattered look. Once he asked: "Another migraine?" She seemed startled, surprised. "You told me about them, remember?" he said. And she admitted that yes, she had another migraine, the Complex seemed to bring them on. But she couldn't stop coming, she said.

"And you, Barney, how are you?" she'd ask on occasion, and he was thrilled when she turned those eyes on him, as if no one else in the world existed except him and Cassie there in the dusk-drenched room.

"I'm okay," he said.

His big fear was that an aftermath would seize him in

her presence. He wanted to be strong and brave for her. Most of all, normal. Once in a while he'd become light-headed and hold his breath, afraid that an aftermath was on its way. Occasionally the car slanting down the hill would flash across his eyes and he'd hold himself rigid, not moving, saying *tempo, rhythm,* hoping his body would not betray him.

"How are your tests going?" she'd asked. "What are they, anyway?" She had a habit of asking a string of questions all at once, like when she inquired about Mazzo. "Are they painful?"

He answered only vaguely, telling her that they were tests involving memory and they were not painful, merely weird, made him dizzy sometimes. He hurried to change the subject, afraid she might pounce on him with her un-ending questions and he'd be unable to resist answering, telling her everything she wanted to know. He didn't want to reveal himself for what he had become, some kind of guinea pig here in the Complex.

His body betrayed him once as they spoke. One minute they were speaking about the Hacienda. Barney had built up to it carefully, framing the question in his mind and then asking it: "Are you going back to that place . . . that Hacienda?" He hated the thought of her shut away in a convent.

"I've taken the semester off. To be with my mother and Alberto."

"You said once that you didn't go there to be a nun," Barney reminded her. Hopefully.

"I don't know what I want to be," she said.

At that moment dizziness assailed him, his body sud-denly light and weightless, and he rose to his feet, the room whirling, nothing to hold on to. Floating above the floor, no feet, Cassie's face floating with him but fragmented, broken into tiny pieces. He clutched at the chair for support, reaching blindly for it. Where are my feet?

"What's the matter?"

Her voice from far away. Light years away.

He worked to move his mouth, tongue, vocal cords, to do what seemed impossible: tell her what was happening.

"Reaction," he managed to gasp at last, squeezing the word out painfully. "Aftermath . . ." Didn't know whether she could hear him, whether he was whispering or shouting.

A moment later—or had it been hours?—he found himself in the chair again, Cassie's hands holding his, her face so close he could see the tiny pores in her flesh, the smell of soap clean and sweet in his nostrils. The spinning had stopped, his feet had been rediscovered and touched the floor, and his hands tingled at her touch. He wanted her never to let go.

"I'm okay now," he said, voice functioning again but a bit fluttery. "That was a bad one. They're usually not that bad."

"What kind of stuff are they giving you, anyway?" she said angrily.

"That memory drug. It has aftermaths, reactions. They come and go." Damn it. He was angry, at himself, his body, the Handyman, the merchandise, for making him collapse like that in front of her. Her, of all people. "Nothing serious," he said, forcing a smile. Had to keep it light.

Cassie withdrew her hands, and he wanted to grope for them but let his own hands remain in his lap.

"We're quite a pair, aren't we?" she said, smiling thinly. "Me with my migraines, you with your aftermaths."

Thinking of Alberto and Billy the Kidney and Allie Roon, he looked at her.

"I know," she said, voice husky and low, barely discernible in the half-light. "We're the lucky ones. . . ."

I'm lucky to know you, he thought.

Later he stood by the doorway, watching her going down the walk, disappearing into the darkness, heard the car roaring away, tried to create the ghost of her outside the window, smiling at him, waving a greeting. No one there. He tried to conjure her face. But couldn't. What did she look like? Her face a blank spot in his mind, like the time he couldn't bring back the image of his mother's face. Cassie's face was now like the missing piece of a jigsaw puzzle.

He hurried to his room in blind panic, sweeping by Allie Roon standing with mouth agape in the hallway. As he entered his room and snapped on the light, Cassie's face emerged in his mind once more—blazing blue eyes and lovely curve of cheek—and he sighed with weary relief. He flung himself onto the bed, dreading the next merchandise session—what if something went wrong and Cassie was wiped from his memory and his life forever?

The Handyman summoned him to the Hit Room the next morning after breakfast. Barney entered the office warily, hoping that the Handyman wasn't planning more merchandise this week.

Sitting behind the bare wooden desk as usual, the Handyman seemed affable and in good humor.

"How are you getting on with Miss Mazzofono?" he asked.

Barney felt his cheeks grow warm.

"Fine, just fine," he said. Let's change the subject, doctor.

"As you know, Barney, I am not a great disciplinarian, and I allow reasonable freedom here. In fact I encourage everyone to move around, go outdoors, to the best of their abilities. But I must tell you that I do not entirely approve of these meetings. Ours is a closed society here. She is a disruptive influence." He didn't seem angry. Sad, maybe.

"Your Miss Mazzofono is indulging in a bit of blackmail. Sweet blackmail from her viewpoint, I think. But blackmail all the same."

Barney waited, didn't know what to say anyway.

"She may have told you, Barney, that her mother is an important benefactor of ours. And we are in need of benefactors. That is why I've allowed Alberto to become a resident here." *Resident* instead of *patient.* "Why I allowed his sister to visit. Do you see?"

Barney nodded, still wordless.

"This Cassandra Mazzofono, she's a beautiful young woman, isn't she?"

"Yes."

"Do you enjoy her visits?"

Another nod, not trusting his voice, afraid he might betray how he felt about her.

"This troubles me, Barney."

Barney's hopes began to capsize. He was afraid the Handyman would end the visits.

"I would not want you to form attachments, Barney. An attachment that may later cause unhappiness. You are the subject of delicate proceedings." *Proceedings* instead of *experiments.* "It would be unfortunate to upset your delicate balance."

"What do you mean—delicate balance?"

"In matters involving the mind, Barney, one cannot discount the emotions. Your emotional well-being is as vital as your mental and physical states."

"What are you trying to tell me?" Barney asked, scared of all this mumbo jumbo about physical states and emotional well-being.

"I want you to be careful, Barney. Do your duty, what this young woman asks of you. But keep yourself remote from her. In your own compartment. Remember that you are a resident here and she is from the outside world. There will come a time eventually when she will have no need to visit here."

The preciseness of the Handyman's manner of speaking kept Barney alert to his words, and his words seemed to doom him now. He knows, Barney thought, he knows I love her, live for her visits. From the beginning he had seemed able to read Barney's mind. Now he could read his emotions. Yet the Handyman's words didn't contain a threat, did they? They were more like a warning, a friendly warning, maybe.

"You may go, Barney." His voice almost gentle.

On his way back to the room, going along the corridors in a haze of uncertainty, he wondered about this strange doctor who was the Handyman. He'd always been almost like a robot, hiding deep within his own compartment, and today he had seemed human. As Barney had closed the door, leaving the Hit Room, he had seen a sad and lonely look on the Handyman's face. He wondered who the Handyman felt sad for—Barney, Cassie, Mazzo, or even himself.

12

BILLY the Kidney was taken to Isolation the next morning for another session with the merchandise. Hooked up to the wires and tubes, pinned down by sensors and clamps, all the doodads necessary for the tests, he looked forlornly at Barney, who was watching through the Observation window. Barney made a thumbs-up gesture. Billy had been confined to bed for more than a week, his condition worsening, all his tests suspended. Maybe these new tests meant that he was getting stronger. Wasn't this a good sign? Then he remembered the Handyman's admonition: This is not a place for hope or miracles. Barney turned away from the window. For a moment he had pictured Ronson lying on that same table, trapped and helpless, like a specimen in a grotesque exhibit.

Allie Roon was waiting in Barney's room, sitting patiently in the chair next to the bed. He smiled at Barney's arrival, the weird smile that split his face in half, one cheek twitching furiously, the other cheek wrinkled like a withered apple.

Allie made an effort to speak. His tongue flicked in and out of his mouth, spit flew in all directions. "L . . . l . . . l . . . e . . . e . . . t . . . t . . . 's . . . s . . ." Barney realized finally that Allie was trying to say: Let's go. Out. Out there into the real world. Barney nodded, took his jacket from the closet and led the boy through the corridor to the exit.

May dazzled his eyes with its brilliance, the grass soft and spongy beneath his feet. He paused and looked toward the street, half hoping to see Cassie emerging from the car she drove to their meetings. He was impatient for the day to pass, hopeful for her arrival, impatient to see her again. Allie tugged at his arm, dancing at his side. "Okay, Allie, let's go," he said.

The breeze was warm and gentle on Barney's face and he took deep breaths, drinking in the air and the scents of the season, scents he couldn't identify but filling his nostrils with pungent aromas. He and Allie Roon made their way to a lilac bush heavy with clusters and fragrance. As they got closer, Barney saw that the lilacs were already past their prime, beginning to shrivel, the season passing too quickly for them to survive, remain living. Spasmodically, Allie pointed to a small flowering tree. Tiny pink blossoms danced on its branches. Barney didn't know what kind of tree it was, realized he knew nothing about nature.

"N . . . i . . . nice . . ." Allie sputtered.

Barney looked from the tree to the lilac bush, considered how one was dying and the other shimmering with beginning life. And a while ago the tree had been stark and lifeless while the bush was exploding with beauty. Sad somehow, one life ending while another began. But he drew a kind of comfort from this knowledge, seeing for the first time the continuity of life, nature at work in the world, providing a never-ending process of life in all its forms. Maybe there was some kind of continuity in people, too. Nature at work in people. Or was it God? He shivered at the thought. An old prayer leaped to his lips. "Our Father, who art in Heaven . . ." He couldn't remember the last time he had prayed. He used to say his prayers every morning and night but had somehow lost the habit. Tempo, rhythm.

Turning away from the tree, he looked at the bush once more and the dying purple clusters. The bush, though, wouldn't die. Just as the flowering tree hadn't really died during the winter but had slumbered on through the seasons, withstanding the rain and the cold. Were people like that, too? Death only a sleep from which they eventually awakened? Not the body, of course, but the soul, soaring into eternity, joining others there.

He raised his head to the sky as if he could find eternity in that endless blue. He thought of Cassie, how she had made him *feel* again, as if she had roused him from a long sleep, sharpening his senses, making him aware of life's joys: his own beating heart or the blossoms on a flowering tree. He shivered with pleasure, glad to be here, his feet on the spongy earth, this same earth Cassie traversed when she visited him.

Allie called to him in an explosion of vowels. He was standing at the fence, pointing to the top, his arm suddenly straight and still, index finger pointing like a pistol.

"What do you want?" Barney called.

But he knew what Allie wanted. He wanted, impossible, to climb the fence.

"Come back, Allie," Barney yelled.

Allie kept pointing, the arm twitching now, his mouth working. "Y . . . y . . . yo . . . you," he called, his eyes bright with anticipation, mouth trying to smile or laugh.

"Ah, hell," Barney said. Realizing what Allie really wanted. He wanted Barney to climb the fence.

"Come on back, Allie."

127

Allie shook his head and stayed at the fence, no longer exuberant, arms twitching at his sides, half turned away from Barney.

He walked over to the boy, angry, not wanting to climb the fence, not wanting to risk injury or being caught by the Handyman or a nurse. He didn't want to do anything that would threaten his meetings with Cassie. Had to play everything safe, not break any rules.

But when he arrived at Allie's side, he saw the disappointment on the boy's face. What the hell difference did it make to Allie Roon if he climbed the fence or didn't climb it? He knew the answer, however. He realized that when he climbed the fence, he was acting for Allie, doing what Allie couldn't do, and somehow Allie was doing it, too.

"Okay, okay," Barney growled, scowling. He measured the distance to the top. It seemed higher today than before. Allie danced a ridiculous jig, his eager old man's face full of hope and anticipation.

Barney found himself scaling the fence, going up faster than he'd intended, renewed strength in his bones and muscles. The wind caressed him as he climbed, as if someone stroked him in his ascent. Allie crooned encouragement from below. If Cassie could see him now. At the top he swung his legs around. Clinging precariously but triumphantly there, he looked down to see Allie trying to clap his hands, missing most of the time, slapping at air, but a wide smile cracking his face open.

The junkyard looked the same to Barney, a forlorn battlefield untouched by spring and the change of seasons. If anything, the ruined vehicles seemed to have shrunk further into the ground. The MG gleamed in the sunlight, a small riot of color in all that drabness and desolation. In his mind's eye he saw the car speeding along the highway, Mazzo at the controls, a white scarf billowing in the wind, and he and Cassie crowded beautifully close together, laughing and singing as the car sped along. But the MG in the lot was only an illusion, not really a car. Like his dream of Cassie's love. Both not real, false and fake.

He looked at the Complex, which seemed to tower menacingly above him. A place of secrets under that slanting roof. In a corner of Barney's mind the glimmer of a vision winked, like a star's quick glitter from afar. He held his breath waiting for the glimmer to grow. Glancing again at the MG, he let the vision burst full flower. He saw for the first time the flight of the Bumblebee, although Cassie had not yet provided him with the name.

Mazzo's condition seemed to improve—temporarily, of course, Barney realized, remembering the Handyman's words—and Barney found that the visits to his room were almost pleasant, as pleasant as any trip to a sickroom could be. Although Mazzo still brooded a bit and seldom initiated a conversation, letting Barney carry the ball, he didn't mind answering questions. About his prep-school days, baseball and football and mountain climbing, the mountain in question Katahdin up in Maine. Mazzo's eyes came alive when he told Barney about the game Stanley Prep won in the last half of the sixteenth inning, a night game, at three o'clock in the morning.

"I suppose you hit a home run to win the game," Barney said. "The big hero." Kidding him a bit.

"Look, Barney, I was good," Mazzo said. "I don't take credit for it. I was a natural athlete. Born that way. All I did was use that talent. The lousy thing is to have talent and not use it." And his face turned dark. "Or not be able to use it."

Eventually, all the conversations ended that way, on a bitter note, but before that happened Mazzo seemed to enjoy reminiscing. Barney listened, bored sometimes but disguising the boredom, waiting for an opening in the conversation to ask about Cassie. When the opening came, Barney moved in quickly.

"How about Cassie?"

"Cassie?"

"Was she good at sports?"

Mazzo shrugged. "I don't know. I don't think so. She was a funny kid."

"What do you mean—funny?"

"I mean, she wasn't just one thing. Sometimes she was full of fun and doing crazy stuff. Like all kids do. And then she'd be up in her room, alone. I was away a lot. She'd go on different kicks. She was a vegetarian for a while. Drove Mrs. Cortoleona—she was our housekeeper, chief cook and bottle washer—up a wall. Then that phase passed and she became a radical. At fourteen years old. Actually walked in a picket line downtown, some crazy protest in front of a supermarket. My mother almost flipped her lid. . . ." Mazzo laughed. Sort of laughed, that is, making a sound that was half laughter and half sigh. "My mother. I used to feel bad for her sometimes. Very proper lady, my mother. Every hair in place. Old New England family. And she's caught in this family—Papa, the wild Sicilian, and Cassie who was always changing from vegetarian to radical and then getting religion. And me. Wrecking a couple of cars, getting suspended from school—good thing they needed me in the backfield or at the plate, or I wouldn't have survived. . . ." He fell into one of his brooding silences.

"Cassie got religion?" Barney asked carefully, playing that same dangerous game with Mazzo as he had with Cassie, not wanting to go too far and yet pressing on.

"She didn't get religion, I guess. She had it all the time. My mother was Protestant, Papa Catholic. He insisted we go to religious classes every Saturday morning. Until we got confirmed when we were fourteen. I hated it. Sitting in the classroom with some old nun talking about the Holy Trinity, all that stuff. I hardly ever listened, and Cassie helped me with the tests. She didn't seem to mind the classes. I used to call her Sister Superior. She didn't seem to mind that, either. She was always a good kid. We got along, not like some other brothers and sisters I knew. Maybe because we were twins . . ." He shrugged deep into the sheets then, closing his eyes, and Barney sat there, in his own silence, thinking of Cassie as a little girl.

Later, another day, Mazzo awakened from a nap looking rested and at ease, his face empty of bitterness or resentment.

"What about that mountain climbing? That mountain in Maine? What's it like on top of a mountain? I never climbed one," Barney said. He didn't really care about mountains, but he tried to be subtle in his questionings, leading up to the topic of Cassie in a roundabout way so that Mazzo would not become suspicious.

So Mazzo told him about mountain climbing and Barney barely listened, uninterested in all the gear that was necessary, although he perked up his ears when Mazzo told him about the time he slipped, fell from a cliff, and hung suspended by a thin rope until he was pulled to safety. "For five minutes, there, I thought I was a goner. If that rope had broken . . ." His eyes became hooded, his lips pressed together thinly. "Maybe it should have happened then. Or maybe that other time . . ."

"What other time?" Keep him talking.

"I got hit by a ball. Beaned. Two strikes on me, bases loaded. Top of the ninth. Everything always happens in the ninth inning. The bastard threw right at me. At my head. Guy named Cranston. Exeter. And I didn't duck or pull back. Because I didn't think anybody would do a thing like that. Jesus, I was stupid. So I stood there, thinking this guy must have put a hell of a curve or hook on the ball because it had to miss me at the last minute. And bang. Knocked me out. I woke up in the hospital. Concussion. Two black eyes. Had to stay there a few days. Worried as hell that my mother and Papa would find out what happened. But the school was covered by Blue Cross or something. And they never knew. Christ, they didn't know half the stuff that happened to me." He fell silent. "I had a headache for, like, two months afterward."

"Did you quit playing?" Barney asked, wondering how he could get the topic around to Cassie.

"Had to keep playing. . . ." Silent again.

Barney saw his opening. Weak, lame, maybe, but an opening.

"Speaking of headaches, how long has Cassie had those migraines?"

Mazzo's head snapped up, his eyes sharp and alert, and Barney immediately realized his blunder.

"How do you know about her migraines? I didn't even know she has migraines."

Blood rushed to Barney's cheeks. His pulse throbbed in his temple. Damn it. He had made the fatal slip that had to be avoided at all costs. Mazzo didn't know about Cassie's visits.

"She . . . mentioned them that day she was here . . . visiting you," Barney stammered, tripping over the words. He was again grateful for his ability to lie.

"I don't remember that she talked about migraines," Mazzo said, unconvinced. But not so much suspicious now as puzzled. "The damn medicine. It does all these strange things to you. . . ."

Barney waited, watching, not daring to move or say anything more.

Mazzo made his usual escape, shrinking himself into the bed sheets, drawing them up to his chin. "I wonder what else I can't remember. . . ."

Barney got out of there as soon as possible, vowing to be more careful in the future. Mazzo might be sick and dying, but his brain was sharp and alert.

And then everything accelerated and the woozy times began. He was taken to the fourth floor again and strapped to the chair and endured the slice of pain in his arm that admitted the merchandise. Dr. Croft, inscrutable as before, hovered over him, and the Handyman lurked somewhere nearby. Barney submitted himself to the proceedings although everything inside of him shouted out in protest. He didn't want to be deprived of memory, did not want to take the chance of having Cassie abolished from his life, risk having her vanish from his perceptions. Yet he knew that his presence in the Complex depended on the tests. If he didn't participate, then he had no reason to be here and that would be even worse, being sent away and never seeing her again. So he let himself go limp in the

133

chair as the merchandise invaded his veins, bringing that dizzying oblivion.

When he awakened, the woozy times began, the funny times when minutes disappeared and the walls shimmered and melted and the ceiling danced. Dazed and dazzled by lights and shadows, he wandered the corridors, swaying and tilting, and seemed to bounce off the walls as he walked. Or didn't walk but seemed to float, filled with the need to see Cassie again, looking for her but not finding her. Feeling lonely and abandoned. Groping his way back finally to his room.

The wooziness diminished at last, and he was able to negotiate his way up and down the hallways without incident, in control again, although he was frequently lightheaded and his legs a bit unstable. Billy the Kidney remained in his room after his most recent experience with the merchandise, door closed, red light glowing, nurses whisking in and out like starched ghosts. They paid no attention to Barney, and he felt like a ghost himself.

And then that strange time was over and he awoke one night, shot abruptly into here and now like a bullet out of a rifle. He raised himself on one elbow, heard the night sounds of the Complex—hum of a motor, sigh of a door closing somewhere, sudden rush of rubber-soled feet—and felt content. No dizziness, no crazy thoughts, no buckling walls and dancing ceilings. Cassie's face floated before him in the darkness, and all his longing returned but filled now with sweetness.

Restless and unsettled, he threw off the sheet, climbed out of bed, nosed his feet into his slippers, and made his way out of the room. It was luxurious to be walking without dizziness threatening to tumble him down, the walls and floors behaving. The wall clock said 11:26.

He paused at Billy's room, ignored the red light and peeked in, saw Billy's form on the bed. Gratified to learn that Billy had returned from Isolation, Barney whispered, "Sleep tight, Billy." Waited, no response, Billy sleeping nice and tight.

He went down the corridor to Mazzo's room, again ignored the red light, and went in. A night light burned feebly on the wall. Mazzo twisted and turned on the bed, moaning, groaning, muttering. The machine to which he was attached blooped and bleeped. As Barney walked quietly to the bed, Mazzo stiffened under the sheet.

"Who's there?" Mazzo asked, alert, alarmed.

"Barney." A whisper.

"Where the hell have you been?" Mazzo asked, voice hoarse, phlegmed.

Barney was appalled at his condition. Just a few days ago he was sitting up, telling Barney about home runs and bean balls. Now he looked fevered again, wasted.

"The merchandise," Barney said. "They gave me more stuff."

"Was it bad?" Mazzo asked, grinding the words out through stiff lips, as if it cost him a lot to speak.

"Nothing to it," Barney said. Then bent toward Mazzo to hear him better. "How's it going? Tough?"

Mazzo began to cough, a hacking, rasping, violent cough that convulsed his body. His hand reached out like the hand of someone drowning, groping for rescue, and Barney grabbed it and held it firmly in his own, crushed it to his chest.

"Take it easy," Barney said.

Mazzo's hand was tightly in his, perspiration like glue fastening their hands together. Barney had bent over at an awkward angle, and his back began to hurt. But he didn't move, remained standing that way because Mazzo wasn't moaning or twisting on the bed anymore. The room smelled terrible—did pain and hopelessness have odors? Barney didn't mind the faint smell of vomit or even the farts that came out of Mazzo once in a while, but those other unidentified odors bothered him, seemed to sink into his pores and spread through his body.

"Christ, Mazzo, what are you doing in this lousy place?" Barney asked, his back killing him but not moving, Mazzo's hand still pressed against his chest. "You could be someplace else, home, maybe. . . ."

Mazzo intensified his grip on Barney's hand.

"I came here to die," Mazzo muttered.

"Everybody comes here to die," Barney said. "But you're fighting all the time."

Mazzo finally loosened his grip and withdrew his hand, and Barney, grateful, was able to unbend. He stood up straight, arching his back, waiting for the pain to subside.

A long sigh came from Mazzo, like a hollow whistle heard from far away. "I came here to die quicker," he said, pronouncing the words carefully, as if he wanted to be certain Barney understood them. "I heard about this place. The experiments. I figured one of the drugs would get me. Kill me. I didn't have the guts to do it myself, but I thought the drugs would do it for me." He grimaced, face sour. "But it hasn't happened," he whispered.

Barney knew now why Mazzo was so different from Billy the Kidney and Allie Roon. What had the Handyman said? How can you know other people's motives for what they do?

Mazzo beckoned him closer.

"Do me a favor," Mazzo said, breath rancid. "Pull the plug, Barney."

"What plug?"

"On the machine." He gestured toward the unit near the bed, bleeping quietly in the half-light, the bleeping so customary here in the room that you barely heard it.

"I can't do that," Barney said, horrified. "That's murder."

"Not murder. You'd be doing me a favor."

Barney turned away, not because of the terrible breath but because of the anger that churned through him, anger at whatever brings people to a point in their lives that they prefer dying to living, ask for it, beg for it.

"Ah, Barney, let me die," Mazzo pleaded.

Barney wanted to lash out at something. But what? The whole world, maybe.

"I thought you wanted to go out in a blaze of glory, Mazzo," he said. "One big wild ride."

The harsh semblance of laughter from Mazzo, not really laughter but a cackle an old man might make, toothless and mirthless.

The vision Barney had seen on the fence, that glimmer from afar, winked at him again.

"Hey, Mazzo," Barney said, suddenly excited. "You're going to have that last ride. Go out in a blaze of glory." A crazy promise, he knew. But he knew at this moment that he could make it come true. Maybe it was the merchandise talking or the wooziness that had warped his reasoning, but he saw it so clearly: Mazzo in the final ride, beautiful and dazzling.

Footsteps in the corridor. Coming close. Closer.

Barney glanced up to see the silhouette of a nurse standing at the doorway. She stepped into the room, eyes widening in surprise when she spotted Barney there.

"Get back to your room this instant," she said, her voice crackling with anger.

A new nurse—he had never seen her before. And he couldn't risk her anger and a possible report to the Handyman.

"Sorry," he said, giving Mazzo a last encouraging look over his shoulder. Mazzo merely turned away.

Back in his room, in his bed, Barney drifted into sleep, weary now, bones aching a bit, his back painful from that uncomfortable stance in Mazzo's room. He would keep his promise somehow. Mazzo would go out in a blaze of glory, and Barney and Cassie and all of them would cheer him on.

13

*B*ILLY," he said. "We are going to steal a car."

"We?" Billy asked, raising his hands in a helpless gesture. Meaning: me, this wheelchair, my legs all shot?

"Yes, we," Barney said. "I'll do the actual stealing, but you'll be the expert on how to pull it off and also act as a lookout."

Billy looked doubtful, but his expression also showed a bit of hope. In a place like the Complex, anything that broke the routine, fractured the hopelessness and boredom, was welcome. Even the impossible, like stealing a car.

"Where are we going to steal this car?" Billy asked, playing along, nothing to lose, what the hell.

"From the junkyard next door."

Billy shook his head. "You're crazy, Barney, know that? Why do you want to steal a car from a junkyard?"

"Not just any car," Barney said. "A particular car. A very particular car."

Billy's eyes gleamed with interest now. Barney could always do that to him, capture his attention and interest.

"What are you going to do with it once you steal it?" Billy asked.

"Give somebody a ride in it," Barney said, delighted

with Billy's curiosity. He was also delighted by something else: a new kind of aftermath. Not the frightening, dizzying aftermath he had dreaded so much but a new one. He'd awakened this morning feeling pleasantly light-headed and tipsy, his body loose and relaxed. He had never been drunk in his life, but he figured this was how being mildly drunk must be. Feeling willy-nilly and sort of woozy. But in control. Able to walk and talk and eat—the return of his taste had also brought back his appetite and food tasted good again, even the institutional kind of food he found on his plate every day. Anyway, anyway. He enjoyed the sensation of tipsiness, drifting down the corridor to find Billy sunning himself near a rear window.

"Who?" Billy asked. "Who's going to ride in it?" A child again, hoping it might be him.

"That comes later," Barney said, thinking that yes, maybe Billy could get to ride in it too. He'd hate to disappoint Billy. "First the car."

"Okay, which car you going to steal?"

"We," Barney said, "you and me, we're going to steal it." Slurring his words a bit, talking lazy but nice and slow, no hurry. "Like a partnership. Partners in crime."

"Wow," Billy said. "But which car?"

"Well, it's not really a car."

Billy's face fell, disappointment draining the eagerness away. "Hell, Barney, you just said we were going to steal a car and now you say it's not a car."

"That's right, Billy. It's a car but it's not a car. Remember that day I climbed the fence? I spotted it from the top of the fence. A red car, looked like an MG."

"That was the day you froze on the fence. Like a statue and I was calling you to come down."

"Right. Well, I went back up again. Went up the fence

140

and over, and looked at the car real close. Know what I found out?" He felt light and bright and clever.

"What?"

"That it was made of wood. An imitation car some kids made in a school in woodworking class. The label said that."

Billy was even more disappointed. "Aw, what good's a phony car?"

"Remember those little cars they have in amusement parks? They weren't real but they were fun to ride. Hell, you must have ridden in one of them. I did." Barney wasn't sure where or when he had driven one but knew he had, all right.

"Sure, I remember," Billy said.

"Well, you had fun, didn't you?"

"But it wasn't made of wood, Barney."

Barney sighed in exasperation. "What does it matter what it's made of," he said, "as long as it works." But he wanted to say more. Needed to tell him how he felt about the car and what it meant.

"Billy," he said, knowing he was breaking the rule and entering Billy's compartment, "why did you come here? To this place?"

Billy looked quickly away, a pink flush invading his sallow complexion. His hands fiddled with the controls of his wheelchair. "I . . . I . . ." he stammered.

"To serve mankind?" Barney asked, knowing the words were high sounding and probably embarrassing to Billy. But true all the same.

"I don't know," Billy said. "There was nothing else to do. I figured what they learned in the tests might help somebody, sometime. I don't know about mankind, though."

"Okay. In other words, you're doing something, right?"

Billy looked at him again. Nodded. "Trying to."

"Well, I've got to do something, too. Or try." It was still difficult finding the words. "The worst thing, Billy, is not doing anything at all. So stealing a car that isn't a car is better than doing nothing."

Billy looked at him doubtfully, frowning.

"Trust me," Barney said, thinking: The best thing is action, not words. Show Billy the Kidney what he meant. Steal the car and let Billy see what he meant. "I'm going to make that car work, Billy. . . ."

Billy still looked skeptical. But there was a hint of interest behind the skepticism.

"Tell me some more," Billy said.

"Before I tell you more, we have to steal it," Barney said. "We also need a plan. And some tools. That's where you come in, Billy. You know all about this place. Where can I find some tools? Like a saw and a screwdriver. Stuff like that."

"You going to build a car or steal one?" Billy said, eyes bright with interest now.

"Maybe both," Barney said mysteriously. "And I'm counting on you, Billy, to help."

Billy snapped his fingers. "The cellar," he said. "I saw a maintenance guy come out of the celler with a toolbox once."

Good old Billy the Kidney. He knew almost everything about the Complex except when he was going to die.

He had never been in the cellar before, had had no reason for visiting it, so he stumbled around the place like an explorer invading foreign territory. The cellar reminded him of a haunted house, white sheets covering assorted pieces

142

of furniture. Barney gingerly lifted a sheet off a chair, afraid he might find a ghost sitting in it. And chuckled when he saw nobody, not even a ghost, was under the sheet.

Just as Billy had reported, the cellar was neat, everything seemed in place. An array of paint cans lined one wall. Lawn mowers and other pieces of equipment, along with shovels and hoes and rakes, hung from pegs on a long board at the far end. The cellar was divided into small alcoves. Peeking into them, Barney saw that most were empty or contained more furniture, shaped like desks and chairs, also covered with sheets.

There had to be a workbench somewhere. And a workbench always had tools, among them the tools he needed—a screwdriver, a hammer, maybe a chisel.

The dust tickled Barney's nostrils and he almost sneezed. He tried not to sneeze, although nobody was here except him. Nobody but us chickens, he thought, feeling light and bright and adventurous.

At the next alcove he saw the green workbench, loaded with tools of all kinds. Thanks, Billy the Kidney.

In the drawers of the workbench he found a variety of tools, all kinds of hammers and chisels and drills and screwdrivers and stuff he didn't know the names of. He took a medium-size screwdriver and a small hammer. He could always come back if he found that he needed more tools.

Best of all, he discovered a room at the far end of the cellar that was completely isolated from the rest of the place. Not an alcove but a room with a door. The room was dusty and dirty, old newspapers piled in a corner, rags tossed here and there. A sagging table, covered with cheap oilcloth, stood in the middle of the room. A few straight-backed chairs, some with missing legs or backs or seats, stood around like crippled beings from another planet.

Barney giggled with delight.

A perfect place to work.

Private and untouched by human hands for God knows how long.

Giggling again—he couldn't remember ever giggling before in his life—and still pleasantly light-headed, he stood at the doorway of the room, grinning happily.

Next item on the agenda:

Car theft.

But first, Allie Roon.

Billy the Kidney had protested when Barney had said that he wanted to make Allie part of the plan for stealing the car.

Disappointed, he had said: "He's no use, Barney. He won't even make a good lookout with all his twitchings. You wouldn't know whether he was trying to give you a signal somebody was coming or whether he was just twitching like he always does."

"Look, Billy," Barney had explained. "He's going to see us coming and going. He'll wonder what's going on. He might start asking questions or nosing around. He could screw it up nice and easy."

Billy's lips formed a childish pout. "I thought we were partners, just you and me, Barney."

"We are partners, Billy. Think of Allie Roon as our assistant."

"He'll have to take orders from me?" Billy asked, getting interested again.

Barney sighed; he got tired sometimes of Billy's childish behavior. Actually, he didn't know why he was insisting on

Allie Roon's participation in the event. He wasn't really worried that Allie would blunder and probably ruin the plan. Somehow it seemed proper to have Allie join in the conspiracy.

"Yes," Barney said, "Allie Roon will have to take orders from you."

"Gee, I don't know," Billy said, still reluctant, shaking his head dolefully but giving in finally. "But I guess it will be okay."

Barney stole his way along the fence, crouched low as if he were a moving target, looking for loose slats. But there were no loose slats. Whoever had built the fence had built it to last, to resist anyone trying to break through the fence. Which seemed ridiculous, of course. Why would anyone want to break into a junkyard? But I'm breaking into it, Barney thought.

He ran his hand over the weather-beaten wood. Weather-beaten but sturdy. Glancing back at the Complex, he saw Billy the Kidney in his wheelchair acting as lookout near the doorway. He knew that Allie Roon stood inside near the freight elevator also performing lookout duties. Unnecessary, of course. But they'd been so eager to be a part of the car theft that Barney had pretended that lookouts were needed at this point. Maybe later, but not now.

He frowned at the fence. Problem: getting the car into the Complex. Impossible to lift it over the fence. Probably impossible to cut an opening in the fence wide enough to get it through. Even if it were possible, he didn't want to risk sneaking a car into the complex. Better to smuggle it in piece by piece, a little at a time, and then reassemble the car later. Slower, maybe, but safer.

145

What he needed was a section of fence, away from the street or the windows of the Complex, in which he could loosen some of the slats. He became discouraged as he moved along the fence, testing the sturdiness of it, looking for weaknesses and finding none. Maybe he'd have to return to the cellar and find a saw. But how the hell would he go about sawing his way through a fence?

Finally, a hundred feet or so from the Complex, almost at the spot where the fence turned a corner, he noticed a section with boards that were not joined as tightly together as the rest of the fence. Two loose slats with a bit of daylight between them. Enough daylight to admit a hammer or screwdriver or even a crowbar if he could find one back in the Complex. Might as well give it a try with the tools at hand. Taking the hammer from his pocket, Barney pried the boards apart. Without having to exert himself too much, he pulled two boards loose from their nails, creating a small opening less than a foot wide. He would have to loosen another slat. But the third board proved tougher, resisting his efforts. The board was newer than the others, evidently installed during a recent repair job. Finally the slat yielded to him, drawing loose from its hold. Barney peered through the opening, then measured it with his hands. Wide enough to pass the sections of the car through. Beautiful. He spent another ten minutes at the fence, nailing the boards back into position but not hammering the nails too tightly so that they'd be easy to remove. Tomorrow he'd begin the actual theft.

The sun was slanting low in the sky when he returned to the Complex. Billy greeted him with professional courtesy, formal in his questions, which reflected how seriously he was taking the conspiracy. What was the condition of the fence? Had it been hard taking the nails out? Was he sure the opening was wide enough for both him and the sections of the car? Barney answered his questions with equal seriousness, playing the game, going along with the act. Although he knew that Billy didn't consider it an act.

Inside, Allie Roon greeted him juicily, spitting and twitching. "H . . . h . . . h . . . o . . . o . . . o . . . o . . . ow . . . ow . . . ow . . . how . . . d . . . di . . . di . . . did . . . I . . . I . . . I . . . d . . . do . . . do?"

Barney thought: How the hell do I know? You were inside, I was outside.

But he told Allie Roon that he had done fine, real fine.

He was impatient to get away from Billy and Allie Roon. He wanted to get back to his room, wash up and change his clothes, get ready for his meeting with Cassie. He hadn't seen her since the wooziness, three long days ago, and hoped she would show up today. His desire to see her was like a wound in his heart.

That day she told him about the Thing.

"It happened when I was just a kid, oh, twelve years old. Actually, I remember exactly when it happened. A Saturday afternoon, July, Alberto away at summer camp in Maine. Papa and I came out of McDonald's. I'd just pigged out on a quarter pounder with a large order of fries. On the way to the car this weird feeling hit me. Like the sun had disappeared, although I could feel its warmth on my face. It was like I was ready to drop through the earth, my breath coming fast. Dizzy, but more than that, as if I was floating in space. And this terrible feeling that I was going to die . . ."

She shuddered and Barney, stunned at her words, listened raptly, afraid to breathe, afraid to distract her and stop the flow of words.

"Papa came around the car and helped me. The light dazzled my eyes. My head whirled. And then, suddenly, nothing. As if all the clocks in the world had stopped. And my heart along with them. And then the Thing ended as abruptly as it had started. Bingo. Everything normal again. Sun shining, heart beating, stomach bulging with all that food and the taste of the fries in my mouth again. That was the first time. . . ."

"And the second?" Barney said, barely knowing that he was speaking the words but knowing the question was exactly right.

"The second was pain. Unbearable. Never knew such pain. What I called my first migraine, although I knew it wasn't a migraine. The doctor knew it wasn't either. But he couldn't tell what it was. Doctor Langley, our family doctor. He did all sorts of tests. Sent me off to a clinic in Boston. Brain scan, all that stuff. But they found nothing. Like an old joke: They X-rayed my head and found nothing in it . . . but the pain was in it. It hit me like lightning, my head almost spinning off my body. God, it hurt. So much that I guess I must have screamed and Papa came running. Rushed me to the hospital. And then it subsided, became not so bad. But it stuck around for quite a while. . . ."

She fell silent then. And Barney waited. He had never seen her like this before, never heard her talk like this before. She had arrived early for the visit, was waiting for him in the reception room when he came ambling along the corridor. She seemed tired, eyes shining almost with fever, said she hadn't been sleeping well, worrying about Alberto all the time. Instead of sitting across from him as usual, she paced the room, like a trapped thing looking for a means of escape but not sure whether escape was the answer. He gave his usual report about Mazzo, watching her closely as she paced up and down nodding her head. Finally she collapsed in the chair, blowing air out of the corner of her mouth with the little-girl aspect she displayed on occasion.

"Anything I can do?" Barney asked. "You look so . . ." He groped for the word. Unhappy? Hurting? Another migraine?

She supplied the word. "Rotten," she said. "I feel rotten and look rotten."

She could never look rotten, of course. Tired sometimes, face drawn, as if she hadn't been sleeping well. But always lovely, even when the loveliness was tattered. Like at this moment.

"Poor Barney Snow," she said, looking at him with the tenderness that melted his bones and muscles. "Heaping you with my burdens."

"You haven't heaped me with anything," he said. Gathering his thoughts, not wanting to say too much, scare her away. "I look forward to these meetings with you."

Her appraising eyes measured him. "It must be this place, Barney Snow, and what it does to me. I tell you things I've never told anybody."

Thrilled, he hugged his silence.

"Like the migraines you're always asking about," she said. "They're not migraines at all."

"What are they then?"

"The Thing."

"What thing?"

"I didn't know myself for a long time. That's why I called it the Thing. For want of a better name."

And that was when she began her recitation, her history of the Thing that had haunted her through the years. Made

149

her a prisoner of phantom aches and pains and depressions that no doctor could trace or diagnose.

"I'm quite a case, right, Barney?" she asked, smiling ruefully. "I should probably be in this place instead of all you guys." She closed her eyes for a moment, her head resting now on the back of the chair. "And yet . . . and yet . . ."

She told him then that she was grateful for the Thing, after all. It had led her to the Hacienda, made her realize there was more to life than the clothes you wore or the food you ate or wanting nice things. Something beyond all that.

Barney felt the chill of dread as she spoke. Cassie locked up in a convent, dressed in the nun's costume of black and white? All that brightness shut away, the blond hidden under a veil.

"Ever hear of stigmata, Barney?" she asked.

The word was vaguely familiar to him, but he couldn't pin down its meaning.

"It's a manifestation. I looked it up. The wounds of Christ or the saints appear on people's bodies. Along with the pain."

The question he wanted to ask was in his eyes, because she laughed a bit, shaking her head. "No. I didn't have stigmata. Although I thought I did. It's a long story. . . ."

It wasn't really a long story, and anyway, he could have listened forever to this strange and lovely girl with the blues-singer voice who had entered his life at a time when he was empty, barren, his emotions as blank as his lost sense of taste. She had filled the emptiness with her visits here to this room. He wanted to keep her talking, keep her here as long as possible. And he concentrated furiously on what she was saying, absorbing her words into his being, so that they'd become a part of him when she wasn't there.

". . . so I looked down at my leg, just under my knee, and saw this stain spreading on my skin, just below the surface. The pain was fierce, a burning pain, and as I looked I saw the stain become deeper, an angry red, an oozing kind of pain as if blood was actually flowing from a wound. Crazy, right? What wound? I'd been sitting in the den, doing my homework, being a good little high-school student, when it happened. I watched the stain grow deeper and winced as the pain grew worse. The stain was about four inches long, jagged, the shape of a crocodile. I limped upstairs, slipped into bed, felt safe there, hoped no one would come in and find me, although Alberto was away at Stanley Prep and Papa was on one of his business trips and my mother was at the monthly meeting of some club or other. I prayed. Prayed for the first time in a long time. Not like the going-through-the-motions prayers of Sunday school. Really prayed. And as I prayed I thought, crazily, stigmata." She laughed, the laughter a small whoop of self-mockery. "It wasn't stigmata. People like me don't get stigmata. The saints do. But those prayers I said, they opened doors for me. I'd never done any praying like that before. I'd always prayed the way you recite lessons in class. But not that time. I really felt as though I'd . . . communicated. With something, someone. Anyway, when I heard about the Hacienda a few weeks later, I talked Papa and Mother into letting me enroll. Even though I didn't know what I wanted to do with my life. And still don't. . . ."

Silence in the room then, and Barney let it gather, afraid to say or do anything to break the spell. He had been allowed to enter Cassie's private world for a little while, and

151

although he was dismayed by the pain she had endured—
was the whole world sick, was there no safe place on
earth?—he cherished the intimacy they had shared.

"I talk too much," she said, breaking the silence. "It's
this place, I think."

He plunged, letting his curiosity get the upper hand.
Not curiosity but concern for her. "Did you ever find out
what the Thing was?"

"No," she said. But too quick and too loud in her response. Then settling back in the chair. "It doesn't bother
me as much anymore. Mostly small headaches now. I can
live with that."

He didn't know whether to believe her or not. Had no
choice, really. Had to believe her.

"Hey, Barney," she said, bright now, eyes glowing
again. "Don't look so glum. It's not that bad."

"But you looked so sad."

She scoffed, shaking her head in that way she had.
"Okay, it gets me down once in a while. But that's life,
isn't it? Don't be sad for me." Her voice husky and vibrant,
her chin tilted challengingly. "Let's not talk about it anymore. How about you? Tell me about you. . . ."

But there was nothing he wanted to say, nothing he
could say. He was afraid that if he began talking he would
tell her about the car and his grand design. And it might
sound crazy to her. She might laugh. And he would be unable to bear being laughed at by her.

Angrily she kicked at the accelerator, sent the wheels of
the car spinning, spitting gravel onto the pavement. Angry
at herself. For letting down before that poor kid, Barney
Snow, telling him about the Thing, for God's sake. She'd
always feared something like that happening during one of

her visits, feared that a visit would coincide with one of her vulnerable moments, when she was defenseless, without any protection at all.

Damn it: She had not wanted that to happen. She had hidden the Thing and its ravages from dozens of people—including Papa and her mother and Alberto, as well as all the doctors, and now she had confessed it all to that boy, responding maybe to that hopeless helpless adoration in his eyes. She was sorry that she had begun those visits to the clinic. She'd found no comfort in them, only corroboration. And corroboration was the last thing she wanted.

The street stretched before her like a tunnel, old maple and oak trees forming an arch, and she slackened the speed of the car. She was reluctant to return home, needed some time to prepare herself for her mother, to calm down a bit. Like an actress preparing for a role. Had to be light and bright, cheerful, hopeful. Had to hide the panic that came upon her at odd moments when her guard was down.

I will not let it get me down, she vowed. I will fight it to the end. This thing that threatened everything.

Still angry, angry as much at the Thing as her confession to Barney Snow, she pressed down on the accelerator again and grinned as the car surged forward. Cassie Mazzofono, demon driver. Outracing the moon above and the sun tomorrow. How she wished she could outrace the Thing.

14

*H*E looked at the car, resplendent in its crimson beauty but grotesque in its fakery, and felt defeated before he began. The screwdriver was in his hand and the hammer in his back pocket. But the whole plan struck him now as ludicrous and impossible.

For instance:

Take this thing apart, carefully, screw by screw, piece by piece, get it back somehow to the Complex, assemble it in the cellar, and then arrange for Mazzo's ride.

Impossible.

Disconsolate, he stood there, hands thrust into his pockets, knowing that Billy the Kidney and Allie Roon were in the Complex, standing guard, riding shotgun, expecting great doings, miracles. And here he was in this terrible junkyard contemplating this fakery of a car.

Sounds reached his ears. Noise, movement. From the front of the junkyard.

Just his luck. Someone invading this distant section where he'd never seen anybody before.

Standing on tiptoe, craning his neck, looking toward the front of the place, where all the action usually went on.

Everything seemed secure and serene. No more sounds. No movement.

And then he giggled.

Giggled out of the aftermaths, and the funny feeling of being tipsy. Giddy and giggling—Barney Snow, of all people, actually giggling—he smiled at the world of busted vehicles and drew the hammer out of his pocket.

But before beginning, he surveyed the object of his intention.

Had to count the parts. The parts that must be separated and then joined together. Let's count the parts.

Two front fenders: check. Hood: check. Two back fenders: check. Trunk:

He looked at the trunk, then lifted the cover and found a hollow space within. Okay, check. Trunk cover, no trunk.

Two doors: check.

Craning his neck now, looking into the car.

Front seat: check. Instrument dashboard: check. Steering wheel: check. Floorboards: check.

Okay, now add up the sections.

Wait a minute. The wheels.

Bending down, still a bit dizzy, he counted the wheels. Four of them.

Didn't all cars have four wheels?

Giggled. So. Now. Count the parts. Add them up.

Forget addition. He knew what he had to do. Get to work with the screwdriver and take the car apart. Sneak the sections into the Complex and put it back together again. A simple procedure, with Billy the Kidney and Allie Roon as watchdogs.

Now he paused before beginning the job, stood for a moment without moving there in the junkyard, surrounded by all the junk. Felt like saying a prayer for some reason. He thought of Cassie and how troubled she had seemed during her last visit. Maybe he should have told her about this great adventure, make her somehow a part of it. Ah, but she was a part of it, anyway, even if she didn't know it.

"Let's go," he said aloud.

He tossed the screwdriver into the air, watched it tumbling and turning and falling, caught it with a hand that was marvelously ready and waiting.

And he began to take the car apart.

The car reminded him of that old song—the hip bone's connected to the thigh bone and the thigh bone's connected to the knee bone—and the song sang in him as he worked out in the sunshine, coasting nicely in the light-headedness that made everything sort of unreal, as if this was happening in a dream.

Despite the wooziness his hands were steady, wielding the screwdriver expertly for the most part, dropping it once in a while, but then he had never been very clever with his hands. The wood was soft, balsa, like the kind used in making model airplanes, and it yielded the screws easily most of the time. Once in a while a screw was stubborn, refusing to come loose, and Barney closed his eyes and concentrated all his strength on getting it out. And laughed in triumph when the screw gave way.

Occasionally there was activity at the front of the junk-yard, sounds of motors and men yelling to each other. But no one approached the area Barney worked in. The vehicles here were especially dilapidated, probably no longer contained usable parts. The air was pleasant, a sparkling spring day, and it was nice working on the car, feeling useful, the breeze bringing the smell of freshness to his nostrils.

He dismantled the front fender and the door on the driver's side first, and when he removed them the remainder of the car sagged dangerously. Barney feared that it might simply fall apart, screws torn from wood, the car splintered and damaged beyond repair. But that didn't happen. The car merely tilted a bit, listing as a foundering ship might list but with no ocean to sink into.

Sweat rolled down his forehead, stung his eyes, causing him to blink, blurring his vision. He rested, sitting with his back to a front wheel. Heart thudding, his body almost rising and falling with the thuds. He knew he had embarked on a crazy mission but didn't care. This was better than wandering around the Complex, bored and restless, bored with everything and everybody, including himself. And it was almost a sin to be bored when life was precious and sweet and so many others were dying.

When he resumed work, he looked at the watch he had borrowed from Allie Roon. He had been working about an hour, and his progress was going according to plan. The plan was to carry out the dismantling and carrying of the parts into the Complex by stages, bit by bit, all carefully timed. Because of the lightness of the material, he could comfortably carry three parts at a time. That meant six trips at a minimum. He would take the sections to the fence, rest there awhile. The next step was Allie's contribution. He had found a room containing spare wheelchairs, not in regular use. He suggested to Barney painstakingly, spitting and sputtering, that a wheelchair could be used to transport the sections from the fence to the Complex. And from the doorway to the freight elevator. The elevator would then carry the sections to the cellar. Simple but risky. The risks small, however, as Billy the Kidney, the master planner, had pointed out, relishing his role as the strategist. The use of the freight elevator was Billy's contribution to the plan. At least that was what Billy thought. Barney had known from the beginning that the freight elevator was strategic, but he pretended that it had been Billy's idea. Billy positively glowed these days, quick to laugh or grin. And Allie Roon's twitchings were almost like joyous leapings.

So, feeling nice and loose and floating with the light-headedness, he set to work again, loosening the screws, tongue in the corner of his mouth when he encountered a stubborn one, giving it his best, humming and singing along, the knee bone's connected to the shin bone, the shin bone's connected to the ankle bone, and here we are, doing the job, getting it done, like Humpty Dumpty, taking poor Humpty Dumpty apart after his great fall and putting him back together again.

Cassie's visits were beautiful now.

Weary from the day's work, he sat before her gratefully, feeling useful, as if he had earned the right to be there with her, doing something, accomplishing something.

When he asked her, hesitantly, about the Thing, she shook her head, dismissing the question.

"Forget it," she said. "I exaggerate at times. A need to be dramatic, I guess. Things are fine." And she blinked those marvelous eyes of hers in comic fashion, a clownish smile playing on her lips.

Warmth flooded him and goodness and love. God, how he wanted to tell her about the car, and his plans for Mazzo's last wild ride. But he could not take the risk. He didn't want anything to spoil the adventure. Cassie was from the outside world. He would hate to appear ridiculous in her eyes.

After he gave her the report on Mazzo—he seemed to be in better spirits and without any pain—she rose from the chair, thanked him, smiled. And just before she left, she reached out and touched his shoulder. A brief brushing of her fingers. As she left, calling good-bye over her shoulder, his hand cradled the spot that she had touched, and he stood there like that until his arm began to ache.

This boy, Barney Snow, kept touching chords within her. Chords of guilt, of course. But more than that. She sometimes suspected that he was more perceptive than she gave him credit for. *Did you ever find out what the Thing was?* he had asked. No, she had replied, lying, of course. And the boy had not believed her. Wanted to but hadn't. She'd never told anyone the secret of the Thing—how could she admit it to Barney Snow in the clinic even though he affected her in a strange and tender way? And the guilt: using him for her own purposes. That was part of it. The deception. The Thing had turned her into a superb deceiver through the years. Particularly after she had learned its secret. She wished, in fact, that she had never learned its secret.

It had happened the night after Thanksgiving two years ago. She was home for the holiday weekend, the home that had always been a winter-holiday kind of house, storybook stuff: blazing logs in the fireplace, bow windows hung with icicles, snow like white frosting on the lawn. Papa was sentimental about holidays, always rushed the seasons, preparing for Christmas before Thanksgiving, cutting a tree up in the New Hampshire woods and nursing it along in the cellar with special secret liquids he concocted. But no tree in the cellar two years ago. No rushing of the season with Papa dead and gone. No holiday mood, either. She'd returned almost reluctantly from the Hacienda; although she was uncertain of a vocation—who was she, Cassie Mazzofono, to think she could be a nun?—she'd found a kind of fulfillment in the cheerful and bustling atmosphere. Why had she thought convents were grim and somber places?

In her room that night after Thanksgiving, she played some old records—mostly Beatles stuff—and reread two Nancy Drews ("Will I ever grow up?") and had just closed the second book (*The Secret of Shadow Ranch*) when she was assaulted with a staggering pain in her left arm, astonishing in its intensity. A pain that echoed the explosion in her head years ago the second time she'd felt the Thing. Now the pain, between wrist and elbow, made her nauseous, acid burning in her throat, knees weak and trembling, eyes dazzled as if the small lamp burning in the room was too bright. The pain brought an image to her mind of a pencil being snapped in two. It lasted for almost two hours while she clutched herself in bed, arms locked around her body, trying to diminish herself, make her body a small target. Finally the pain subsided, became muted, then disappeared altogether, although her arm continued to throb as if a giant pulse were beating beneath the surface of her flesh. Finally she fell into a deep dreamless sleep.

She awoke the next morning, still in her jeans and sweater. Showered and then shampooed her hair, arm still sensitive and throbbing.

And went downstairs to learn the secret of the Thing.

Alberto stood at the den window looking outside, then turned to greet her. His left arm was in a sling. He had a

160

sheepish grin on his face. "Jerry Belson was driving, Cassie," he said. "His car was totaled. Lucky I only got a broken arm...."

She managed to keep her face from falling apart.

Coincidence, of course, she told herself later that day, the kind of impossible thing that happens all the time, flouting all the odds. But then she turned detective, like some kind of demented Nancy Drew, and led Alberto through sly interrogations.

Waylaying him in the kitchen as he gulped down a piece of Mrs. Cortoleona's pizza while waiting for some girl to pick him up (the fractured arm didn't inhibit Alberto's social life), she pinned him down with questions.

"What year were you at Camp Wickwackee down in Maine?"

Tomato sauce bubbling on his lips, he said: "Camp Wickennona." Added, "I don't know. All those camps were alike."

"No, they weren't. Come on, think."

Rolling his eyes, wolfing down the pizza, chewing vigorously, he thought. Or pretended to.

Finally, with her prodding, they pinned down the year. Cassie nodded her head with grim satisfaction.

"Anything unusual happen that summer?" Cassie asked. "On a Saturday? Early afternoon?"

"You crazy, Cassie?" he asked. "How can I remember what happened on a Saturday that long ago?"

"This would be something unusual," Cassie said, patient and persistent. "Maybe some kind of accident."

He poured himself a glass of milk, showing off how clever he could be with one hand.

"Think," she commanded. And prompted him. Had he been injured, sick, threatened?

"Jeez, Cassie," he complained. "Why all the big interest? You sound like some kind of nut."

"Were you in some kind of danger? You've always done crazy things. . . ."

"Okay, okay," he said, always giving in to her. "Let's see. . . ." Closed his eyes for a moment. Then they flew open. "Wait. That was the summer I started climbing."

"Climbing what?"

He looked disgusted. "Mountains. What else do you climb at summer camp? This mountain in Maine. Katahdin. Real big. A bunch of us went up, crazy, without a guide, didn't have proper equipment." His eyes widened. "I remember now. I slipped. At the edge of this big chasm, and actually dropped. Out in space, dangling there by this thin rope. Cripes, I thought I was done for. Never been so scared in my life." His face turned pale as he spoke. "I actually thought I was going to die . . ."

. . . while Cassie in the parking lot outside McDonald's, crammed with a quarter pounder and a large order of fries, had shared his danger and anguish and dread, more than shared, experienced what he was experiencing as his mirror image, his other self.

During that Thanksgiving weekend she tracked down other incidents, searching her own memory, pinning down exact or approximate times she had been struck by the Thing and matched them to Alberto's experience. He was an athlete, always getting battered and bruised, tackled roughly. Ever cut your leg, Alberto, below the knee, deep cut? He still had the scar, showed it to her, told her how he'd always kept this kind of stuff hidden from Papa and Mother. Hey, what's this all about, Cassie? I'm doing a term paper on athletic injuries, she told him. He seemed satisfied, his mind on other things, like the student nurse he'd met in the emergency room the night of the accident.

She learned that the Thing and its effects were not reciprocal. Alberto could not recall unexplained aches or pains. Cramps had often accompanied Cassie's menstrual flow, but Alberto scoffed at the idea of stomachaches and cramps. Posing in a parody of muscle-beach characters, he said: "Look at this body. Narry an ache or pain."

Oh yeah, Cassie wanted to say, remembering the hundreds of times she'd absorbed a vicious blow to the head or neck or chest, mystified then and terrified, but knowing now the reason. A sudden thought alarmed her: Suppose Alberto had fallen that summer day, plunged into the depths of that canyon in Maine? She had shared the sensations of his danger. What else would she have shared? If he had fallen to his death . . .

She recoiled at the thought, panic racing along her bones and sinews, rushing through her veins and arteries. Calm down, calm down. Maybe she ought to talk to someone, make a furtive appointment with Dr. Langley, present him with the evidence of her investigation. But she'd feel silly exposing herself that way, certain he would dismiss her as a hopeless neurotic or explain it all away as psychosomatic.

Before returning to the Hacienda that Sunday night, she wondered whether she should tell Alberto, risking his ridicule and disbelief. If she couldn't tell him, then she should at least warn him to be careful. Take care of yourself, buddy. Think twice before sliding into third base or climbing another mountain. Whither thou goest, I will go. But she didn't tell him anything.

Before going off to the Hacienda, she made a trip to the

163

library. She remembered dimly a movie she'd seen long ago on late-night television, an old adventure derived from a book, about two brothers sharing a condition similar to hers and Alberto's, a tale of derring-do, swordplay and galloping horses. She'd reached back in her memory but been unable to remember the title of the movie or the book. She knew it had something to do with brothers. Or cousins. The title teased at the edges of her mind, flirting, beckoning. Brothers something, Brothers Karamazov? No, that was Tolstoy. Carpathian Brothers? No. Something brothers. An Alexandre Dumas *Three Musketeers* kind of thing brought to the screen.

At the library she was dismayed to find in an encyclopedia that there were *three* Alexandre Dumas entries—father, son, grandson—studied the array of titles, in French yet, some recognizable, anyway, *Le Comte de Monte Cristo* and *Les Trois Mousquetaires* and finally, the name of the movie leaping before her, not from the encyclopedia but from a memory dislodged from her brain. *The Corsican Brothers.* In which twin brothers had shared each other's wounds and injuries. The library did not stock the book. She searched secondhand bookstores in the next few months and then stopped looking altogether. What solution or solace could she find in a book?

Returning to the Hacienda after that Thanksgiving holiday, she decided to play it cool. She knew that at least she didn't harbor some strange and perverted disease in her body. Alberto was a strong and healthy person, if a bit reckless. But what young guy wasn't reckless as he played the games of youth? Anyway, he wasn't a child anymore, and the hazards of adolescent antics in summer camps were over. Eventually he'd lose interest in contact sports and settle down. She felt immeasurably cheered. She also found a kind of peace at the Hacienda among the murmuring nuns and the other students and loved those quiet moments in the chapel when she did not really pray but knelt there, content, almost happy.

Until.

Sitting in the car, in the driveway, looking up at the house that she used to call home—was the Hacienda her real home now?—she was tempted to drive back to the clinic and confess to Barney Snow how she had used him for her own purposes, as a source of information, listening to Alberto's symptoms and comparing them with her own. Ah, but what use would confession be? And whether or not she saw him, her symptoms would continue—the headaches, the fever that seemed to course through her body most of the time, the awful feeling of disaster lurking ahead and, of course, the question that tormented her every waking hour: What happens to me when Alberto dies?

15

*T*ROUBLE."

Allie Roon had never before uttered a word without tortured pronouncement complete with flying spit and darting tongue, but this time the word came out of his mouth without hesitation, no vocal fireworks of any kind.

"What kind of trouble?" Barney asked, rising from the bed, stretching luxuriously. He had slept beautifully last night, weary bones and muscles soothed by sleep, aided by the nightly capsule, of course.

Allie became self-conscious again, arms jerking and mouth working futilely. "C . . . c . . . co . . . co . . . come . . . come . . ." he managed to say finally.

As he followed Allie Roon down the corridor, Barney's sense of well-being began to disappear. He'd awakened this morning with the memory of Cassie's face bright and clear and also with the knowledge that he had done a good job yesterday taking the car apart, of accomplishing something instead of passing the day uselessly.

Allie led him to a window that looked out on the rear grounds of the Complex. Furious activity met his eyes as painters came and went in the yard, carrying scaffolds and ladders and other paraphernalia, apparently preparing to

166

paint the building. They shouted to each other good-naturedly while a large man checked items off sheets of paper. He was the only person out there without smears of paint on his clothing, his beefy face red in the morning sunlight.

"Damn it," Barney said.

Billy the Kidney came wheeling up, the bearer of more bad news. "They're using the cellar to store their cans and brushes and stuff. They'll be in and out of there all day long."

Shouts from the men outdoors pierced the window, punctuating Billy's news.

"H . . . h . . . ho . . . ho . . . how . . . ?" Allie Roon began.

Barney finished the sentence for him, something he ordinarily didn't do, figuring Allie should be given the right to end his own sentences.

"How am I going to do it? Right, Allie? Sneak the car into the cellar with all that action going on?"

"I knew we'd get screwed up," Billy said. "Nothing ever goes right."

Anger surged through Barney.

"Shut up, Billy." He needed time to think.

"There's going to be people running all over the place. Inside and outside," Billy said, whining now like the child he so quickly became when things went wrong.

Allie began to croon a sad song.

Jesus, Barney thought, I'm not going to let this happen. Refusing to be discouraged, to let his great plan explode in their faces.

"Let's not jump to conclusions," he said, "before we find out what's really going on. I'll find a way. We haven't come this far for nothing."

His words transformed Allie, who stopped his sad

crooning and managed to arrange his lips into a smile, head nodding eagerly. Billy turned his wheelchair away, trying to hide the disappointment in his face.

"Where you going?" Barney asked.

"Nowhere. I've got no treatments today."

"Okay," Barney said. "I want you to do something. Keep a watch on the painters." Probably a futile gesture, but he figured Billy would feel better if he had something to do, something to make him believe the theft was still on. "First of all, find out where they're starting to paint. Maybe they'll be in the front of the place and I can still get the car in the back."

"Okay," Billy said, wheeling away. But calling over his shoulder: "Nothing ever goes right, nothing."

Allie begged for attention, arms signaling like a spasmodic traffic cop.

"And you, Allie," Barney said, doing some rapid thinking, trying to find something to keep Allie occupied and happy. "Listen, keep watch at this window. Count the painters. Find out how many there are. That may be important."

The boy nodded eagerly. Barney patted his shoulder. "Don't worry, Allie. We're not calling it quits yet," he said, speaking with a confidence he didn't really feel. But he couldn't let them down, could he? Couldn't let Mazzo down, either. And somehow Cassie was mixed up in all this.

By the time he had finished his eggs and toast, tasting the food but not hungry suddenly, Billy was back, wheeling rapidly toward Barney across the dining area.

"Good news and bad news, Barney," he called.

"Okay, give me the good news first," Barney said, wiping his face with the paper napkin.

"The good news is that they're not painting the back of

the building or the front of the building or the side where the junkyard is," Billy said, bright and enthusiastic, proud of his swift investigation. "They're setting up their stuff and junk on the other side."

"Good job, Billy. Now the bad news."

"They're using the cellar to store their paint and drop cloths. They're going to be in and out of there all the time, Barney. How can you put the car together with all that going on?"

"At night, maybe," Barney said, not giving up, not yet, if ever.

"Not at night, Barney. They check the beds all the time. And this place is so quiet that anything unusual would be noticed."

"Okay, okay," Barney said, impatient.

"Besides, some painter might find the car down there. What would happen then?"

"Christ, Billy, you're a real pessimist, know that? You always look on the black side. The cellar's not the only place to work on the car. How big is this building? Six stories high, isn't it? Must have a hundred rooms. Probably all the rooms aren't occupied. I don't need much space. They must have storerooms all over."

"Wait a minute," Billy snapped. "How about the attic? Every building's got an attic."

"Now you're talking, Billy. Now you're thinking positively. That's what we need."

He walked beside Billy as the boy wheeled himself along the corridor, realizing that Billy didn't try to walk anymore. The thought saddened him. But he turned from the sadness. Think good things, he told himself.

"I'm going to do a little exploring, Billy. I'm going to sneak up to the attic and see what's what. Maybe it'll be better than the cellar."

They spotted Allie Roon keeping watch at the window, counting the painters as they trudged through the back-yard.

"What's Allie doing?" Billy asked.

"Counting the painters."

"Why?"

"I want to know how many painters there are," Barney said lamely.

"You're crazy, you know that, Barney?"

"Maybe," Barney said, wondering if Billy was right, that he was crazy, after all, out of his mind. "It helps if you're crazy in a place like this."

Billy laughed, as if Barney had made a joke.

But Barney wasn't joking. He felt, in fact, like crying.

He waited for the quiet hours of early afternoon, when the Complex seemed to fall into a deep slumber after the frantic busy morning of treatments and examinations. The corridors were empty, doctors and nurses having retreated into their own recesses, patients napping or lying quietly in their beds.

Barney waited a few moments outside the freight elevator. He had never used it before and distrusted new gadgets, paraphernalia, equipment, anything that ran mechanically. Finally, he pushed the button and the doors slowly parted. It was an old elevator with a wooden floor and wooden slats for walls. Like an elevator he had seen once in a factory, although he couldn't remember where. He stepped in, saying, Tempo, rhythm. The control panel listed the usual stuff along with the numbers of the floors. Barney pushed 6. The doors closed, creaking noisily, which did not cheer him up too much. The rise was slow and laborious, the machinery grinding away someplace. He could see the brick walls of the shaft between the slats. He felt queasy, wished for the old feeling of wooziness again to take the edge off his apprehension. The elevator arrived at the sixth floor, bumped and lurched as it came to a halt. Barney held his breath until the doors parted once more. Grateful, he stepped out of the elevator without hesitation, and into the attic.

It was like stepping into the rib cage of some prehistoric beast. The floor, walls, and ceiling unfinished, wooden studs and joists visible. Dust motes danced in dim light coming from the single skylight in the slanting roof. The ceiling slanted in a single sharp slope. An open stairway led to the skylight.

Barney stepped cautiously forward, testing the floor for durability. He had to step over the studs, which were placed about two feet apart. The floor seemed to be sturdy enough. Walking on the studs, as if doing a balancing act on a high wire, Barney made his way to the wooden stairs. He tested the strength of the bottom step and was satisfied it could hold him. He began to climb the stairs gingerly, testing each one before continuing. The skylight was located at the highest point of the ceiling. Reaching the final step, Barney stepped out, again carefully, warily, onto a small platform. He looked down, the open elevator door directly beneath him. The skylight glass was covered with soot and dirt, admitting little light. Barney reached up and turned a small knob at the base of the skylight. He swung it outward, admitting a blast of sunlight that dazzled his eyes. Cold air rushed at him as he poked his head out. He squinted against the dazzle of light, looked down at the pitched roof, felt dizzy, and looked away to the landscape.

The view commanded the junkyard, a row of bleak tenement houses, and in the distance, on the side of a hill, an old cemetery with tombstones like small teeth scattered on a rug. The sharp slant of the roof drew his eyes again and

171

he held on for dear life, afraid he would somehow tumble over the sill and go hurtling downward. Trembling, he tore his eyes away from the slope and took one last lingering look at the landscape before he drew back onto the platform, heart beating fast, breath in quick gasps, eyes watering from the bright sunshine. Standing there, looking down at the deserted and abandoned attic, he knew this was a perfect place for his purpose. For the first time that day he felt that the project could—and would—succeed.

In the elevator once more, buoyed by the success of his mission, Barney felt adventurous, didn't want to return to the boredom of the downstairs area, where he'd have to wait for Billy and Allie to wake from their afternoon dozings. He realized how seldom this elevator was used and felt master of it. Looking at the panel of buttons once more, he pressed 5, for no reason at all, just for the hell of it. He felt like exploring, to see what was happening on the fifth floor. But as the button glowed brightly, the 5 echoed in his memory, the glowing number pulsing to the rhythm of his heartbeat, the 5 imprinted on his mind as if stamped there a long time ago. As the elevator reached the fifth floor—Barney had been only dimly aware of the descent—a memory flashed across his mind. He knew without any doubt what lay beyond the door, saw the long narrow hallway, bright blue, knew the sound of footsteps on the blue tiled floor, saw a white door with the numeral 9 on it, a 9 in dull brass.

The elevator doors parted, groaning as if in protest. Barney stepped into the hallway like a sleepwalker. Saw, unsurprisingly, the blue walls as expected, and the brighter garish blue of the floor. Saw the closed doors all along the narrow corridor. Heard the elevator door squeaking closed behind him as he began to walk down the hallway to Room 9. Found no Room 9. Other numbered rooms, 4 . . . 6 . . . 8.

Disoriented now, puzzled. Wheeled around and realized what had happened. On those other visits to this floor and this hallway, he had emerged from the regular elevator, located on the wall opposite the freight elevator. Now he saw the 9 door. But paused. Did he want to go in there? Funny thing, he knew what the inside of this office looked like, knew he would see the plain gray metal desk, the filing cabinet also steel gray, the digital clock on the wall, the single chair in front of the desk. But there was a room beyond the office. And the key to the door of that room was in the top left-hand drawer of the desk. All this knowledge came to him as a series of small flashes in his mind, like slides on a screen.

Sucking in his breath, he opened the door, stepped into the darkness of a room without windows. Closed the door and touched the light switch, knowing its location on the wall next to the door. The fluorescent light brought the room into harsh view, gray everywhere, desk, floor, filing cabinet. His eyes were drawn to the white door that led to the inner chamber. Where he had been before. Didn't know when, didn't know why. But *knew* he had been there. He walked to the desk, pulled open the drawer, found the key, a single key on a small silver chain. The key was cool to his touch.

He inserted the key in the lock, heard the satisfying click, turned the knob, and swung the door open. Another windowless room. He groped for the light switch, found it, flipped it, and light flooded the room. He stepped inside and there were no more flashes. He was here and now. A bank of television monitors, blank and dull, on the wall to his right. To his left, panels that resembled the control room of a radio or television station. Facing him, on the wall opposite the doorway, was a huge television monitor or movie screen, blindingly white. The whiteness pro-

173

duced the flash again, *him in the car and the car slanting down the street.* In front of the screen a green sheet covered—what? He knew and he did not know. The flash again, *rain on the windshield and the glistening pavement.* Tempo, rhythm, he whispered, as he approached the object hidden by the sheet. Drew the sheet off and stared at what had been revealed before him. Moving mechanically, mind blank, he slipped into the seat. He placed his hands on the steering wheel, studied the dashboard, swept his eyes along the windshield. He was sitting in a car that was not a car, only the front seat and steering wheel and dashboard and windshield, like the kind you find in amusement parks to test your driving ability for a dime or quarter. He had sat in this car many times—but when? why?—and he knew what to do now. He touched a button on the dashboard. A humming in the walls, growing louder. The huge screen in front of him glowed green, and the seat began to rock under him as if he were sitting in a real car and the car had started to move. Then the screen burst into life and he found himself in the middle of his nightmare.

The windshield wipers began to swing, back and forth, swishing, back and forth, and the screen became the slanting cobblestoned street of his dream, the wetness and the streetlights reflecting on the stones, and the roar of the motor and the pounding of the rain and the howling of the wind. He gripped the steering wheel frantically as the car began to rock furiously, his foot reaching for the brake pedal he knew wouldn't work. His eyes were fastened on the street, that glistening tilting street, and he knew what to expect: that figure stepping off the curb exactly as she had done a million times.

In the dream but not in the dream, in the car but not in the car, he wanted to close his eyes to shut out the street

174

before him on the screen but was unable to do anything, unable to do anything but hold on, gritting his teeth against the rocking of the car and the sound of the engine and the buffeting wind and rain.

His hand traveled a thousand miles as he reached for the button on the dashboard. Pressed the button. The screen began to break up into a jagged jigsaw puzzle, scattered images clashing and colliding, the sound fading, the car slowing down, everything gentle suddenly, the images gone from the screen and the screen glowing green again, the wind giving one last sad shriek before falling away into silence. His hands trembled, his body shook as he let the meaning of the room and the car and the screen reach full flower in his mind. His nightmare had been manufactured in this room, in the simulated car and the movie on the screen.

He rested his head on the steering wheel, trying to calm his racing heart, trying to keep from running in panic out of the room and down the corridor and into the streets.

He felt the presence behind him a moment before he heard the voice.

"I am sorry you had to learn about it this way, Barney," the Handyman said.

Barney didn't move, didn't want to move, didn't want to open his eyes, didn't want to know what had happened, what *was* happening to him. But in the darkness of his closed eyes he was in the car again, slanting down the street.

And the only way he could flee the nightmare was by opening his eyes and facing the Handyman.

16

*L*ET me tell you what a screen is, Barney," the Handyman said.

"I know what a screen is," Barney replied, angry, but the anger hiding something else inside him: a growing, numbing fear. To hold back the fear, he forced himself to concentrate on what the Handyman was saying and keep up his part of the conversation. "There are a lot of screens, doctor. Movie screens, window screens." Pleased with himself. In control.

"Yes," the Handyman agreed. "And still others. For instance, the screen that keeps people hidden while they dress. You have seen them in films, perhaps. You find them in the dressing rooms of theater people."

Barney nodded, impatient but concealing his impatience, waiting for the explanation the Handyman had promised a few moments ago in that terrible room upstairs. "Come," the Handyman had said, "let us leave this dreadful place and go to my office, and I shall tell you everything." He had held out his hand to Barney but Barney hadn't taken it, had kept his arms stiffly at his sides. Feeling betrayed and deceived, he had walked silently beside the Handyman as they went to the elevator, the regular one, and descended to the first floor. And now, here in his office, the Handyman seemed to be playing games with words—all this talk about screens—with Barney deciding to wait him out, take it easy, tempo, rhythm.

"Screens are also used in the functions of the brain," the Handyman said. "Memory in particular."

Dropping the word *memory* like a coin down a well, an expectant look on his face as if waiting for Barney to hear it land. And maybe explode like a bomb on landing.

"You remember, of course, how I explained to you about short-term memory and long-term memory. How we retain what happened yesterday and forget what happened, say, twenty years ago."

"Yes," Barney said, waiting, watching, trying to fathom what was going on in the Handyman's brain, behind those brilliant green eyes.

"But do we really forget, Barney? Is it possible, after all, that there is no such thing as forgetting? That what we learn throughout our lifetime remains recorded permanently in our brains?"

"Then why can't we remember everything?" Barney asked, curious. More than curious: knowing this was leading somewhere and it involved him.

The Handyman smiled briefly, apparently pleased by Barney's display of interest. "Because the memories are blocked out. For any number of reasons. Perhaps as time goes by the blocks become heavier and heavier, thicker and thicker, so that it's more difficult to penetrate a block and retrieve the past. These blocks are mysterious. And they seem to change character as time goes on. For instance, old people suddenly begin to remember what happened fifty years ago and yet are hazy about what happened yesterday. The fact that they remember dis-

177

tant events indicates that memories may be permanently in the mind, hidden behind blocks."

But what about me? Barney wanted to ask. Where do I fit in?

"I explained to you earlier how chemicals can alter the functions of the brain," the Handyman went on, but slower in speech now, choosing his words carefully, like a man stepping through a field of broken glass. "Chemicals have been found to affect the memory. A scientist in Europe discovered during experiments with laboratory mice that those that were forced to learn new skills—such as finding their way through a maze or learning to balance on a trapeze—produced a chemical in their brains. A marvelous discovery, Barney, linking a chemical to learning and memory. A landmark event. Later, a scientist here in our own country took the opposite course. He injected mice with a chemical that interfered with the production of the learning chemical. Using this interfering drug, he found that mice that had learned new skills promptly forgot them. In other words, the scientist found that he could block out a short-term memory—the skill the mice had learned the day previously—by injecting the counter-chemical. This was the beginning of our studies of memory, and the control of memory by chemicals."

"Am I a mouse in a maze?" Barney asked.

"You are much more than that, Barney. You are a precious human being. If we did not regard you as such, we would not have subjected you to the tests. It is unfortunate that you found your way to the laboratory upstairs, which has caused me to disclose this information prematurely."

Unfortunate. Another one of the Handyman's words. Meaning: too bad, tough, your luck has run out.

"Screens," Barney said, running from his thoughts—his

thoughts like mice in a maze. "You were talking about screens."

"Exactly," the Handyman said. "You have anticipated me. We have arrived at the point where the screen becomes involved." He seemed unsure of himself now, pausing, tugging at his beard, eyes moving away from Barney for the first time. Sighed briefly, then eyes back on Barney again. "A screen, in terms of the memory system, is a device to hide a memory, an image. A chemical is utilized to wipe away this particular memory, in this case a small isolated patch of short-term memory. A screen is then substituted to suppress the original memory. Your screen was the experience of the car ride. While under the influence of a chemical, you were exposed to the experience of the automobile, seated in the improvised car, exposed to the events on the monitor. This experience became the screen—and the screen, Barney, was for your protection, blocking out the original memory whenever your mind threatened to retrieve it."

"You mean all those times I dreamed—even while awake—of the car going down the hill and me driving it, that meant the old memory was trying to break through and come out?" Scared to death at his question. Tempo, rhythm.

"You have said it well," the Handyman said. "The screen performed beyond all the projected expectations. There were occasional lapses. Some losses of control. Before you came here. But the proceedings here and, in particular, Dr. Croft's work, succeeded admirably. Those earlier tests disturbed other facets of your memory. But only to a minimal degree. Occasionally you had trouble recalling a minor memory. This was a sort of fringe reaction. We subjected you to a form of hypnosis, with posthypnotic suggestions, to reinforce the chemical and the screens. You complained once that you could not recall your mother's face, that it was like the missing piece of a jigsaw puzzle. We supplied the proper screen."

"Wait a minute," Barney said, alarmed, wanting to leap to his feet, wanting to scream in fact, but keeping calm, letting the blood flow. "Back up, back up. . . ."

"What do you mean—back up?" the Handyman asked. Frowning, puzzled.

"What you've just said. Back up to it. You said: those earlier tests. Before I came here. But I was given the first memory test *here*. Just a couple of weeks ago. When Dr. Croft arrived."

As Barney spoke, he saw the Handyman change before his eyes. For the first time the Handyman seemed to have lost his composure. His mouth was opened slightly and those eyes, usually so penetrating, were clouded over, as if a film veiled them. Had he mentioned those earlier tests without intending to, or was he realizing for the first time the effect the knowledge would have on his patient? Barney didn't know, knew nothing but this terrible fear growing in him, like a siren howling in his mind, screaming through his veins and arteries. He didn't like this perplexed Handyman he saw before him. He wanted the familiar all-knowing Handyman to return, to laugh off Barney's question—"Do not be absurd, Barney"—and to say that it was all a mistake, another test, more merchandise to test his reactions.

But the old Handyman didn't return. This new and troubled man sat behind the desk, deep in thought. As if waiting.

And now Barney knew what he was waiting for. He was waiting for Barney to ask a question and Barney knew what the question was. He had told the Handyman to back up but he hadn't backed up far enough. Hadn't gone as far back as the original memory.

"What was the memory you blocked out, doctor?" Barney asked, and his voice sounded like that of a stranger, a thin and quivering voice.

The Handyman rose wearily from the chair, leaned against the desk for a moment, and walked to the paneled wall, opened a small door that had been part of the wall a moment before. He withdrew a pitcher of water, poured a bit into a glass, took a pill from a small bottle, placed it on his tongue and swallowed it.

"You see, Barney?" he said, indicating the bottle. "We are not monsters here. We are human beings. We get headaches—I am subject to migraines—but we always hide these things from our patients. Sometimes I think that is a mistake. It makes us appear immune. And we are not immune. We are not gods, either, although some pretend they are." He directed the eyes, brilliant once again, at Barney. "Yes, you had earlier tests before you arrived here. Three, in fact. You received the original screen there."

"Where was I before I arrived, doctor?" Barney asked, voice still small, almost a whisper. "I can't remember."

"I know you can't," the Handyman said, kindly, gentle. Barney feared the gentleness.

"Was that other place screened out, too?"

"I realize there is no easy way to tell you this, Barney. So let me say it plainly, the way you always insist. First, however, let me point out that you volunteered for this project. You were eager to participate at that other place. Your eagerness provided the first objective: to choose a subject who would benefit immediately, if perhaps only temporarily, by the experiment."

"Go on," Barney said, letting the blood flow, tempo, rhythm.

"You see, Barney, that place you came from, which you cannot remember, was a hospice. A facility for persons suffering from terminal diseases."

Barney closed his eyes, wiping out the Handyman the way his own memory had been wiped out. He held himself stiffly, afraid to move, afraid that he might break into a thousand pieces if he tried to move. He said, "Oh, no," in a frail and futile attempt to deny what he now knew to be true. He was like the others here, after all, like Billy the Kidney and Allie Roon and Mazzo, who used to be a bastard. He was one of them.

17

*T*HE trick now was not only to live in separate compartments but to divide *himself* into separate compartments, so that the left hand did not know what the right hand was doing and his mind would be separate from his body. Actually, his hands worked together, each contributing to the task before him, taking the car apart and moving the parts into the Complex, then into the elevator and up to the sixth floor. His legs walked, carrying his body to the junkyard, and his hands manipulated the screwdriver and the small hammer and the chisel he found useful to pry loose stubborn sections.

His mind was separate from these operations, dictating the actions to his body mechanically, the way a computer orders the movements of the machine that it is. He tried to make himself into a machine, functioning smoothly and efficiently, no unnecessary motions, his mind working keenly and analytically, planning ahead, solving the problems as they arose—like stationing Billy the Kidney at Old Cheekbones' desk to divert her with carefully prepared questions while Barney pushed the wheelchair loaded with automobile parts across the corridor and into the elevator.

He kept his mind separate from his body and he banished his emotions altogether. Didn't know how he managed to do this but did it. Realized his emotions were tied to thoughts, and, thus, certain thoughts triggered certain emotions. He kept those thoughts from developing. His screen, most of the time, was the car itself. Planning the theft, timing the movements of parts from junkyard to the Complex, envisioning the grand design and the final outcome. He pictured his mind as a series of rooms—all right, compartments—and there were certain compartments he did not enter. Except sometimes. Sometimes he could not keep the doors closed to all the compartments, and he found himself remembering, his memory, ironically, intact about certain things. Like that talk with the Handyman.

"You were doing me a favor, right, doctor?"

"If a certain patch of knowledge had to be erased, why not the most terrible knowledge of all?"

"You mean, I was going to die anyway and climbing the walls about it?"

"You were not resigned, Barney. Those stages I told you about when you first arrived? You went through them all but did not reach the stage of acceptance."

"So you took the knowledge of my condition away."

"The test was successful. With qualifications."

"What do you mean—qualifications?"

"I mean that it was impossible to maintain complete control."

"You mean you erased too much?"

Silence from the Handyman.

"Like my early life that I can't remember? My mother's face that I can't recall sometimes? Where I lived before coming here?"

The Handyman's face was like stone, gray like the side of a cliff.

While the plan proceeded beautifully, Allie Roon spitting and twitching and dancing and laughing, Billy the Kidney saying it was good to be on a caper again as Barney stole in and out of the Complex.

Timing was the key, avoiding the painters who were concentrating on the far end of the building, ducking Old Cheekbones, who seldom looked up from the papers that occupied her, but having close calls occasionally. Once at the elevator door, a maintenance man stepped out, pushing a floor waxer before him, regarding Barney curiously as he stood there behind the wheelchair loaded with automobile sections, the sections luckily covered with a sheet. But presenting a strange sight anyway. The maintenance man swerved quickly away and Barney was grateful for the thing about Section 12 that made people avoid it. The isolation of the section made the project go more smoothly, took away some of Barney's apprehensions about discovery.

He looked up once to see the Handyman at the far end of the corridor. Barney had just stepped out of the elevator, pushing the empty wheelchair. Their eyes met, even at that distance, and held for a moment, and then the Handyman turned away. Barney wondered if the Handyman suspected what was going on, the Handyman who seemed to know everything. Or almost everything.

"I've been in remission, then?"

"Yes. They did not realize at the time of the first test that you were about to go into remission. Or did not anticipate that the test might induce remission. Remission has its peculiar mysteries. Emotions perhaps play a role."

"How long will the remission last?"

"That is impossible to tell, Barney."

"It could end ten minutes from now?"

"Or it may continue indefinitely."

"Those aftermaths you always talked about, doctor. Were they really aftermaths or the thing itself?"

By thing, *he meant the thing that was killing him. Slowly maybe, postponed for a while, but still killing him.*

"Perhaps a bit of both."

And now the car began to take shape beneath his hands as he sneaked up to the attic at all times of the day and night, when the coast was clear or everybody slept, timing again, flirting with discovery. When he had finally laid the car sections on the floor, they resembled the pieces of a toy bought for the child of a giant, waiting now for the giant to come along and assemble them. Barney felt like a giant as he began his work, whistling, chewing the insides of his cheeks, concentrating on the job, keeping his mind blank, the doors closed, his hands busy, busy hands are happy hands, like the sister in school said one time. What sister? What school? Didn't know. Didn't want to know at this moment. Didn't want to think. But had to think, of course, impossible not to think, especially about the Handyman.

"Why did you pick the car as the screen? The car going down the hill?"

"The image required power, Barney. The power to block the truth about your condition. Emotional power. Fear, apprehension."

"The girl in the screen? The one who stepped off the curb, whose face I never saw. Who was she?"

"You were meant not to see her face."

"Why?"

"Because then she became every girl to you, every girl you might have loved or desired, or longed to love and desire. Thus, it did not matter who she was."

"But there's more to it, isn't there?"

Pause. "Yes, Barney."

"My parents. It was something to do with my parents."

"Your parents died in an automobile accident, Barney. Not as in your screen. The automobile in which they were riding went out of control, struck a pole, overturned, and ignited."

"So a car was linked in my mind with something terrible. Terrible enough to blot out something just as terrible. Or worse."

"That is a simplification, Barney. But yes, it is the truth."

"How old was I when they died?"

"Seven years and eight months."

"Where did I live?" Somehow he knew.

"A series of foster homes." Like Billy the Kidney.

"Is my name really Barney Snow?"

"Yes, Bernard J. Snow. J. for Jason. Your father's name was Jason. Your mother's name was Emily."

"My mother's bracelets. And her face that comes and goes. Are they screens, too?"

"The visual screens were supplemented with audio screens."

"You mean there are bracelets somewhere in that room upstairs?"

"The bracelets exist only as sounds on a bit of tape."

"Did my mother really wear a lot of bracelets?"

"There is no evidence to indicate that she did."

"But you had to invent something to link me with her?"

"For your protection, Barney."

"What about her face? The face I see sometimes. Is that someone else's face?"

"No. A photograph of your mother was enlarged."

"And flashed in front of me?"

"Projected on a screen."

"So that it burned itself into my mind?"

187

The Handyman nodded.

Barney did not want to hear any more. The emptiness of not knowing was better. Here and now was better. In the Complex. With the car. A mission to carry out.

Sometimes he ascended the wooden stairs and threw open the skylight, resting his chin on the sill, letting the wind assail his face, studying the outside world, the bleak landscape of abandoned buildings and the distant cemetery. He looked at the junkyard and thought of the resemblance between the junkyard and the Complex, both filled with busted and broken things. A door opened in his mind: He was going to die. He looked down the slanted roof and pondered how easy it would be to tumble over the sill and let himself plunge below. But he pulled back, dazed and numbed. He had a job to do first. Later. Maybe later.

Billy the Kidney began to regard him suspiciously, studying him keenly, eyes narrowed, thin face taut. Barney tried to avoid him, busy in his comings and goings. Until Billy trapped him as he emerged from the elevator.

"Hold it a minute, Barney."

"I'm in a hurry." Avoiding Billy's eyes.

"What's the matter, anyway? Is something wrong, Barney?"

"Nothing's wrong. I've got a lot of work to do."

"You're a liar," Billy said, eyes flashing, flashing as always with the pain but something else in the flashing now. "Did something happen to the car?"

"The car's fine. Coming along beautifully."

"Then what's the matter?"

Stubborn Billy. Better play the game with him. "Okay. I'm kind of tired. Feel lousy. All that work, maybe. And I can't sleep at night."

Billy's eyes were watchful, still suspicious. Then he relaxed, face softened. "I wish I could help, Barney."

"You've already helped, Billy. Listen, it's almost finished. Then I can take it easy."

He was telling the truth. The car was growing as if by magic in his hands and Barney felt like a creator, fitting the pieces together, watching it take shape once more, the crimson catching the skylight sun and spinning it before Barney's eyes. He swore sometimes when the work didn't go well, when he dropped the screwdriver or it missed its mark and gouged his hand. The screwdriver tore into the webbing of his left hand, bringing blood, and he had no handkerchief or Kleenex and the blood mixed with the color of the car and he smiled at the thought, his own blood staining the car, becoming a part of it. But the blood started the thoughts coming, seeping into the compartments.

"We can send you away, Barney."

"Where would I go?"

"A place more comfortable than this, since your tests have been terminated here. We are not designed for comfort here. There are places more cheerful than this, staffed by knowledgeable people who can provide the best of all possible care. This facility is nothing more than a huge laboratory."

Barney was silent.

"Think about it," the Handyman said.

Barney thought about it and knew that he could never leave the Complex. This was the only home he could remember, and the only people in his life were here, Billy the Kidney and Allie Roon and Mazzo. And, most of all, Cassie. Cassie who had brought beauty into his world, and love and brightness. He also had this mission to complete, the building of the car and Mazzo's last ride. And Cassie, too, was a part of all that.

How could he ever leave this place?

His visits with Cassie were more precious than ever now. Basking in her nearness, inhaling the clean soap smell of her, he was able to deny what the Handyman had told him. He didn't feel like the others when he was with her, not like Billy and Allie Roon.

Sometimes she looked unhappy, weary, when he gave her his report about Mazzo and realized, guiltily, that although these visits were a pleasure for him, they were difficult for her. He tried to spare her the truth about Mazzo, that he seemed listless now, drifting away, almost uncommunicative. During the entire adventure of the car, his biggest fear was that Mazzo might never take that last ride. He checked his room constantly, made inquiries of the nurses, and stole into his room sometimes and whispered to Mazzo, lips close to his ear: "Hold on, Mazzo." So he faked it a little in his reports, becoming expert at it, fooling her, and he also talked to her on another level in which he did not use words or even whisper, telling her silently what he could not say aloud: I love you, Cassie. I'm dying, Cassie.

"What happened to your hands?" she asked.

Barney looked down, startled, saw the scratches on his flesh, small cuts from the screwdriver and the torn web between his thumb and index finger. He looked back at her, lost for an answer, couldn't tell the truth. But what could he tell her?

"I'm doing some mechanical work." Stupid answer.

"What kind of mechanical work?" she asked, curious, of course.

"On a car." Damn it.

"A car?" Surprised, skeptical. "They've got a garage here to work on cars?"

"No, not a garage. But a place to work on a car." He was getting in deeper and didn't know how to get out.

"Where's it located?" She seemed genuinely interested.

He responded to that interest, beginning to glow. For once they were talking about him, not Mazzo.

"In the attic."

"The attic?" she asked, voice curling in surprise, or maybe disbelief. "This place has an attic?"

"Sure, a big one. Floor's not finished, but it's safe to walk on."

"Let me get this straight," she said, the tough-guy huskiness in her voice again. "You've been working on a car in the attic of this place?"

"Yes," he said, getting fidgety, sorry he'd brought up the subject, knowing how ridiculous it all sounded.

"How did a car get up into the attic?" she asked, patiently now, as if she were addressing a small child.

"Well," he began lamely. He should have kept his mouth shut. Now there was no way out without telling her everything. Well, almost everything. "It's not a real car. It's sort of a model car. You know, like the ones that come in kits?"

"Oh," she said, relieved, as if that explained everything.

"But it's life-size," Barney said, telling himself to stop talking, drop the subject, but unable to do so. "I mean, it's the size of a regular car."

"And it came in a kit?" Something about her eyes, as if she wasn't sure whether to laugh or not. "That must be some kit."

"No, not a kit," he said, hastening to correct that impression. "I stole it." Pause. "From the junkyard next door."

"You stole it?" Incredulous now.

So he told her about it. How he'd spotted the fake car and decided to steal it. How he had taken it apart and brought it into the Complex and then sneaked it up into the attic in the freight elevator. How he had almost completed assembling it. How Billy the Kidney and Allie Roon had acted as watchdogs. And all the time he talked, he knew that when he finished the explanation, he would face the big question she would ask. Unless she decided she was dealing with a madman and ran screaming out of this place. He ran out of words, finally, studied his hands, wishing he could hide them someplace.

And she asked the question.

"Why?"

The word hung on the air and he squirmed in his chair.

"Why did you do all that, Barney?"

As usual, his name on her lips warmed him, the warmth spreading through his body like balm and benediction.

He knew he had to be careful now, had to play it safe.

"To take a ride in it."

Her earlier expression of incredulity returned. The look that said: I am talking to a maniac.

"I mean . . ." He groped for proper words. "I mean take it out into the corridor or maybe down to the cellar and give it a push and jump in and take a ride." Looking sharply at her, knowing how crazy it all sounded. "In a place like this, you have to do something." And yet, he found that he didn't want to apologize for what he had done, crazy as it seemed. Explain, yes, but apologize, no.

"I don't even know if the wheels will turn," he said, unable to stop himself again. "I've got nobody to push me. It wasn't built to be driven."

"Like the bumblebee," she said.

"What bumblebee?"

"Any bumblebee," she said, voice light again, speaking

192

to him in normal fashion now, not as if he were a child or a madman. "A bumblebee isn't supposed to fly. The law of aerodynamics or something. Its body is too heavy and it's the wrong shape. The wingspread, too, is wrong for its size and shape. That makes it impossible that it should fly." Amused now, shaking her head. "But know what? The bumblebee doesn't know about the laws of aerodynamics. So it goes ahead and flies, anyway. And, they say, manages to make a little honey every day."

They burst into laughter, joining together in sudden rowdy merriment, sharing the vision of the bumblebee in flight and the fake car shooting down the corridor. Cassie bent forward, her hand touching Barney's knee, setting him on fire.

"I'll push you, Barney Snow," she said. "I'll give you a ride in your Bumblebee."

"It's not for me," he said, the words coming out of his merriment and her touch on his knee, his guard down once more.

"Who's it for, then?" she asked.

Barney didn't answer, couldn't answer. He'd said too much already. And he was getting tired, weary, a small headache pulsing above his eyes.

"You're always doing things for other people, aren't you? The telephone for Billy. The visits with Alberto for me. And now stealing that car for somebody else."

She looked at him with admiration in her eyes, as if he were a knight in shining armor.

"It's nothing," he said, determined not to tell her, afraid that he might tell her everything. And she'd laugh.

"You're one of the good guys, Barney Snow," she said, taking his hands in hers, clasping them tightly so that he didn't know where his hands began and she herself left off.

A moment later she was gone, taking back her hands,

calling "Good-bye, Barney" over her shoulder, her smile radiant, as if for him alone. He stood without moving in the failing afternoon light, his love so huge that he felt he couldn't contain it and would explode at any moment into a thousand beams of light.

He had begun a special kind of vigilance, on the alert, on the watch. Object: his body and its functions. He checked himself constantly for signs and symptoms, clues, changes in his body's behavior that might signal that remission had ended and the invader had arrived. He called it the invader, this thing that was dormant now inside him and could leap to life at any moment. Hadn't the Handyman said that even emotions played a part? He had asked the Handyman what the symptoms would be when remission ended. "It is best if we do not anticipate," the Handyman had said.

Barney was studying his arms when Bascam appeared at the doorway. "He wants to see you," she said, inscrutable as ever. He was thankful for her inscrutability, would have hated to see pity in her eyes. Maybe her coldness was a blessing, after all, a gift she bestowed upon the patients here.

The Handyman sat as usual behind the desk, fastidious, hands clasped, unmoving.

"I'm afraid, Barney, that we are past the moment for choices," he said.

"What do you mean?"

"I told you earlier that we do not have the facilities here for providing the care you require, both at the present time and later. However, I felt it possible for you to remain here for a time. I know you have your friends here and the visits from the young woman. But it is beyond my control now, Barney. The authorities have decreed that you must leave for a more hospitable environment."

"I don't want to leave, doctor," Barney said, panic rising in him.

"There is nothing we can do to prevent your departure," he said, his voice gentle. And the gentleness made his words more terrible.

"This is the only world I know," Barney said. His past a blank and his future blank as well. Tempo, rhythm, he told himself. Past, tempo. Future, rhythm.

He saw a flicker in the Handyman's eyes at the same time he realized he was pronouncing *tempo rhythm* silently. Had his lips moved? He said the words aloud: "Tempo. Rhythm." On a hunch.

"What is this you are saying?" the Handyman asked.

"Tempo, rhythm, doctor. I say these words, tell myself to keep tempo, rhythm, when I start getting panicky. When I start thinking about where I came from or my life before coming here. Are they screens, too, these words?"

The Handyman lifted his shoulders and let them fall as if in surrender. "Yes, Barney. It was decided to experiment with auditory screens—the bracelets, of course—as well as the visual. In order to give you more protection when the memory of your condition encroached upon you."

Barney felt as if he had been manufactured here, like some kind of Frankenstein's monster, assembled from bits and pieces like the car he was assembling in the attic, only he was not made up of pieces of wood like the car or parts of bodies, like the monster, but of pieces of tape and film, images printed on a screen, sounds burned into his ears.

"What else did you do?" Barney asked.

"Nothing else," the Handyman said. "Believe me."

Maybe he was lying. Maybe a lie was better than the

195

truth. Maybe he was better off not knowing everything they had done.

"Barney, let me tell you something, although I may be overstepping my bounds in doing so," the Handyman said, looking down at the bare desk as if what he wanted to say was written there. "You asked me a moment ago: What else did you do? I did nothing, my boy. You were sent to me from that other place. Dr. Croft and I did our best. But the decision to use you in the experiment was not mine. We carried on the work that was started elsewhere."

Maybe he wasn't a monster, after all.

"You have always had my complete sympathy," he said.

"Is that why you gave me the run of the place? And allowed Cassie Mazzofono to visit?" Barney asked.

The green eyes were still cold as always as they looked at Barney. But his voice was gentle as he said: "I can say no more, Barney." Maybe the eyes weren't the windows of the soul, after all.

"Thanks for whatever you did, doctor."

The Handyman became businesslike again, sitting erect at the desk, clearing his throat. "This new facility will provide you with all the comforts, Barney. Please trust me in this."

"But all my friends are here, doctor. Why can't I just keep on living here?" Barney asked, shooting the works, not wanting any more merchandise but willing to take that risk if it meant remaining at the Complex.

"We have procedures we must follow, rules and codes," the Handyman said. "I told you this long ago. Those in authority are unwilling to put you to further risk."

I'm not going, Barney said. But not aloud. Said it silently to himself like he said tempo, rhythm. I'm not going. He was tired of being controlled by other people, faceless people whose names he didn't know, whose faces he couldn't recall. He would play the game of leaving but he would not go.

"When do I have to leave?" he asked. Asking for the sake of asking. Playing for time.

"In two or three days, perhaps. Arrangements are now being made. Papers being processed."

"Is it far from here?" Keep talking, keep asking, use the words as screens to block the Handyman from finding out what he was going to do.

"A few hours," the Handyman said brightly, obviously relieved at Barney's show of interest. "A city north of Boston."

"I see."

"I think you will like it there."

"I hope so." I'm not going.

The Handyman stood up, as if to terminate the conversation, but then sank down again in the chair. "Barney," he said, hesitant. "Would you like to see a priest before you leave? No doubt there will be priests in that new place, but I have a friend here who could visit with you, give you reassurance."

Startled, Barney said: "Why?" and saw what the Handyman was getting at. "You mean because I'm a Catholic?" He winced, closing his eyes. Of course he was a Catholic, had a faint recollection of candles burning, the peculiar taste of the wafer in his mouth, the Body and Blood of Christ, the priest at the altar and then: nothing. Trying to grope for the memory but encountering blankness, terrifying blankness, like snow, suffocating, obliterating snow. Tempo, rhythm, he cried, hearing his voice—had he spoken aloud? His eyes flew open, establishing himself here in the Complex. Tempo, rhythm. That was his religion now, the religion that had been created for him in the tests. Instead of a prayer, tempo, rhythm. He looked at the Handyman, shook his head. "No, I don't need a priest." Glad to hear that his voice was steady, did not betray the panic inside him.

As he left the office, he realized that he would never know whether the Handyman had been his friend or his enemy. Maybe neither one. And what was he to the Handyman? A subject. A project. A mouse in a maze. A piece of tape. A slice of film. In other words: nothing.

He completed the Bumblebee that night. The final hinge attached, the final screw in place. The car stood erect, garishly scarlet in the merciless light from the unshaded bulb in the ceiling but beautiful all the same.

Billy the Kidney whistled with delight, sitting in the wheelchair, the footrest holding the elevator doors open, gazing at the car in wonder.

"You did it, Barney. You put the car together."

"The Bumblebee," Barney said.

"There you go," Billy said, "still not calling things by their right names." But too happy to be annoyed.

"A bumblebee is not supposed to fly, Billy. But it does anyway. It flies all over the place." He stroked the hood of the car lovingly. "And this car is like that, a bumble-bee. . . ."

That vision in the junkyard, like the winking of a far-off star, leaped to his mind's eye, quickening his pulse. He looked down at this marvelous object he had taken apart and re-created, this Bumblebee of his own making. And he knew now what that last wild ride would be.

18

*T*HAT night he didn't swallow the capsule. He tossed it into the toilet bowl and watched it swirl away into the bowels of the building. He had been afraid to sleep, afraid the invader would come, find its way through his body while he slept. He felt that he could keep it away if he stayed awake, on guard, alert. He tossed on the bed, images flashing in his mind, faces he didn't recognize, dream figures that were probably from another time and place or maybe screens, and he didn't know which was which, his mind a jigsaw puzzle with missing pieces, impossible to put together.

Two or three days, the Handyman had said. He had to play a delicate game, make his move at exactly the right time. But not too soon. He needed to see Cassie again. Tomorrow and the next day, at least. And if he was lucky, the day after that. Then what?

He wondered what it would be like to be dead. Blank, zero, nothing. Wasn't he blank now, a zero, a cipher? But not dead, of course, because his heart plodded on within his chest and his breathing went on, inhale, exhale. And anyway, death meant either heaven or hell, didn't it? Heaven and hell and purgatory. The nuns had taught him that. What nuns? Where? When? A face flashed before him, pale face enclosed in some kind of starched white collar that concealed ears and hair, and lips moving, saying something about heaven, hell.

He leaped from the bed, afraid, afraid of thinking. Christ, afraid to sleep, afraid to be awake. Stood up uncertainly, put on his robe and slippers and fled the room. Two o'clock in the morning, slipping down the silent corridor, a wraith in the night, past the closed doors and the red lights, shivering in the heat of the Complex, crazy, but everything topsy-turvy. Paused at Mazzo's door. Why here? Because. Because he felt close to Cassie when he stood near Mazzo's bed, saw echoes of her in Mazzo's face and eyes.

Mazzo moved spasmodically beneath the sheets, restless and agitated. As Barney drew near, Mazzo peered at him balefully, as if looking out of a dark and forbidding place.

"What do you want?" he rasped, insolent and hostile, like the old Mazzo, Mazzo the bastard.

Shit, Barney thought, I should have stayed in my room.

"How are you?" he asked, trying to be light and bright as usual and wondering why he tried.

"How the hell do you think I am?" The words came through cracked and swollen lips, carried on a breath that was rancid and foul, causing Barney's stomach to lurch.

Barney looked around the room, waiting for his eyes to get accustomed to the darkness so that he could find what he was looking for. Finally, he saw it: The tube like a thin black snake between Mazzo and the machine.

"How long would you live if I pulled the plug?" he asked, leaning into that foul and soiled breath.

Mazzo laughed, a bitter bark that brought up phlegm

from his throat. He spat into a small basin tucked under his chin.

"Couple of hours. Maybe three," Mazzo said. "Anyway, that's what they said. Then I'm blown away." Coughing now, struggling, chest heaving. "You going to pull it?"

"I might surprise you sometime," Barney said. He was appalled to find Mazzo looking so bad, at the end of his rope, sweating and struggling to breathe, funny sounds coming out of him as he struggled to speak. How long could he last, even with the machine plugged into his body?

"Get out of here," Mazzo said. "You don't belong here anyway."

"Yes, I do."

"You're crazy, staying here. Is that how you get your kicks?" Eyes blazing with anger as well as fever.

"I belong here, Mazzo. With you. And Billy and Allie and all the others, whoever they are, in this rotten place."

"Go away," Mazzo said, hunching his shoulders, shifting his body, adjusting his bones and muscles to the spasms that gripped him as he moved, or made the effort to move.

"I can't go," Barney said. "Not yet. Because I'm like you, Mazzo. Like you and Billy the Kidney and Allie Roon. Can't you hear what I'm saying? I'm dying, for Christ's sake, just like you."

He instantly regretted the words. Terrified. As if speaking them had put the final seal on his doom. Until he had uttered the words, a small part of him had cried out his immortality, and now it vanished, like smoke pulled into tatters in the air.

With effort, with groans and twisting and fartings, Mazzo drew himself up on his elbows, squinting through fevered eyes, face wet with perspiration, hollow cheeked, breath foul.

"What in the hell do you mean—like me?"

"Just what I said. I am dying. What do you want, a written guarantee?"

Mazzo's eyes glittered in the dim light. He raised himself on the bed, gathering himself somehow to a half-sitting position. His fetid breath filled Barney's nostrils but Barney didn't move, tried not to breathe it in, impossible, waited there for whatever Mazzo wanted to say.

"You goddamn fake," Mazzo said.

"I'm not a fake."

"We were dying and you said you weren't. The great Barney Snow. The fixer. Faking it all the time."

A terrible smell now filled the air as Mazzo stiffened in the bed, farting, maybe soiling himself. Barney didn't care, he cared only about making Mazzo see that he wasn't a fake.

"Mazzo, Mazzo. For crying out loud, listen to me. I'm really dying. I didn't fake it. The Handyman did. I came here not knowing I was going to die." He didn't want to go into all the details of the memory experiments, not now, not at this time of night. "It's a long story, Mazzo. But believe me. I didn't know about it. I am not a fake."

"You poor bastard," Mazzo said, smiling. But a mirthless, joyless smile, as he let himself settle back carefully on the bed.

Barney remained there, the stench in his nostrils, mind empty, heart empty, everything empty, his entire being vacant, like an unoccupied building. He had no desires at this moment, to either stay or go, laugh or cry, sleep or remain awake. He was nothing, a shell, an empty vessel.

Waiting. Waiting for what? Waiting to be filled. Filled with what? A small fear awakened in him, like something evil hatching out of an egg.

Mazzo stirred, murmured something Barney couldn't understand, his hand reaching out, clutching at the air, clutching at nothing. Barney took his hand. So wet with perspiration, it seemed like he'd just immersed it in hot water. Mazzo's fingers closed on Barney's hand with surprising strength.

"I'm here," Barney said. Didn't know why he said it. Didn't know why he stayed here.

"I know," Mazzo said. Without inflection, so that Barney didn't know whether he was being sarcastic and hostile or merely acknowledging Barney's presence.

After a while Mazzo loosened his grasp and his breathing became regular, no rasping or rattling in his chest. Barney's back hurt from standing all that time in an awkward position, his hand and Mazzo's locked together in midair. He gently placed Mazzo's hand on the sheet over his chest, shivering slightly because it seemed the kind of thing you do to a dead person. Depressed, still vacant and empty, he made his way out of the room and encountered Bascam in the corridor.

"Don't you ever go home?" he asked out of his weariness and depression.

Her countenance did not change. Still without expression, her face one-dimensional, unreadable.

"This is my home," she said. Now the slight blush again, like on the day she had suggested that he smell the lilacs.

"You live here?" Barney asked.

She didn't answer. Didn't nod her head or acknowledge his question. Merely looked at him.

And Barney knew. Instantly.

"Are you in remission, too?" he asked.

She nodded her head, so slightly that it seemed she barely moved. But he saw the answer in her eyes. He wondered if the tight hair pulled into the severe bun at the nape of her neck was a wig. From chemotherapy. Everything in the Complex not what it seemed.

"I'm sorry," he said.

Want to go with us? In the Bumblebee? The crazy thoughts emerging from his utter exhaustion.

"Did you know about me?" he asked.

"Not at first," she said. "No one knew. Only Dr. Lakendorp."

"I'm not giving in," he said stubbornly.

"I'm not either," she said.

And slipped past him, padding down the corridor on rubber-soled shoes.

Blotches.

Like small explosions beneath the surface of his flesh, evil stains seeping through his skin.

Standing before the mirror, stripped to the waist, he observed pink smudges on his chest and arms, deeper than pink, angrier, reddening in spots. He touched the blotches, feeling for pain, but his flesh didn't seem to have changed. He touched a spot where a small blister had formed, near the nipple on the left side of his chest. The blister was moist, but then so was his entire body.

He had awakened strangely light-headed but pleasantly rested after the deep sleep following his encounter with Bascam. The room had tilted slightly as he moved, and he had welcomed the half-tipsy feeling of the wooziness. He

204

had gone to the mirror on light and airy steps and pulled off his T-shirt.

That was when he saw the first blotches.

The invader was here, slinking through his body, slithering through his bloodstream.

I shouldn't have fallen asleep, he said, but knew that was crazy. Remission was over. Time to put the show on the road. Which sounded brave with bugles blowing but he wasn't brave. He was waiting for the reaction, waiting for panic to come.

It wasn't until he saw the angry red smudge on his forehead, as if someone had smeared him with paint, that he uttered a cry, a wordless sound a small animal might make, trapped and injured and enemies closing in.

He could hide the blotches on his arms and legs with clothing but not his forehead. Everybody would see it, like a badge announcing his identity. If this was the last day here—and he knew it was as soon as he saw the first blotches—he had a lot to do. Had to get ready for the last ride. Say good-bye to Billy the Kidney and Allie Roon without having them know he was saying good-bye. Spend those last few minutes with Cassie.

The stains on his face meant that he had to keep away from people. Everybody in this place would recognize immediately what the blotches meant. And he didn't want Billy to know. Or Allie.

He dressed quickly, needing to hide the blotches. Then he stared at those telltale smears on his forehead.

Tears sprang to his eyes and he turned from the mirror in anger, the room whirling slightly. Not tears. He didn't want tears. He didn't want to cry, he never cried. He was angry because of the threat the blotches presented to all his plans. He had an entire day to get through, meaning an entire day to be faked. How do you fake a whole day? Where do you hide? How do you make yourself invisible?

He walked tentatively back to the bed, testing his legs, the room settling down with him as he sat. Checked his pulse: heart beating a bit faster than usual but that could be expected along with the anger and the disappointment and dismay. He was in control again, wiped the moisture from the corners of his eyes—he had been successful in holding back tears—and knew he had to gather his resources now. Had to use his wits, the old Barney Snow in operation. Felt warm all over, a moist suffocating kind of warmth. Eyes hot, too, now.

Better lie down, Barney, take it easy, conserve your strength. The invader's here, all right, but nobody knows how fast it will move. Got to play a waiting game now. Tempo, rhythm. Said the words aloud: "Tempo, rhythm." Felt better saying them, for some reason. Like a prayer. "Tempo, rhythm."

Billy sailed into the room, maneuvering his wheelchair directly to Barney.

"Listen, Barney, when am I going to ride in that car?"

"The Bumblebee," Barney said automatically, waiting for Billy to raise his eyes and see his forehead.

"Whatever you call it," Billy said. "I acted as a lookout. I helped steal that car. And now you've got it up there in the attic like it's your exclusive property."

"Give me a little time," Barney said, stalling. Look at me, he thought, look at what's happening to me.

"Hey, Barney, nobody's got much time here, you know that." The flashing in Billy's eyes, the old flashing of pain blinking off and on, like neon lights.

"Okay, Billy, let me think about it. Conditions have to be just right." Look at me, will you?

And Barney realized that Billy *had* been looking at him all along.

"Okay," Billy said, mollified, blowing air out of the corner of his mouth, the docile child again.

As they sat talking, Barney saw that the dying really didn't look at other people. Maybe they were too busy enduring their own agonies to attend to anybody else's. It was as if a kind of blindness overcame them, mental more than physical, allowing them to blot out what they didn't wish to see, focusing attention on themselves, ignoring the rest of the world. That was the blindness that affected Billy, that made him see Barney and yet not see him. When Billy finally left, Barney relaxed. His eyes still felt raw and fevered and his body moist with peculiar warmth, as if he were lying in a steaming bath. But he knew now he could fake his way through the day, hiding, drifting from room to room, avoiding Bascam and the others, keeping out of the Handyman's way—this all depended on not getting a summons from the Handyman, of course—until his meeting with Cassie late this afternoon. And, somehow, he would have to fake her out.

He felt faint late in midmorning, splashed water on his face in the bathroom, stood uncertainly at the door of his bedroom, wanting to rest but fearful of discovery if he got into bed.

Damn it. Always something threatening his plans, his grand design. The flight of the Bumblebee so near and yet so far away.

The Bumblebee. That was the ideal place to hide. In the

attic. In the front seat of the Bumblebee. Behind the wheel.

A perfect place to hide until his meeting with Cassie. Her face blossomed in his mind and then wavered and dissolved, fading into a mist. The way he felt his own face dissolving as the fever did its work.

The attic was hot, but a dry heat that was a pleasant contrast to the warm moisture he carried with him wherever he went.

He climbed into the car, clutching the wheel, rested his head on it. Dust motes exploded in the slant of sunshine.

He dozed now and then, waking fitfully sometimes. He forced himself to stay there. Mouth dry and parched, wanting a drink of water to soothe his throat. But staying there. Hanging on.

He was grateful that he did not plunge into the nightmare of the car and the street and the faceless girl. He was also grateful that there was no mirror in the attic, so that he could not look into it and see the new ravages of the invader on his face.

19

"Y OU look awful," she said, hurrying through the door, letting it close behind her with a slam.

But she looked awful, too. Eyes bloodshot, face flushed as if from fever, huddled in her blue blazer, shivering a bit, arms folding across her chest.

"How are you?" he asked warily, disheartened by her appearance. He wanted everything to go well during this last meeting with her, had it all rehearsed in his mind what he was going to say, but she looked so sick and wretched that he was thrown off-balance.

"I've caught a miserable cold," she said, sniffling, grimacing, rubbing her forehead. "But what about you? You don't look so great."

"A virus of some kind," he said, prepared for her question, following the script he had outlined for himself. "Even the nurses are getting it."

"Looks more like leprosy than anything else," she said half humorously in that husky wise-guy voice. She squinted at him. "Or maybe measles." Leading him toward the reception room, she said: "I shouldn't have come today. I'm probably spreading germs all over the place."

He sensed that she was making deliberate small talk,

feinting with words, her mind elsewhere, not on what she was saying. And he did the same thing, sitting across from her, giving her his report about Mazzo. Told her that Mazzo was the same, no change at all, seemed to be drifting even while lying in bed, no apparent pain; but all the time drinking her in with his eyes, thinking how beautiful she was even with the cold, the fever in her eyes—if it was fever—making them more blazingly radiant. His own eyes were burning, as if small fires had been lit in them. And his body was still warm, oozy with perspiration, more than perspiration, as if the juices of his body were bubbling forth through his pores.

At last he ran out of words, nothing more to say, and sat there looking at her. She seemed forlorn, as if she had been abandoned. He hated to see her looking that way, wished he could do something to take away her sadness but couldn't, could only sit here, waiting for time to run out, knowing he'd never see her again after today.

Reluctantly, he went into the talk he had prepared.

"They're sending me away," he said.

"Where to?" she asked, responding immediately, making him soar the way she always did when she focused her attention on him.

"A place north of Boston."

"When are you going?"

"Tomorrow." Keeping his voice steady.

"Is it going to be a nicer place than this?" she asked. "You've got to admit that this isn't the most luxurious spot in the world."

He shrugged, had to be careful, had to stick with his outline. "Any place is better than here, I guess," he said lamely. Groped for the next words, found them. "This new place has all the comforts."

She squinted at him again. "Are you sure you're okay, Barney? Did something go wrong with those tests of yours?"

"I'm fine," he said. "Just fine." Making his voice light and bright. He had to make her believe he was fine. Had to appear strong and healthy to her. "It's just this virus." Continuing with his scenario, he said: "I'm finished with the tests, and the doctor has arranged for a transfer to a place where I can recuperate faster."

"That's great," she said. "Listen, maybe I can stop by and visit you there sometime."

"Why not?" Barney said, enjoying this game of pretending, seizing the moment and holding it. "The doctor can give you the address."

He paused, gathering his thoughts for the big finale he had planned.

"Cassie, I want you to know how much I enjoyed meeting you and talking to you."

"I enjoyed it too."

He plunged:

"I think meeting you is the best thing that ever happened to me."

There. He'd said it. Didn't dare say more. Didn't want to blurt out how he really felt and how helpless he knew his love was. Because then she'd feel bad for him. And her pity would be worse than anything else.

"Why, thank you, Barney," she said, smiling, pleased, holding him in her gaze. "I don't know what I'd have done without you." Her words singing in him. "Without your reports about Alberto, my mother and I would have been lost. You don't know how much they meant to us. To me. And I'm sure your friendship has helped Alberto through some bad times."

He said nothing, didn't need to say more, proud that he had convinced her he was leaving the Complex, afraid that he might spoil it all if he said more. But aching to say more. To tell her how much she meant to him, how he'd had nothing to cling to but her presence in his life.

Not trusting himself, he felt a need to move and he stood up. She stood up, too. And he realized that this was hurrying her departure. Yet he wanted her to go, to get out of here before he did something crazy, like confessing his love for her and trying to kiss her or telling her the truth: that he was dying and she could never visit him in that place north of Boston because he wouldn't be there.

In a desperate move to detain her, he said: "How about you, Cassie?"

"How about me?" she said, tilting her head, like a little girl again.

"That Thing you spoke about. Is it still bothering you?"

"Oh that," she said. "It was my imagination, I guess. Everything's fine, Barney."

"Are you going back to the Hacienda?"

"I don't know. I always felt safe there. But I have to wait."

He knew what she had to wait for. For Mazzo to die.

"Listen," she said. "How's the car coming along? You know, the one in the attic."

They both laughed. As if there were other cars in the Complex.

"The Bumblebee," he said.

"Yes, the Bumblebee," she said, smiling at him like a conspirator.

"Well, it's finished. Finished it last night."

"Does it work? Did you take a ride in it yet?"

"Maybe tonight," he said. "Or tomorrow." Then remembered his story. "Before I leave."

"Tell me, Barney. Who did you steal it for? Who did you build it for? Who's going to ride in it?"

He didn't answer, couldn't answer. He was afraid that if he started talking about the ride, he would tell her everything. He couldn't take a chance on that. All of him ached to tell her about the ride, but he had to remain silent.

"Alberto," she said, husky voice a whisper. "You built it for him, didn't you? You're still doing things for other people, aren't you, Barney? And you're going to give Alberto a ride in your Bumblebee."

Suddenly, surprisingly, she kissed him. Her lips on his lips for a brief moment, her body pressed against him, immersed in the clean soap smell of her. Him, Barney Snow, big ears, scruffy hair, bowlegged. And dying. Kissed by this girl, Cassie Mazzofono, whom he loved, who was looking at him now with such tenderness and affection and maybe even a flash of love, gone as quickly as it came but shining out of her for a sweet instant here in this twilight room. He stood before her in the faded hospital clothes, burning with fever, duped and deceived by the Handyman, certain to die. Yet this was the one great moment of his life.

"Oh, Barney," she said, voice tremulous, eyes a bit moist. "Thank you."

"You're welcome," he said. Kicking himself. *You're welcome.* Why couldn't he have come up with something memorable, a phrase she'd remember forever, like the last words in a movie when the lovers had to part? But they weren't lovers, were they? "Hope your cold gets better." *Hope your cold gets better.* That was even worse.

And then she was gone. A quick smile and out of the

room, around the corner and into the hallway. He heard her heels clicking on the floor, like that first day. Then the outer door opening and closing. He wanted to rush after her, risk everything, tell her everything, call out to her: Come back, I love you. But only stood there.

That was the moment the first shaft of pain entered him, a fire in his groin, like a hot knife melting into his flesh. He clutched at his stomach and it lurched sickeningly. He was afraid he would vomit and soil himself at the same time. Telling himself, tempo, rhythm, he closed his eyes, held himself stiff, hoping that this stillness would keep the pain and the nausea from getting worse.

Yet, as he stood there in the agony of this thing that was killing him, he had the taste of Cassie Mazzofono on his lips and the knowledge that he had pulled it off, sent her out of here without telling her what was happening to him, his condition, the screens, and the pathetic thing his life had become. Because of that, his life, whatever was left of it, wasn't pathetic after all. But kind of noble, somehow.

20

*O*UT of the room and down the corridor, eleven
o'clock at night, he knew he cut a ridiculous figure, walking crablike, half bent over, one shoulder higher than the
other, like some grotesque hunchback on the prowl. He'd
learned very quickly that pain can be accommodated by
the body if the body adjusts to meet it. Little tricks. He
had found ways to stand or sit or walk that reduced the
degree of pain, his bones and tissues shifting and arranging
themselves so that he could navigate with a minimum of
pain. Didn't know how he had learned so quickly but he
had, as if some previous experience was helping him now.
Who knows? In the part of his memory he could not recall,
maybe certain information lurked and was being fed to
him subconsciously. Maybe he had learned to combat pain
in that other place before he came here and was an old
veteran now.

He paused, crouching, before Allie's room. Pushed the
door open. Allie was asleep, old man's face in repose, all
twitchings gone. Barney stood by the bed, watching, listening. Poor kid. Would never get to ride in the Bumblebee. Allie's breathing was so shallow that his chest did not
seem to be rising and falling. Barney bent close, adjusting

his body to do so, placed his ear near Allie's mouth and felt the hot breath in his nostrils.

"Good-bye, Allie Roon," he whispered.

He felt silly talking to somebody fast asleep like that. At the doorway, feeling silly again but somehow good about what he was doing, he saluted the still small figure on the bed.

Still hunched over, he made his way to Billy's room, moving sideways sometimes to lessen the pain, as if he could shift the pain here and there inside him to less vulnerable areas. Outside Billy's room he straightened up as much as possible, adjusting his body to a more normal posture. There was a chance that Billy was awake, and he wanted to appear normal to him.

"Barney, what are you doing here?" Billy the Kidney asked as he approached the bed.

"Making the rounds."

Saying good-bye.

"What time is it, anyway?"

Time for the Bumblebee.

"Eleven or so. I don't know."

Billy pulled the sheet up snugly to his chin. "It's chilly in here. You chilly, Barney?"

"A little," Barney said. Actually he was hot, a heat that radiated throughout his body, fed by something inside him. But he didn't want to alarm Billy. If Billy thought he was the only chilly person in the room, he'd start worrying.

"Can't sleep, Barney?" Billy yawned.

"Right."

No time for sleeping.

"I'm tired, but I can't sleep either."

"Know something, Billy?" Careful now. Had to say it right. Didn't want to spoil anything.

"What?" Voice drowsy.

"I admire you very much, Billy. For being here, in this place, when you could be somewhere else. And for not talking about the pain. I see the pain in your eyes all the time, sometimes worse than others, but you never say anything. You complain about other things, you're a pain in the neck at times, but you never kick about your pain. Just take it."

"I'm just dumb, I guess," Billy said. "Too dumb to complain about it."

"You're not dumb, Billy. You're brave."

Billy's voice became sharp again. "Hey, Barney. You okay? You look kind of funny the way you're standing there. And I didn't see you all day long. Did you get some new merchandise or something?"

"Yeah, and it's got a strange effect, it makes it hard for me to walk." Amazed, as always, at how easily he lied. "I've got to be going, Billy."

Good-bye, Billy the Kidney.

"See you later, Barney." Closing his eyes, snuggling deeper into the bed.

Barney stole through the doorway, glad to be out of Billy's sight so that he could let down a little, allow his body to change and shift to accommodate the pain. He found to his relief that the pain had subsided somewhat. Instead of singing through his body like a high-pitched sound that could shatter glassware, the pain was more like a quiet hum now, murmuring through his bones and muscles and tissues, a dull ache, better than the thousand knives.

He found Mazzo a lump in his bed, sleeping quietly, small snores making his nostrils quiver, mouth half open. He looked so peaceful that Barney hated to disturb him, bring him back to the world, bring him to the Bumblebee.

217

He touched Mazzo's shoulder and Mazzo was instantly awake, alert, on guard.

"Don't you ever sleep?" Mazzo asked, annoyed.

Good. Mazzo was his usual unpleasant self.

Barney bent close to his face.

"It's time to go, Mazzo. Time to go."

"Go where?" Mazzo asked. "You crazy or something?" Irritated, patient, turning away.

"Out. Going out of here in a blaze of glory."

Looking at Barney over his shoulder, he asked, "What the hell are you talking about? We're not going anywhere."

"Remember when you asked me to pull the plug?"

Mazzo moved his body to face him, up on one elbow now, still sullen and suspicious but a spark of watchfulness in those fevered eyes.

"Did you ask me to pull the plug?"

Mazzo nodded.

"We're going to do more than pull the plug, Mazzo. We're going for one last wild ride."

Mazzo groaned and sank down in the bed, like a ship settling into deep waters.

"Go to bed, Barney. Stop telling fairy tales."

Barney grabbed his arm, careful not to disturb the tube connected with a doodad above Mazzo's wrist, but grabbing all the same.

"Listen to me, Mazzo," Barney said, his own voice hoarse and raspy now. "I'm calling your bluff. You're the guy who said you wanted to end it all. You also said you wanted to go out in a flash. Well okay. We're going to do it together."

"You look like hell, you know that?" Mazzo said, pulling loose from Barney's grip but raising himself on one elbow again. "Okay, tell me about it, what you're talking about."

"You're going to have to see it to believe it, but trust me, Mazzo. We're flying out of here tonight, flying high." Barney indicated the machine humming in the corner. "After you get disconnected from this thing, you have about two or three hours, right?"

Mazzo nodded, watching Barney closely as if he had to read his lips to understand what he was saying.

"Isn't it connected to a monitor in Observation, too? I mean, if you get disconnected from it, somebody will notice, won't they?"

"I don't think any alarm bells go off or anything. But I don't know."

"It's a chance we have to take," Barney said. In command now, brain working sharp and true, no wooziness. Maybe the pain helped, helped clear the fuzziness, the way iodine burns away infection. "All we need is ten, fifteen minutes." He looked down at Mazzo. "Will you trust me, Mazzo? Will you do what I say?"

"What have I got to lose?" Mazzo asked, sighing, resigned. "Can you get this thing off me?"

Barney's fingers trembled as he removed the needle, closing his eyes at the final loosening, a coward about stuff like that. Feeling faint, he gripped the bed, watching the machine and watching Mazzo, wondering if his separation from the life-giving unit would kill him here and now. Nothing happened. The machine continued to hum.

"Let's make it fast if we're going to do it," Mazzo said, impatient. He looked feeble, however, as he threw off the sheet and turned his body. Slowly, he raised himself up, letting his legs dangle off the bed. His feet looked dainty, like small white fish.

"Can you walk?" Barney asked. "Want me to find a wheelchair?"

"I can walk," Mazzo said, shrugging away from Barney's

touch. "Just give me a minute." Scowling, breathing heavily. "How far do we have to go?"

"To the elevator. The freight elevator down the hall, about fifty feet and around the corner."

"The elevator? Christ, Barney, I hope you know what you're doing."

I hope so, too, Barney thought, getting Mazzo's slippers and robe from the closet.

When Mazzo launched himself from the bed and stood on those delicate, fragile feet, Barney held his breath. He feared Mazzo's body might crumple, unsupported by his legs and feet. Mazzo swayed a bit for a moment or two, standing unsteadily, like a drunk leaving a bar.

"Let me get a wheelchair," Barney urged.

"Screw you, Barney Snow. I can walk."

And he took small tentative steps toward the door, wobbly, delicately, but going forward bit by bit.

"Well, then, let me help you at least," Barney said, putting his arm around Mazzo's waist. "You don't have to prove how tough you are." Barney's own movement brought a spasm of pain in his groin, and he almost leaned against Mazzo for support.

"This better be good," Mazzo said, eyes blazing. "Your breath smells terrible."

"You don't smell like sweet violets yourself," Barney said.

And Mazzo laughed. Not the usual harsh bark of derision but a real laugh with merriment in it. "Look, ma, I'm walking," he said, but straining a bit, legs still uncertain.

Stepping into the corridor, Barney peered down its length. No one in sight.

Mazzo followed his gaze. "Looks like a long way to that corner," he said.

Barney tightened his grip around Mazzo, and Mazzo

leaned a bit against him, allowing Barney to support him.

They made a strange caravan as they inched along the hallway, hugging the wall, turning the wall into support for Mazzo on his other side, Barney on the outside. Mazzo's feet got tangled in each other on occasion, as if they had to learn how to walk all over again.

The nature of Barney's pain changed as they walked along. Tiny bolts of pain shot through his body now, small lightning streaks, causing him to catch his breath, weakening his knees. He felt like a lightning rod in a wild thunderstorm, his heart leaping inside him, his body twitching sometimes like Allie Roon's. Tempo, rhythm, Barney told himself.

"Let's take a rest," Mazzo said at the halfway point, panting, gasping for breath.

Barney was suddenly doubtful about the venture. If Mazzo was running out of strength at this point, could he get through the entire ordeal? Shoulders twitching, eyes brimming over with moisture—not tears, moisture, he kept telling himself—he studied Mazzo.

"Want to go back?" he asked.

"Let me get my breath, will you?" Mazzo growled.

"Mr. Personality," Barney growled back, but cheered by Mazzo's refusal to return to his room.

A door swung open behind them. Barney looked over his shoulder, saw Billy the Kidney's wheelchair emerging through the doorway. And then Billy himself manipulating the wheels. Craning his neck, Billy called softly: "What's going on out here? Where're you two going this time of night?" Excited, eyes flashing but not only with pain.

"You can't come," Mazzo said petulantly, starting to move again.

"Hey, Barney, can't I come?"

"You don't even know where we're going," Mazzo said, slouching forward against the wall, voice breathless, face glistening.

"You don't know either, Mazzo," Barney reminded him. And then: "Wait a minute."

Listening. To footsteps approaching from down around the corner, the familiar rubber-soled sound of nurse's shoes.

"Freeze," Barney commanded. "Somebody's coming."

They waited, frozen, a ridiculous tableau, Mazzo flat against the wall like a three-dimensional painting, Billy leaning forward in the wheelchair as if sitting on the lap of a metal monster, and Barney himself, almost spinning on one leg, poised between the other two, like a ballet dancer. A nurse appeared at the end of the corridor, carrying a small basin in her hands, walking delicately as if she were afraid to spill whatever was in the basin. If she turned left, she could come face to face with them. If she turned right, she was probably headed for another section and would not see them. Yet Barney felt as if she could see them in the periphery of her vision but like so many other people didn't want to see them.

They waited, endlessly.

She turned right and was gone out of their sight.

The tableau came to life.

"You're supposed to be in bed," Barney admonished Billy the Kidney. "A few minutes ago you were off to sleep."

"I got to thinking about you, Barney. You looked so weird." His eyes searched Barney now, studying his face, his crablike posture. "You still look weird. What's the matter?"

"Never mind that," Barney said, impatient and angry. He'd already said good-bye to Billy and he was on his way to the Bumblebee and he didn't want any delays on the way. "Go back to bed, Billy."

The dawn of comprehension lit up Billy's eyes. He looked at Barney and Mazzo and shook his head. "You're going to ride the Bumblebee," he said, dismal with disappointment. "And you weren't going to let me ride too."

"For Christ's sake, let's get going," Mazzo implored Barney, breaths coming in gasps now, eyes like glazed glass.

"Okay, Billy," Barney said. "You can come and watch."

"Watch? I want to ride," Billy said, excited now, rubbing his hands together with glee.

Barney glanced down at Billy, pondering the situation. He couldn't afford to spend time on long explanations. It was best to take Billy along and let Billy do whatever he wanted to do. He was tired of making decisions for other people.

"Okay, come on." While Mazzo shook his head in disgust.

They rode the elevator in silence, Barney and Mazzo resting, gathering breath and strength after the strenuous walk along the corridor while Billy the Kidney was watching them curiously but not asking questions, opening his mouth once as if to speak but silenced immediately when Barney directed his eyes to him and shook his head. Barney's pain had changed again, seemed muted now and subdued except for occasional lightning bolts that made him leap and twitch.

The doors parted creakily as usual. Barney stepped into the attic with Mazzo but didn't turn on the light right away. He wanted Mazzo to get the full effect. "Close your eyes," he whispered in Mazzo's ear. Feeble light from the elevator fell on the Bumblebee but he wanted Mazzo to see it for the first time in all its glory, fully illuminated.

223

Mazzo squeezed his eyes shut. "Hurry up, will you?" he said.

Billy the Kidney climbed out of his wheelchair after positioning it to hold the doors open. He looked at Barney in rapt anticipation.

Barney switched on the light.

"Lo and behold," he said. "The Bumblebee."

"Jesus Christ," Mazzo said unbelievingly. "A car." Astonishment in his voice. "What the hell is a car doing up here?" He turned to Barney. "What's it got to do with us? Are you crazy, Barney?"

The Bumblebee was beautiful, glowing red in the crosslight between the ceiling bulb and the spill of light from the elevator. Ready and waiting for the big trip.

"Maybe I'm crazy," Barney said, "but that doesn't mean it's not going to work."

"It's the Bumblebee," Billy called, crooning the name as if he were singing a song.

"What's he ranting about?" Mazzo asked. "What's this all about anyway?" Dismayed now, weary. "You unplug me, get me up here with all this talk about going out in a blaze of glory, and then you show me a car. In an attic. You've flipped your lid, Barney." He narrowed his eyes, studying the Bumblebee. "And it doesn't even look like a car. It's a fake, for Christ's sake."

"It's a long story, Mazzo, and we haven't got time for details," Barney said. "But trust me. You're right, it's not a real car, not a car that anybody'll ever drive. It's a car that flies, like a bumblebee."

"The Bumblebee," Billy crooned again.

"How the hell does a car like that fly?" Mazzo said, sounding as if he were about to cry, from disappointment and failure and exhaustion.

Barney pointed to the skylight. And the platform. And

the stairs. "Simple, Mazzo, simple as pie. We carry the car up to the platform, open the skylight, and launch it into space."

"Are you crazy?" Mazzo said, aghast. "Get me back to my room, Barney."

"Look, Mazzo, want to go out in that blaze of glory? Sixty miles an hour and then nothing? All done, all over? Okay, here's your chance. The car's not heavy at all, it's made of soft wood, balsa wood. We get the car up to the platform, you and me. Not that big a deal. Ever see the roof on this place? It's like a ski jump. The skylight's at the top. We get in the car, Mazzo. And we sail off the roof. Six stories up and off we go. We fly. The Bumblebee flies and we're in it and where it lands nobody knows and nobody gives a damn." He found himself breathless and shaken now, the pain all over him, not inside now but outside, like a thousand bugs feasting on his flesh.

Through the fever and the pain that ravaged his body, Mazzo looked and listened in his ruin and desolation, eyes bloodied, flesh glistening. And Barney saw a flicker of understanding in those eyes and realized Mazzo was seeing what Barney could see, sharing the vision with him: the marvelous flight of the Bumblebee, out into the night, soaring off the roof, a small soaring maybe but enough to set them free, joining the stars and the moon and the planets.

"Jesus," Mazzo said, his voice an awed whisper.

"I want to go too," Billy cried. "Is there room for me?"

"You don't want to go," Barney told him.

"You sure we can get it up there?" Mazzo said, measuring the distance between the car and the platform.

"Listen, I got the car in here. From the junkyard next door. Took it apart piece by piece and got it up here. And then put it together again. Allie Roon and Billy here

225

helped. And I didn't do all that to stop now, Mazzo. The Bumblebee's flying tonight, with or without you."

"Hey, Barney," Billy called, and it was his turn now to be awestruck. "How come you're going? You got nothing to go out like that for. You're different than us."

"He joined the club," Mazzo said. "He's one of us, Billy."

"Aw, jeez," Billy said, on the verge of tears. "Not you, Barney. Not you too."

"Let's cut out the talk," Barney said. "Time's passing by. Somebody's going to be checking your rooms any minute now. Maybe that monitor sounded an alarm and they're already looking for us. Quit stalling, Mazzo."

"It is true, Barney?" Billy implored.

"Yes, it's true," Barney said, in a hurry now. "I only found out a couple of days ago. I've been in remission."

Tears in Billy's eyes. Barney didn't want to see Billy cry. Turning away, he said: "What do you say, Mazzo? Put up or shut up."

"I'm going, too," Billy said, face set, chin firm, determined.

"There's no room, Billy." He tried to say it gently. "It's a two-seater."

While Mazzo stood there studying the car. Or maybe the events of his life were passing before his eyes.

"I can cram myself in the back," Billy said. "I'll find room."

A sudden sheet of pain overwhelmed Barney, lifting him almost on tiptoe, taking his breath away. Heart pounding, vision blurred. "Okay, okay. But let's go." Turning to the blur that was Mazzo. "You coming?"

"I'm coming, I'm coming."

Barney blinked, his vision cleared, everything in focus again.

"I am, too," Billy cried.

"There's no room for you," Mazzo said.

"Look, Mazzo, I helped Barney steal the Bumblebee. Didn't I, Barney? And I deserve to go. Don't I, Barney?"

"It's not a joyride, Billy. Do you realize what we're doing?"

"I know, I know. And I want to do it, too. You're my friend, Barney. The only friend I've got. And if this is how it's going to be, then this is how it's going to be. What's the big deal staying here, in this place?"

Barney felt like swearing. He was responsible for himself, and Mazzo was old enough to make his own decisions, but Billy the Kidney was another matter.

"Maybe you'd better not come," Barney suggested, gently, making himself patient while all the time he wanted to get on with it, do it, before somebody hit the elevator button and decided to investigate.

"I'm dying too, you know," Billy said, sniffing. "I probably been dying longer than you have."

Christ, Barney thought, and wasn't sure whether he was swearing or praying.

"Okay, then," he said. "But don't take chances helping us with the car. Wait till we get it up there on the platform, then I'll help you climb the stairs."

Billy let out a whoop of delight, and Mazzo gave Barney a baleful sour look.

"Let's go," Barney said, with a whoop of his own.

Like slow motion.

Or moving underwater, walking on the bottom of the sea.

Barney and Mazzo moving the Bumblebee, picking it up and walking with it between them—Barney walking backward holding the front of the Bumblebee and Mazzo bringing up the rear—sharing the burden that wasn't a burden really, not heavy, something that linked them together, finding as much support from the Bumblebee as they gave it. Stumbling a bit over the naked studding, swaying and wavering at times, they faced each other as they went toward the stairs, letting the sweat drip down their faces, crinkling their eyes to prevent the moisture from blurring their vision, concentrating so much on this marvelous event, this great undertaking, that there was no place for pain or anything else. Arms and legs moving in unison, as if Barney and Mazzo had been rehearsing this for weeks, shifting weight and balance as they went along. While Billy the Kidney cheered them on, shouting encouragement but not really shouting, whispering the shouts, Billy underwater, too, so that you expected to see bubbles coming out of his mouth and float toward the ceiling.

They finally arrived at the stairs.

Exhaustion overcame them now. They set the Bumblebee down carefully across the floor studs. Barney did not realize how heavy it was until released from its weight. His arms were light and airy, felt almost transparent.

"Steep," Mazzo said, squeezing out the word between ragged breaths as he looked at the pitch and height of the stairs.

Barney nodded, incapable of speech, conserving his strength. Even talking required effort. Funny, no pain suddenly, a dull aching that enveloped his body but no more sharp knifelike pains.

"Wow," Billy called from the doorway, "you guys are really doing it. Halfway there, Barney, halfway there."

Barney looked back at him, managed a wan and weary smile. Even his lips seemed tired.

Gasping, Mazzo said: "Can't stop now." Pausing, blinking sweat out of his eyes.

Barney said: "Sixteen steps." Wiped his forehead with a trembling hand. "We lift the car. . . . I go first." Better for Mazzo to push from below, less awkward for him, easier. "Three, four steps at a time." Barney knew he'd have to climb the stairs backward and crouch uncomfortably to carry out his part, but he knew nothing could stop him now, nothing.

"Let's get going," Mazzo said, impatient, eager to get on with it.

"Okay."

This time it wasn't walking on an ocean floor but a grunting, groaning ascent, climbing a wooden slatted mountain while they tugged and shoved and pushed the Bumblebee between them. The wooden stairs creaked under their weight. Barney strained to maintain his balance as he mounted the stairs backward and crouched forward to tug the Bumblebee upward. If he relaxed his grip on the bumper, the entire weight of the car would rest on Mazzo down below. The weight of the Bumblebee seemed to have doubled since they had carried it across the attic floor. Barney felt the muscles in his shoulders and back straining against the weight. Sometimes his foot slipped as he raised it blindly to find the next step in the ascent. He'd compensate with the other foot, shifting his body perilously, risking loss of balance.

Billy didn't cheer anymore. He stood in stupefied wonder, as if he couldn't believe his eyes. Barney paused once to look at Billy, and dizziness caused his head to spin and he almost lost his grip on the Bumblebee. Mazzo's strength astonished him; he kept thrusting the car upward relentlessly, silently, calling up his reserves, the discipline of his athletic years maybe paying off. Barney wanted to call encouragement to him, to tell him that he was doing fine, but he didn't dare—he had to save his own strength and energy for the task at hand.

Barney finally made it to the platform, swinging one leg onto it and then holding on desperately to the car as he swung his other leg upward. In doing so, he relaxed his grip on the car and it dropped a bit, only a few inches or so but with enough force and weight to cause Mazzo to cry out in anguish. Barney took hold of the Bumblebee and held on for dear life. With Mazzo pushing and shoving, doing the job by himself now as Barney lay panting and fighting for breath on the platform, the car nosed up to the platform. Barney grabbed at it, pulling and hauling furiously, while Mazzo struggled to obtain a foothold and pulled himself up by sheer determination, veins on his forehead bulging like worms beneath his skin.

Now: The two of them on the platform with the Bumblebee between them, both triumphant, exhausted, grinning at each other, but the grins terrible, lacerated by pain and fatigue, Mazzo's flesh gray as if the flush that always tinted his skin had been wiped away with a cloth.

"Can I come up?" Billy called from below.

Barney risked moving, looking down, dizzy, lungs bursting as if he'd been holding his breath too long. He heard his voice saying: "Not enough room . . . wait. " It was like somebody else's voice, raspy, coming from far away.

Mazzo pointed to the skylight.

Barney nodded. Couldn't stop now.

He reached up and unlatched the skylight, pushed at it with all his strength. The skylight swung open, up and away, and Barney secured it with a steel rod that kept it from swinging shut. He raised himself and glanced out, saw the night for the first time from this vantage point, the sweep of sky spinning with stars, the moon radiating silver, turning the sloping roof into a glittering ski slide, the lights

230

of Monument center glowing in the distance, staining the sky with gold. The wind caught at Barney's mouth and he swallowed it hungrily. Suddenly he simply wanted to stay there, drinking in the night, bathing in the wind. Didn't want to go any further, do anything more. But knew he had to.

Reluctantly, he hauled himself up, leaned against the sill for a moment, then swung himself up onto the roof, arms and legs in a furious scrambling, his body pushed to the utmost. In his final desperate effort to gain the roof, he felt something break inside of him, not bone or ligament, but a fracture of something deep within, never to be repaired or restored. He clung to the roof, feeling the sandy shingles pressing against his body, his hands clutching the sill.

"Here it comes," Mazzo called.

Barney was astonished at Mazzo's effort, heaving the car upward from inside so that Barney saw the car's bumper and hood lifting up like a ship raising its prow in the air before the final plunge to the bottom. The front of the car hovered above the sill, poised perilously, and Barney gritted his teeth, getting ready to catch it as it swooped down. The car fell heavily and brutally, like a tree crashing to the ground, Barney absorbing its weight on his shoulders, holding on, past pain now or even fear of sliding off the roof, embracing the Bumblebee, wet cheek pressed against the glistening wood. Looking up, he saw that the car was being supported on the roof by the two rear wheels, which were still inside the skylight, hooked against the sill. Big test now: letting go of the car to see if the rear wheels would continue to keep it from rolling free. Barney pulled away from the car, releasing it from his grip, held his breath. The Bumblebee did not move, remained in position, pointing downward, ready for flight.

Raising himself up, scrambling to his knees, he peered

231

inside the skylight and came face to face with Mazzo, eyes inches apart, both still grinning those terrible crazy grins, exhausted, spent, bodies singing with the ache of all that exertion but triumphant in this desperate beautiful moment.

Barney motioned to the night and the sky, and Mazzo boosted himself with a mighty effort onto the roof, leaning against the trunk of the car, looking out at the night, shaking his head in disbelief. Raising his face to the sky, he laughed, the sound so startling and musical that Barney, caught by surprise, almost lost his balance as he leaned back to look at Mazzo. Mazzo glanced down, face radiant in the moonlight, and Barney saw, for a blazing moment, Cassie in his face. Cassie and the melting eyes. Cassie and that husky tender voice. Mazzo laughed again, the sound like silver coins in the night.

Barney thought of that marvelous moment when Cassie had looked at him with such admiration, making his life golden for a precious moment. She had made him see the sweetness of living, made him look with awe at blossoms on a tree branch, gave him a sense of life going on, from one person to another, from trees to flowers, from one season to the next. Dazzled by the thoughts, groping for their meaning, his love for Cassie singing inside him—a hopeless love, maybe, but bringing beauty to his life—he reached out and touched the Bumblebee, this impossible object he had stolen and taken apart and re-created with his own hands. Looking away to the golden glow of the town on the rim of the sky, he knew that he didn't want to die. He wanted to cling to life and breath. Didn't know why but knew he must. Maybe because Cassie inhabited this strange and terrible world. It was the only world he knew, and he was tired of the unknowns.

"Barney."

His name on Mazzo's tongue was a sound with a wound in it. Mazzo began sliding down the roof, slowly, inching toward Barney, arms clutching at the air. The wind rose, stiff and biting, as Barney rose up to grasp him. Mazzo trembled as Barney gathered him in his arms, supporting him, preventing him from slipping any farther. Mazzo was heavy as he rested against Barney, face turned away. Mazzo his enemy and now his friend. Mazzo who wanted so much to die. But I don't want to die, Barney thought. I thought that I was one of them, Mazzo and Billy the Kidney and even Allie Roon, but I'm not. Even though he was here on the roof with this absurd car he called the Bumblebee. Maybe he was absurd, too, taken apart and put together by the Handyman like some kind of Humpty Dumpty. But he was still Barney Snow. And he wanted to shout out at the night: I'm not resigned the way the Handyman says everybody here is resigned. Not willing to accept it all without struggling, fighting.

Mazzo's voice in his ear, a hoarse whisper: "I don't think . . . I can make it . . . into the car." Words faint, like ghosts. "Won't fly . . . can't fly."

"The Bumblebee's going to fly," Barney said, lips close to Mazzo's ear.

Mazzo's face was sour, the old Mazzo face of bitterness and scorn. And then his eyes softened. "But we got here . . . didn't we . . . Barney?"

Barney nodded. We got here. And he realized that getting there had been the important thing. Not the flight, although the Bumblee could still fly. For them. Hey, Mazzo, the Bumblebee is going to fly and we don't have to be in it. The Bumblebee will fly for us and we'll be a part of the flight because we made it possible, you and me, me by building it and you by giving me a reason to build it. We're all mixed up in it—you and me and Billy the Kidney and

233

Allie Roon and, yes, Cassie, too. He knew he was hysterical, barely coherent, didn't know whether he was talking or shouting or just thinking these thoughts, didn't know whether Mazzo could hear him or not but it didn't matter. What mattered was the Bumblebee and the flight.

"Barney."

Mazzo's voice again but this time something strange in it, a difference in the tone and timbre now, like the last strokes of a bell lingering in the air.

He turned Mazzo's face toward him and cupped it in his hands, saw Mazzo's mouth move in an effort to speak again. But no sound came. Mazzo's eyes were glazed, like specimens in a jar, not looking at him, not looking at anything, unseeing. Mazzo's body was suddenly still against him, the way a stone or a rock is still.

"Mazzo," Barney whispered, his own voice now with a bruise in it.

He knew Mazzo couldn't hear him, couldn't hear anything. Wouldn't ever hear anything again.

From far away Billy the Kidney's voice shouted his name. He looked up to see Billy not far away at all but peering out at him.

"What's going on?" Billy asked, eyes wide and wondering.

"The Bumblebee's about to fly," Barney cried, but still not knowing whether he was talking out loud, whether he could still make his voice heard.

"What do you want me to do?" Billy asked eagerly.

Good old Billy the Kidney.

"Lift up the rear wheels," Barney called, pronouncing the words precisely, enunciating them slowly and carefully, knowing that he probably didn't have the strength to repeat them.

"Right," Billy said, rubbing his hands together.

"Get the wheels onto the roof," Barney gasped, still holding on to Mazzo but shifting his body now so that he could stretch his legs under the front wheels of the Bumblebee to prevent it from plunging downward as soon as the rear wheels touched the roof. He wanted to do this correctly, properly. He heard Billy grunting as he lifted the wheels over the sill. And then felt an immediate crush of weight against his legs, so heavy and sudden that he didn't know whether he could hold the car back. Or hold himself from rolling off the roof.

The Bumblebee and he and Mazzo on the roof. Digging down for whatever reserves of strength remained in him, using even the broken thing deep inside of him, Barney managed to make his legs rigid, keeping the Bumblebee stationary, blocking its descent.

Billy called: "Hey, Barney. When are we going to fly?"

Didn't Billy understand? They didn't need to fly. The Bumblebee would fly for them. He couldn't speak now, couldn't stop to explain it all to Billy. Tell you later, Billy the Kidney, tell you later. Trust me—did I ever lie to you?

He turned Mazzo's head toward the Bumblebee, positioning himself carefully to meet the increasing weight upon his legs, and then slowly, agonizingly, beyond exhaustion and pain, beyond everything, he began to draw his legs back, arms encircled around Mazzo, head raised to the night.

"Here we go," he yelled with all that was left in him.

He heard his voice loud and clear, skipping across the night and the moon and the stars. Triumphant, brave, beautiful.

And the Bumblebee flew at last.

21

SHE awoke suddenly, leaping from sleep, startled and disoriented, because she hadn't realized she'd dropped off. Last thing she remembered was floating, drifting, listening to an old Simon and Garfunkel tune, "The Sounds of Silence," on the radio, headachy, a bit troubled. Troubled by the Thing, of course, which was always with her now but also by that poor kid, Barney Snow. Funny, pathetic boy. That desperate cheerfulness of his. And the car he was assembling in the attic of that place. To give Alberto a ride. She sometimes doubted that there was a car, thought it real only in his imagination, but a small part of her delighted in the possibility of its existence.

Stirring in the bed, reaching to turn off the radio that emitted only small static sounds now, she decided she would buy him a farewell gift and drop it off at the clinic tomorrow before he left. She was also determined to see Alberto again, to insist that he admit her and Mother to his room. Without Barney Snow as a go-between, the link to Alberto was broken. And—

She was caught in midsentence, midbreath, caught and held, breathless, trapped, immobile, no pain, weightless, transparent like glass, but also breakable like glass. Then

236

she was released, mobile again, and now a stab of pain, quick and sharp in her chest, and a flutter of the heart, her breath returning, the air rushing in to fill a deep cavity within her, arms and legs trembling, head light, the room swimming away from her. She had never felt like this before.

And she knew.

Knew what was happening.

To Alberto at the clinic.

Knew he was dying. At this moment.

And she, too, dying then.

But, strange, no panic, and no pain, just this breathlessness, as if she were the eye of the hurricane, waiting, dangling in time and space.

She managed to make the Sign of the Cross with a trembling arm. *In the Name of the Father and the Son and the . . .*

But wait.

Must be more than prayer.

Must pray, yes, like at the Hacienda. All the time she'd been there she'd been praying, even while doing chores maybe, but hadn't known it at the time. But something must come out of the praying.

Like now.

God, please help Alberto. Make it easy for him, don't let him have too much pain or panic. Don't let him be alone. Be with him. Give him someone through You.

And me.

God, I don't want to die.

She curled up in the bed, making herself a small target, knees drawn up to her chin, arms locked around her knees, waiting. But she didn't want to simply wait, didn't want to lie here like this, defenseless. Must do something, fight, anything. Even that poor kid, Barney Snow, did something. Put a car together in the attic. Like a bumblebee. Even if only in his dreams.

I don't want to die.

She waited to hear her voice echoing in the room, resounding throughout the house, waking her mother and Mrs. Cortoleona, but realized she hadn't spoken aloud, had screamed the words silently, but they were true, nevertheless.

I don't want to die.

And I won't die.

She raised herself from the bed, threw off the quilt, felt the cold touch of the linoleum beneath her feet, sat there like a boxer in a corner of the ring waiting for the bell, ready to fight.

She felt caught and held again, breathless, trapped. Still, in the way a clock is still when it stops ticking. She fought the stillness, sensed danger in it, struggled, twisted away, rose from the bed *I don't want to die* stalked with stiltlike legs to the bureau *I will not die* felt again the stab of pain, held on to the bureau with her hands, held on to life with all the strength and will that she could gather. Dear God.

Then a last flutter, heart beating in a rush, blood pounding at her temples. And nothing. Emptiness. A void.

And she knew with a calm and cold and certain knowledge that Alberto was dead. His life extinguished, obliterated the way light becomes darkness at the snapping of a switch.

Anguish filled her as she stared at herself in the bureau mirror, saw her mouth open but wordless, her eyes wide with the despair and desolation that gripped her, overwhelmed by the knowledge that Alberto, her brother, her twin, her other self, was dead, gone.

What about me?

But suddenly it doesn't matter about me.

Turning from the bureau, she was alive to a thousand sights and sounds springing to life around her. Could hear her veins and arteries churning through her body, her heart pulsing its marvelous rhythms, aware of light and color, everything vivid and dazzling, the glow of the lamp stunning her eyes, the air sweetly stinging her flesh, her body singing like a harp string plucked by knowing fingers. Whose fingers?

Ah, but she knew Whose fingers.

And that's all she needed to know.

22

*T*HE Bumblebee never stopped flying.

He had a trick he had learned, and the trick was the blinking of his eyes and in the blinking came the memory of the Bumblebee, gliding down the roof as if in slow motion, sleek and gleaming in the moonlight, gathering speed, wheels flashing as they turned.

He remembered clinging to Mazzo's body, ignoring Billy's voice calling from the skylight, and watching the Bumblebee's course, unstoppable, not to be denied this flight to glory.

Free of the roof, the Bumblebee hung in the air for a sweet split second, suspended in time and space, the way a dancer pauses in a soaring leap, breathless, denying for a precious moment the laws of gravity, untouchable and unspeakably beautiful.

Then the Bumblebee disappeared, one moment there and the next moment gone, as if removed from Barney's sight by some marvelous, mysterious act. He listened for the crash of the Bumblebee, the smashing and splintering of wood as it struck the ground below. But heard nothing. He laughed, delighted, knowing that the Bumblebee still flew, soaring out into space, unending in its flight.

In the bed he now occupied he was surrounded by a grayness, and out of the grayness came faces. The faces were always sad and unsmiling. He wanted to tell them: Hey, laugh, or at least smile a little, because the Bumblebee is still flying and we made it fly. Often, in the grayness, he searched for something, lost, beyond his reach. A face he had known. He tried to summon the face but couldn't. Her face. But there was only a blankness in the grayness and a terrible loneliness and longing. He wanted to cry out for—who?

He watched and searched and listened in the loneliness, and heard another voice. It was voice that was familiar, but he could not identify it. *Is there anything I can do to help, Barney?* But the voice couldn't help. It was the wrong voice, anyway. There was another voice that could help, a low sultry voice like a singer he had heard once but could not bring back now. Nobody could help anymore. Only the blinking could help.

He was grateful for the blinking. He didn't know what he would do without the blinking. He got ready for the blinking by saying his prayers, *In the Name of the Tempo and the Rhythm,* repeating the prayer over and over, *In the Name of the Tempo and the Rhythm,* and then blinking rapidly, furiously, blink: *Tempo,* blink: *Rhythm,* and that's when he saw the Bumblebee again, breaking through the grayness and the loneliness, glowing and glistening as it moved off the roof and across the sky, out into the stars and the planets and beyond, always beautiful, always flying, always his.

ROBERT CORMIER, one of America's leading authors of young adult fiction, began his career as a newspaper reporter over twenty-five years ago. He has twice received the Associated Press award for the Best News Story in New England and has been involved in all phases of journalism.

In addition to three novels for adults, Robert Cormier is the author of three best-selling young adult novels, as well as *8 Plus 1*, a collection of short stories. Published in 1974, *The Chocolate War* won resounding critical acclaim and was named an ALA Best Book for Young Adults. *I Am the Cheese*, a *New York Times* Outstanding Book of the Year, ALA Best Book for Young Adults and Notable Children's Book, is now a major motion picture. *After the First Death*, an ALA Best Book for Young Adults, is his most recent novel for Pantheon Books.

Robert Cormier lives with his wife, Connie, in Leominster, Massachusetts. They have a son and three daughters.